HardScape

VIKING
Mystery
Suspense

Books by Justin Scott

author of HardScape

Mysteries

Many Happy Returns *(MWA Edgar Nominee Best First Novel)*
Treasure for Treasure
The Widow of Desire

Thrillers

The Shipkiller
The Turning
Normandie Triangle
A Pride of Royals
Rampage
The Nine Dragons
The Empty Eye of the Sea *(Published in England)*

HardScape

a novel by Justin Scott

VIKING

VIKING
Published by the Penguin Group
Penguin Books USA Inc., 375 Hudson Street,
New York, New York 10014, U.S.A.
Penguin Books Ltd, 27 Wrights Lane,
London W8 5TZ, England
Penguin Books Australia Ltd,
Ringwood, Victoria, Australia
Penguin Books Canada Ltd, 10 Alcorn Avenue,
Toronto, Ontario, Canada M4V 3B2
Penguin Books (N.Z.) Ltd, 182–190 Wairau Road,
Auckland 10, New Zealand

Penguin Books Ltd, Registered Offices:
Harmondsworth, Middlesex, England

First published in 1994 by Viking Penguin,
a division of Penguin Books USA Inc.

10   9   8   7   6   5   4   3   2   1

PUBLISHER'S NOTE
This is a work of fiction. Names, characters, places, and incidents either are the
product of the author's imagination or are used fictitiously, and any resemblance
to actual persons, living or dead, events, or locales is entirely coincidental.

LIBRARY OF CONGRESS CATALOGING IN PUBLICATION DATA
Scott, Justin.
    Hardscape: a novel/by Justin Scott.
        p.   cm.
    ISBN 0-670-85212-0
    1. Private detectives—Connecticut—Fiction.—I. Title
    PS3569.C644H37   1994
    813'.54—dc20   93–2050

Printed in the United States of America
Set in Minion
Designed by Virginia Norey

For My Father

A. Leslie Scott
A series at last, Pop, home in our small towns

HardScape

Hardscape
is what you see in winter
when flowers are dead and branches bare.
It forms the character of a house,
like the bones behind a face.

1

I had a gut feeling that Alex Rose had not really driven his Mercedes all the way from New York to buy a weekend home in Newbury. It had been a while since I'd been a New York player, but, like my Armani suits mothballed in the attic, I had kept the instincts. I disobeyed them and offered to show him the Richardson place, hoping he was real. With the recession still twined around Connecticut, stubborn as poison oak, and the high-end country-house crowd pondering "fair share" taxes and hourglass loopholes, I had time on my hands and fifty listings for every buyer.

I drove him in my Oldsmobile, singing the praises of Main Street.

Our homes are set far back. A sweep of green grass separates curbs from sidewalks, and hundred-year-old elms and sugar maples arch overhead. Customers love it. It's the street they had in mind back in kindergarten when they crayoned their first house with smoke squiggling from the chimney, a flower and a picket fence.

Rose sat silent as ice sculpture, blind to snug Colonials, elegant Federal mansions, snow-white churches, even our famous flagpole.

The only commercial structures in sight were the barn-red Newbury General Store, the Newbury Savings Bank, housed in a structure as conservative as its lending policies, and the picturesque Yankee Drover Inn. There was my Benjamin Abbott Realty shingle, and a couple belonging to my competitors. And that was about it, thanks to my grandfather, who wrote the zoning laws, and my father, who enforced them.

Modern conveniences, I explained—like the Grand Union, video rental, gas station, and the bikers' bar—were hidden at the bottom of Church Hill Road. Rose grunted. I told him our flagpole was the tallest in Connecticut. He didn't seem to care.

He was a big man who led with his belly, a well-fed forty-five or so, health-club tanned and burly, soft brown hair fertilized by Rogaine. Poring over my aerial maps, he had studied me with busy, hooded eyes.

He *dressed* like a house hunter, outfitted for "the country" in Bean boots and a corduroy shooting jacket with a leather rifle-butt patch and extra pockets for his bullets. He also looked like he could *afford* to buy, judging by the S-class land yacht parked at my office. So I kept driving and hoping.

Out of town, Route 7 runs along the river, matching it bend for bend with a forty-five-mile speed limit and dotted lines on the straights. I passed a Toyota loafing along at fifty, then slowed down for the Calvary Horse Farm.

"They give riding lessons for the kids," I ventured.

". . . Of course, there's plenty of room on the Richardson place to keep your own horse. Ellie boarded some 'til she died."

Four miles south of town I turned onto Academy Lane and, after a mile of it, onto a dirt road named Richardson Street, which was lined with ancient maple trees decaying from age, neglect, and the thrip. Still, they made a grand tunnel between two of the loveliest hayfields in the county.

"This used to all be Richardson land, but it's been sold off. The house has six acres, with another fourteen available."

Rose's silence doomed his charade. Any buyer worth a mortgage would ask whether the open land would be developed with a bunch of tract houses. Ordinarily, my answer went, "Before 1990 I'd have had to admit development was likely. But those days are gone. The town will continue its very slow growth, but no big developments— Here we are!"

The neglected though elegant farmhouse was relatively new by

Newbury's calendar, built thirty years after the American Revolution. New wings and Greek Revival detail had been added on as Richardsons prospered, until the decline of New England farming left subsequent generations with a house too big to heat, much less paint. What had kept this faded beauty standing when many were lost was a New York City Richardson turned financier who had maintained it as an exquisite country home from the 1920s into the early 1960s. I directed Rose's attention to the faint lines of brick paths through the thorn-tangled gardens. A cherry tree grew out of the clay tennis court, and the skating pond was reverting to marsh.

"Adlai Stevenson used to visit his mistress here. Or so they say. Her estate was out there, through the sycamores."

Rose turned a full, slow circle, confirming we were alone. I pulled out my big ring of keys.

"There's a beautiful brick keeping room that overlooks the skating pond. I swear on a winter day you can still smell the hot cocoa."

"Do you know a lot of people around here?"

I told him I'd been born in Newbury.

"You know the Longs? Jack and Rita Long?"

I knew who he meant. And like everyone else I knew about the thirty-seven-room stone house they had built just across the Morrisville line, which people called "The Castle." Fred Gleason had sold them a hundred acres and celebrated that winter in the Caribbean. The Longs had built in some sort of Victorian turreted style, with crenelations and, for all I knew, a moat of alligators. Jim York had decorated a few rooms. He reported that the Longs spent freely and paid their bills, sterling qualities in any client.

"Friends of yours?" I asked. "I'm surprised you didn't ask Fred Gleason to show you houses. Fred was their agent."

Rose pretended not to hear me. "He's a guy about my size, dark hair, little mustache. Maybe a little overweight. She's a terrific-looking brunette."

"I don't know them."

It was none of Rose's business that I had met Jack Long, briefly, and seen him in action at a land trust meeting. He had a firm handshake and looked you over real quick, pigeonholing you and assessing your worth. I thought he was a little pushy, throwing his weight around, and quick to remind people that, as a businessman, he knew "how these things work."

On the other hand, Long was genuinely interested in the local effort to protect open space and had, I'd heard from Fred, put his money where his mouth was with a generous contribution to the buy-up kitty. Such is not always the case with the big bucks weekenders, so I had no problem overlooking his arrogance as typical busy-guy behavior.

The New Yorker had also, in the short time he'd been in town, become the hero of the guns-and-ammo crowd whose shooting range faced shutdown until he bought up adjacent property to prevent development of homesites in the line of fire. All in all, a man who got things done.

Rose wouldn't let it go. "They come up on the weekends. Maybe you've seen them in town, buying the *Times*."

I was tired of the game. "Assuming you mean what *I* mean by a terrific-looking brunette, I'm sure I'd remember meeting her. Are they the reason you're looking for a house in Newbury?"

"Tell me about yourself." The hooded eyes opened wide, hardening his big, blocky face.

I said, "I've got a better idea. Why don't you tell me what you already know about me and I'll fill in the spaces."

"What do you mean?"

"I mean you've dragged me out here under a pretext to talk about these Longs, which means you want something from me, because you think you know something about me. Tell me what you think you know."

Rose planted his feet and folded his arms. His shooting jacket looked too new and a little silly. I was wearing my basic realtor's uniform—chinos, a country-gentleman tweed jacket that looked thirty years old, and penny loafers with rubber soles for wet grass. I had a cap and windbreaker stashed in the car in case of a change in the weather.

We stood toe to toe a moment—an unarmed hunter and a country gent without estate—then Rose gave me a smirky wink that made his big face go lopsided like an eighteen-wheeler stopped on a soft shoulder.

"You asked for it," he said, and, to my surprise and growing anger, recited my dossier.

"Benjamin Abbott III. You were born here, went to grade school here. Your old man ran the real estate office. He was also first selectman, which is sort of like mayor. You attended the Newbury Prep School, as a day student, then the United States Naval Academy at Annapolis. You served in Naval Intelligence, resigned your commission when your obligation was up, went to work on Wall Street. Am I right, so far?"

He had missed twelfth grade when Great-aunt Connie persuaded my father to pack me off to Stonybrook Military Academy, ostensibly to prepare me for Annapolis, but mostly to keep me from getting into trouble with my cousin Renny. Renny was considered a bad influence, like "your hoodlum friend outside" in "Yakity-yak." Only Renny and I knew it was the other way around.

Rose treated my silence to another smirk, and headed for the good parts: "On Wall Street you made a bunch of money running mergers and acquisitions, got nailed in the Michigan Machine insider trading scheme, and went to jail."

"I didn't break the law."

"But you did time."

"I sure did." I felt invaded. He had slid a knife under a scar and peeled it.

"When you got out, you came home and took over your father's business. His contacts put you first on line with the old money and the big estates that go to probate court."

I wondered how a bloody nose would look on his shooting jacket. Rose backed up a step.

"Don't you want to know why I'm telling you this?"

Of course I was curious why he'd driven a hundred miles to annoy me. "Not as much as you want to tell me."

He backed up another step. His eyes got nervous, but before I could make him more nervous, he surprised me again. "I'm a private investigator."

I had pegged him for a lawyer, from his bad manners and his car. He could have been a doctor, but the Mercedes did not have MD plates. And I knew he wasn't a Wall Street guy; they're friendlier, salesmen at heart. I was a salesman at heart. But I wasn't feeling friendly. "Who's paying you to dredge up my past?"

"I'm offering you a job."

"A job? What do you mean, a job? Doing what?"

"Mr. Long is my client. I want you to shoot a video of Mrs. Long screwing her boyfriend."

I laughed.

"You think I'm joking?"

"I always assumed there were professionals who did that for a living."

"There are, and were she balling this guy in New York I would employ them. But I don't know anyone I can trust to go rooting around up here in the woods without getting caught by the local cops."

"That's not a problem," I said. "We have one resident state trooper to patrol sixty square miles of township. Tell your people they're safe as long as they don't fall into his radar trap."

"I'm serious," said Rose. "The Long house is way out in the boonies. I need a local man. A real 'woody.' I'll pay you two thousand dollars for a half hour of clear videotape."

"Two thousand?" I laughed again. "I'll introduce you to a woody who'll do it for two hundred and burn the house down for another fifty." I had in mind one of the Chevalley boys.

"I want a man with a head on his shoulders, not some damned redneck swamp Yankee."

He was mixing his regional slurs. I let him, just as earlier I had not interfered when he mispronounced Newbury like the fruit instead of the cheese. Neither a berry nor an event in a graveyard, we are, properly, *Newbrie*.

"I'm not a cameraman."

"It's just a Sony camcorder. A kid could use it."

"I'm trying to tell you as clearly as I can that I'm not interested in taking dirty pictures." Actually, I was intrigued. I could certainly use two thousand dollars, and playing detective sounded like fun, provided one didn't break one's neck falling off the lady's roof. But I had enough troubles, reputation-wise, without it getting around town that Ben Abbott had turned into a Peeping Tom.

"Three thousand dollars."

I walked to my car. "I've got to get back to town, Mr. Rose."

He got in and we drove out of there, and it was my turn to be silent. Rose got talkative. He remarked on the trees, the river, the horses, even the hard kick in the back when I passed a station wagon on a short straight. "What kind of car is this?" This last, an artless prelude to fulsome praise, as its name was printed in raised letters on the dashboard.

"Oldsmobile." Cars I would talk about.

"I didn't realize they were so powerful."

"Caddy engine. Bored and stroked. Eats BMWs for breakfast—Son. Of. A. *Bitch!*"

"What's wrong?"

I slowed down and pulled over, my mirrors sparkling like the Fourth of July. Trooper Oliver Moody, who should have been down at the high school at this hour instead of hiding behind a Northeast Utilities truck, swaggered out of his state police cruiser, already writing the ticket with my name on it that he kept in his glove compartment. He danced me through the procedure, enjoying every moment, handed back my license and registration, and advised me I could pay the eighty-dollar fine at Town Hall.

Rose said, "I thought they didn't ticket locals."

"We're not friends."

Oliver burned rubber out of there with an ironic salute, and I continued driving, silently, into town.

"I know what you're thinking," said Rose. "You're thinking that back when you worked on the Street three grand was chump change."

Actually, I was thinking I could get the barn winterized.

At the flagpole, Rose said, "Four thousand dollars and that's my final offer."

The money was sounding better and better. I couldn't deny I could use it. Nor could I deny the occasional restless night when Newbury was quieter than death and my decision to come "home" to put my life back together seemed a sort of voluntary house arrest. I was far from saying yes, but why not pump Rose a little to find out what was going on?

"I ask you again, why me?"

"For crissake," Rose exploded. "You want me to paint a picture? Mr. Long goes first class. He believes that he gets what he pays for. He doesn't question my fees, he only expects me to get the job done. He can afford it. Are you beginning to register what I'm talking about?"

"You bill him cost-plus."

"Exactly like you when you ran leveraged buyouts. There's so much money flying around who's going to question fees?"

"And I'm 'first class' because I went to prison?"

"The word is you did time because you wouldn't rat on your friends. Loyalty's valuable. The fact you got out alive says you learned to handle yourself. That's an asset, too."

"Tell your boss if he ever finds himself in a similar position, treat it like Outward Bound."

"The jail thing is my opinion. What turns Mr. Long on is your ONI background. He ate that up."

"It takes a civilian to really appreciate the military."

"He fought in 'Nam."

"Tell him I spent most of my time investigating sex-bias complaints."

"Terrific training for P.I. work—you could probably get your license. Wha'd you investigate the rest of the time?"

I didn't answer.

"Thought so," said Rose. Another eighteen-wheeler wink implied we both knew that real men do not betray secret submarine landings on the Baltic Coast. For all his heavy-handed flattery, I still wasn't a hundred percent sure why he wanted me. That might be part of the fun. And I had a feeling if I opened the door without speaking, he'd up his offer.

I opened the door.

"Five thousand."

2

The wildest thing my father ever did in his good and orderly life was marry my mother, Margot Chevalley—bastardized "Chevalier" in New England, where folks never needed black people to dump on because they already had the French.

Centuries before the railroad, Newbury had a wrong side of the tracks, named Frenchtown. Mother's people farmed outside of Frenchtown, on a hodgepodge of swamp and cold north slopes. After my father died she moved back to the farm, leaving me the big white Georgian house on Main Street, with the shingle out front, office in a glass porch, and a red barn in the back yard.

Alex Rose, P.I., wrote a down-payment check for five thousand dollars and extended it with a flourish. "Sorry I can't do this in cash."

"Makes no difference to me," I said. "It's going straight to the bank."

"Mr. Long likes his paperwork."

He opened a leather shoulder bag he had brought in from his Mercedes and took out the camcorder. "Maybe you want to practice a little in the back yard, but it's real simple. It's got a little computer that adjusts for your hand shaking."

"Why would I be shaking?"

He answered me seriously, explaining that everyone's hands shake and that when the Japanese made the camera so small it could be held in one hand, they discovered that they had to compensate for that one hand shaking. He demonstrated.

"What's that red light?"

"Indicates you're taping."

"I don't think that's a very good idea."

"So you know it's working."

"You've indicated that you want me to shoot through a window at night, while hiding in the woods. Let's assume that in the midst of entertaining her boyfriend, Mrs. Long glances at the window, perhaps to enjoy their reflection in the glass, and sees instead this little red light in the woods."

"Okay, I see what you mean. Put some tape over it."

"Terrific idea." I was indeed loving this whole concept less and less. It seemed I'd gotten caught up in negotiating a price instead of questioning the deal—an old 'Eighties habit that apparently died hard.

"You know, I don't get the point of this. New York and Connecticut are both shared-property states. What does Mr. Long get out of a video of his wife cheating on him? She still has the protection of equal distribution. She won't lose it all for getting caught."

Rose looked superior and said, "Divorce law is a little more complicated than that, Mr. Abbott."

I was about to retort that realtors, who end up selling the debris of broken marriages, are intimately familiar with divorce law, but at that second a scrawny eleven-year-old with a shy, crooked-tooth grin darted into my office like a muskrat. "Mom wants to know if you'll have supper with us tonight."

"Tell your mom thank you very much. I would be delighted. And what can I bring? You come back and tell me. This is Mr. Rose, up from New York looking at houses. This is my neighbor, Alison Mealy."

Alison froze.

I said, "Say hello to Mr. Rose and shake his hand."

Rose had the wit to extend his hand, and the child did her part.

She saw his camera, and her eyes grew big. I handed it to her. "Go take some pictures of your mother cooking supper."

Rose blanched as his camera went out the door at a high rate of speed. He watched Alison run down the driveway.

"She's taking it into the barn."

"She lives there."

"You rent it out?"

I said yes, because it was easier, though I was surprised that in his snooping around town about me he hadn't heard several versions of how Alison and her mother happened to live in my barn.

Rose said, "Do you own a gun?"

"Why?"

"Something small you could carry with you?"

"What for?"

"This guy Mrs. Long is seeing has been known to get a little violent."

"A little violent. You mean like if he gets pissed off because he sees a man in the woods taking his picture through the window?"

"Obviously, the best thing is don't get caught. But just in case, you might be well advised to be prepared."

I slid his money across the desk, toward him. "I feel well advised to turn down the job. Thank you very much. If you're ever in the market for a home in Newbury, please call for an appointment. As you know, Abbott Realty has a lock on the older, finer, bigger places." I stood up and extended my hand.

Rose looked appalled. "Wait a minute. We have a deal."

"We have not shaken on it. You put money on my desk and then tell me I need a gun. There was no gun in the original deal. So we don't have a deal."

"The gun was just an idea. Some people like guns. Obviously, you don't."

"I love guns. I admire good machinery. If I wanted to shoot people I would be a policeman. Goodbye, Rose. You got the wrong guy."

I felt relieved. The more I thought about taking pictures of some poor couple making love, the more it sounded like a lousy way to earn a buck. Even five thousand bucks.

Rose looked sick, like a guy who had blown a really big deal. That was puzzling because what the hell were we talking about, but a silly little job anybody who wanted to could do? In fact, he seemed so worried and upset that I got curious. "Are you Long's investigator for everything, or just the divorce?"

"Anything he needs."

What I was beginning to understand was that Rose was a high-priced gofer, the sort that guys who can afford to keep around for convenience. In this case, he'd get the video and dig up other stuff in New York and *then* carry their evidence to a shark divorce attorney, who'd hint that maybe Mrs. Long would forgo her half of the stock option. At least that was how men got out of marriage when I worked on the Street.

Rose proved to be a shrewd, high-priced gofer worth his fee. He grinned. "Your little neighbor needs braces."

"What?" I can usually count on my face not to advertise what I'm thinking, but when the detective came that far from left field, I must have looked as dumbfounded as the hero of a Ross Perot infomercial. I didn't know what the hell Alison's teeth had to do with a sexy home video.

Rose, however, saw a connection he could run with. "The little girl who lives in your barn needs her teeth fixed before she grows up ugly."

I regained control of my face, but not the situation. He was right. Alison made a cute tomboy, but she would end up hiding her smile as she got older. "So?"

"I got a client who's the absolutely number-one orthodontist in New York City. East Side parents register their kids at conception to get an appointment. You do the job, I'll take care of the girl's teeth, transportation down to New York, visits on the weekends at his country house in New Milford. Whatever works. We're talking thousands here, fella, if you had to pay for it."

Many thousands.

"Who is this guy?"

"What guy?"

"That Mrs. Long is sleeping with."

"Just a guy. Somebody she and her husband have known a long time."

"What's his name?"

"You don't need to know, fella. None of your damned business."

I made a point of looking very dubious.

Rose laughed. "What, you think maybe I'm setting you up to video somebody famous?"

"That would be one reason to offer so much money."

Rose sighed elaborately, like a bored fight manager reminding a semiconscious client that his right was never his best lead. "I thought I already explained that Mr. Long pays for first-class service— Look, Abbott, I'll tell you what. Make you a deal."

I waited.

Rose winked. "If it turns out she's screwing President Clinton or Robert Redford, don't film 'em. If not, do the job, take the money, and give little Alison a break. She'll thank you for the rest of her life."

I knew when I was beaten. So did Rose. He said, "They'll be at the house, tonight."

"Then I'll do it tonight."

"That's the spirit."

"Spirit's got nothing to do with it. The moon's getting full. Any brighter and they'll spot me."

I walked Rose to his car and ran his money over to the bank. Then I called up John Butler and told him I was ready to insulate the barn.

I had accepted the supper invitation from Alison's mother with no illusions. Janet Mealy was a thin pale weary country girl of twenty-six, old beyond her years. She had borne Alison at fifteen, trading a drunken father for a drunken husband. She had worked waiting tables in a diner up on Route 4 and had had a few factory jobs in Torrington, a wolf-at-the-door existence where all could be lost with a single missed paycheck.

For a brief interlude of hope and tranquility, her husband had landed a job driving a Newbury snowplow, only to get jailed soon after for stealing parts from the township garage. From there it was a quick tumble to welfare and sudden homelessness.

I'd come across them last spring out on Route 7, hitchhiking, hoping to find work in a New Milford motel that I had already heard was going out of business. I was definitely not in the market for roommates. But the sight of Janet Mealy's stringy hair turning dark in the rain, the bundle of plastic shopping bags at their feet, and her bone-white arm wrapped fearfully around Alison's shoulder, pretty much eliminated any options in the matter. I took them home and put them in the barn, which had a crude whitewashed apartment last lived in by my great-grandfather's stable hand, Haughton Moody.

Janet was old New England, daughter of ten generations of hardscrabble farmers, and always addressed me as "Mr. Abbott" in deference to my family, my house on Main Street, and the social gulf that stretched between us. She expected me to call her "Mrs. Mealy" to honor her marriage and her hope that Alison's father might one day come home sober. Alison, of course, called me "Ben" as soon as we became friends, but the quaint titles of courtesy her mother and I shared allowed "Mrs. Mealy" and "Mr. Abbott" their privacy and dignity.

Talk around town ran the gamut nonetheless.

Horny gossips said the barn was a front and Mrs. Mealy actually slept in my own fourposter, while busybodies with a Marxist bent claimed that she worked as a slave, cleaning the houses I tried to sell. The truth was it had been her idea to clean the empty houses I had on the market, which amounted to some light dusting. We would drive out in excruciating silence. She'd demolish spider webs while I mowed the lawns with the vague hope that some buyer would appear by magic, exclaiming, "What perfect grass! How well-dusted! We'll buy it!"

So I had no illusions about supper. Mrs. Mealy inclined toward prepared foods, like frozen baked potatoes. Gently as I could, I would try to demonstrate how two of them cost more than a five-pound sack of the real thing. But she was proud, or maybe the fancy packaging made her feel good. We ate frozen baked potatoes, fried preformed hamburger patties, and fresh spinach, which I had taught Alison to pick from my garden and rinse of sand. Dessert was the specialty of the house, Cool Whip on Jell-O.

We trooped after supper to my house and popped into the VCR the footage Alison had shot of her mother cooking. Janet Mealy hid her face in her hands, then peeped between her fingers when Alison said, "Mom, you look great." And she did. After a painful moment of ducking the camera, she turned into a star, tearing open the potato package, frying the burgers, with sidelong glances at the camera. Her big, sad eyes were her prettiest feature and they shone on the screen. Alison, who had been plowing through my paperbacks all summer, searched for the right word. "You're *exotic*, Mom."

"Hush."

Suddenly Alison herself jumped into the picture, making faces as the lens zoomed in and out.

"How'd you do that?" I asked.

"The remote, silly. See the thing I'm pointing at the camera?"

I saw she was waving a remote-control device, demonstrating her natural aptitude for electronic gear—and reminding me that somehow I had to get hold of a secondhand computer for the kid, and some tools so she could take it apart. She had already fixed my VCR with a screwdriver and a hammer, so I felt she had some future in the field.

Alison wanted to watch the tape again. I left them to it, anxious to get over to Morrisville while there was still daylight enough to get the lay of the land. I loaded a fresh tape into the camcorder and changed into jeans, a dark sweater, and my Raichle Swiss climbing boots, which I had purchased way back when for a junk-bond seminar in Aspen and wore these days to split firewood.

I stepped outside to spray my hair and hands with Deep Woods OFF! and spread some on my face. Then I went upstairs and took a couple of pocket flashlights from my night table. There was a gun in the drawer. My father, who had collected guns, slept with a .38 beside the bed as he got older. It was a fine old piece, ideal weight to pack while filming lovers from the woods, but I left it.

I am next to helpless with a handgun. My father kept promising to teach me to shoot, but he didn't, and it fell to my uncles, who favored hunting weapons. Besides, I seriously doubted that Mrs. Long's fella would come gunning for me, and if he did the best defense would be to bolt into the dark or politely raise my hands. If he came out throwing indignant punches, I wouldn't need a gun.

Route 349 runs east from the flagpole over the hill to Morrisville. North of the road lies Frenchtown, south is a long, rolling slope, home to the bigger estates and horse farms, a section divided by an invisible and totally meaningless Newbury-Morrisville line. Many places straddle the line. The Castle was just east of it, down a dirt road with woods on one side and pasture on the other, neatly defined with white board fences.

It was immediately apparent that the Longs were not suffering from recession. Money had been spent, and was still being spent on upkeep and expansion. Before I reached the house I passed restored barns and silos that made a postcard picture, catching the golden light of a soon-to-set sun. Then the woods on the left began to sheer up the slope opening to broad meadow that blended into a wide lawn that rose to a stone fantasy straight out of *Ivanhoe.*

It really did have a turret. I'd always assumed the talk of a turret was an exaggeration, but up one corner rose a round stone tower, with a conical roof and narrow windows suitable for sheltering archers. I wondered how they'd slipped it by the building inspector. Newbury had a thirty-seven-foot height limit to keep the countryside from being blighted, but the Longs' must have topped sixty feet. Actually, it worked, nicely, even with no moat.

Ninety-nine percent of the new houses I try to sell have been "landscaped" after they're built. It's the commonest mistake, and the most glaring. One look at the Longs' place and you knew that a savvy landscape designer had sited it before a bulldozer was allowed on the property. What could have looked like an oversized, pretentious pile had been rendered romantic—not by the silly crenelations or the too-tall turret, but by being placed perfectly on the edge of the woods. To the south the upstairs rooms would enjoy wonderful views of the hill rambling down to the river. But in back the woods cozied things down to a pleasant scale. Grand, but livable, in a stand of dark, dark cedars. The back rooms, I imagined, would feel like a tree house, the sloped forest looming kindly and mysterious.

I saw two problems right away. The lady's bedroom was probably in front, to take advantage of the views, while my best shot would be shooting down from the woods. Second problem was what to do with the car. Everybody knows everybody's car around here. I drove back to 349, cruised around until it got dark, then stashed it behind one of the Longs' decorative barns and walked.

The night was soft, warm, and quiet. We'd had our first frost earlier in the week, and it sounded as if a lot of the bugs had packed it in for the winter. A mosquito found me, but the OFF! held her off until she eventually lost interest.

I had rerigged the camcorder's shoulder bag so I could strap it around my waist, leaving my hands free, and clipped the penlights into the breast pocket of the jeans jacket I wore over my sweater. The Raichles made more noise on the dirt road than running shoes would have, a tradeoff for the support they'd give on rough ground.

A car came up behind me. High beams reflecting on the overhead electric wires gave me plenty of warning to get behind a tree. Oliver Moody's cruiser, working late; but then Ollie always did like haunting the back roads. I watched his taillights with one eye closed until he was gone, then eased back onto the road, like an outlaw.

It had been a long time since I'd gone walking in the dark, probably as long ago as before I'd got my license. As kids, we'd walk forever on weekend nights, hoping something would happen. Newbury was a great place for little children and adults. But were you between the ages of fifteen and thirty Newbury could be dull as a cement wall, unless you had the balls to cook up some excitement. It was kind of fun to have mine back—yet another reason I had agreed to take this job against my better judgment.

The few dimly lit windows in the Castle were mostly on the second floor, hinting that Mrs. Long and her boyfriend were heading for bed. I stuffed my pants cuffs inside my socks against the deer ticks and cut across the meadow to the lawn, which was smooth as a putting green. I circled behind the house, hugging the woods as I climbed the slope.

A figure—it looked to be a man—passed across a second-floor window, thirty feet from where I was catching my breath after the steep climb. The house was tucked so close to the woods and the slope was so steep that I was literally standing above the second floor, looking down through the back windows.

He came back the other way, carrying a pair of wineglasses. I crouched down to scope out the floor plan. He had apparently come up a back stair from the kitchen—this was all happening in the center of the house and the window I saw him in seemed to light a hall-way. I headed left along the woods, paralleling the direction he had gone. At the end of the house an odd, square structure bulked up out of the pitched roof. I puzzled out that the crenelations were a false front, behind which the roof pitched down to the second floor. The thing at the end was a big, square dormer.

White light exploded in my face—bright as the sun. I dived into the woods, thinking that they had seen me and turned on the security floods. Blinded and confused, I crawled through shrubs and bri-ars, fleeing by animal instinct for the deeper shadows. I banged into something solid, a huge tree, scrambled behind it, and tried to figure out where to run next.

But no one shouted. No attack hounds bellowed up the slope. No one started shooting. I peeked around the tree and saw that the light source was not security floods, but a wall of glass, lit from within. The square dormer that spoiled the roofline housed an artist's stu-dio, a huge, lofty bare white room. Clearly someone had finally taken the architect in hand and said, Okay, you've got your turret, your crenelations, your moat and goddamned drawbridge, now what I need in the back of this fantasy is an old-fashioned Green-wich Village studio with high windows facing north; no one will even see it unless they're sneaking around in the woods.

I found myself liking the house more; the studio lent it purpose. There was something no-nonsense about it. A huge canvas was propped on an enormous easel, draped with a bedsheet. Next to it, a small easel that held a blank sketchpad faced a low platform.

A pair of shadows leaped on the walls. For a moment, I was back in Manhattan, beside a perfumed woman in a darkened theater, waiting for a play to begin.

3

Naked, the boyfriend, the one Rose said tended to violence, looked like a guy who enjoyed working out. His shoulders, broad chest, and upper arms were heavily muscled, his waist and hips model-trim. He was not, however, a professional model. He mounted the platform a little clumsily, threw his arms apart in a self-conscious way, and grinned at someone who I assumed cared for him, because otherwise a ready and willing erection was going to go to waste.

He looked very happy—a young, happy, naked clean-shaven guy with white-blond hair. I was reaching belatedly for the camcorder when Mrs. Long strode into view, her back to me, and fully clothed in a long, flowing silvery blouse over jeans. Only her feet were bare. Rose had called her a brunette, which hardly conveyed the Oriental splendor of the inky black hair that fell shining down her back.

By the time I unlimbered the camera, Mrs. Long was hard at work with a pencil. Zooming the lens over her shoulder, I could see the drawing as clearly as she could. She quickly established the bulge and swell of the muscles on his chest and worked her way down his flat belly. I panned the sketch, the easel, unzoomed to take in her standing before it, swept the studio, then zoomed in on his body and face. I got back to the sketch in time to see her hesitate.

She had done his waist and brought life to his legs with uncommon skill, catching their main lines before she concentrated on his muscles. He was still standing as before, a little awkward, and undoubtedly uncomfortable. Holding the pose with his arms apart, he must have been getting tired, if his wilting erection were any clue. It was there at the groin that she had hesitated.

Suddenly she went for the face. I let go the trigger. He had a broad, almost round face, but on drawing paper only his pathologist would ever know him. Instead of his face, she sketched his skull. She drew cheekbones, but no cheeks, brow ridges, but no brow, no hair, no eyes, only their sockets. She did his teeth in jagged strokes, a bony jaw, and the short, split bone of a fleshless nose. I shivered. She was so skilled she seemed to peer through his skin, into his future.

She put down her pencil and started toward him. By now my camera was dangling from one hand. He too was down to half mast. He watched her come toward him and smiled with an anticipation he might not have felt had he seen how she had rendered his face. I was beginning to wonder about Mrs. Long, but her boyfriend had no doubts. He jumped down from the platform, scooped her into his arms, and kissed her. They kissed awhile, which I dutifully recorded, though from the back he could have been kissing any woman with beautiful black hair. They broke at last, and now when he hugged her, I could see by his expression that he probably wouldn't give a damn what she sketched on paper.

She pushed him back onto the stage, gestured that he should spread his arms again. I fired up the camera, anticipating her next move by the one remaining blank on her drawing paper. Sure enough, slowly unbuttoning her blouse, she let it slither off her shoulders. There are fashion-model square clotheshorse shoulders, and there are courtesan shoulders like Rubens painted. Mrs. Long had round, white courtesan shoulders. How she looked in front could be assumed by her boyfriend's eager "Yes, yes, yes," clearly audible through the open casement window.

She laughed and did a little shimmy that could have gotten her a job dancing hiphop for Madonna. Her shirt slid off her back, a smooth, white, very beautiful back with twin rounds of muscle softly rimming her spine.

"Yes! Yes! Yes!"

"Don't move!"

She stepped closer, bent her head.

Her hair blocked the camera, but there wasn't a divorce court in the nation that wouldn't get the picture. Her boyfriend cried out. He reached for her. She pushed his hands back in position. He laughed. Mrs. Long stepped back, leaving him rigid and glistening, and whirled to the easel.

It was my turn to cry out—an up-from-the-gut gasp of astonishment at my first glimpse of her face. I had never seen a woman so beautiful or so happy. She had a heart-shaped feminine face with a high brow, wide-set cheekbones, a strong nose, and enormous blue eyes. There was a fine quality to her bone structure that made me think of Norwegian blood, despite her jet-black hair. Blue eyes, black hair, maybe Irish, maybe Scots, who knew? Who cared? Her lips were full and wet, and when she laughed she radiated joy.

I ripped the video cartridge from the camera and threw it into the woods.

I felt redeemed, for a fraction of a second: I had come too close to doing a terrible thing to a couple of happy people—a far worse sin than sacrificing little Alison's braces—and I saw Rose's spy job for the dirty job it had been all along.

Then the damned tape hit a tree—with a surprisingly loud *bonk*—and bounced onto the lawn. The cartridge was made of black plastic, except for the white label on the face, and sure enough it landed face up, gleaming in the light from the window. If they didn't find it, the lawn-mowing guys would hand it to the husband.

Mrs. Long had apparently caught the *bonk* through the open window. I heard her say, "What was that?"

I scrambled after the cartridge, hugging the woods. I was nearly to it, crouching across the cut grass, when she cried, "Raccoons! Raccoons. Turn on the light."

Fortunately, he didn't know his way around the house that well, and it took him an extra moment to find the switch, during which time I slid down the slope, grabbed the videotape, and started scrambling for cover. I almost made it. In fact my head and shoulders were in the dark space between two bushes. Then he found the outside floodlights switch, and suddenly the back yard was bright enough to land helicopters.

"Look! It's a *bear*."

"That's no bear. It's some son of a bitch hiding in your woods. Hey!"

"No."

"Yes."

Deep in shadow, at last, I glanced back. He was leaning out the window. She was pulling him back. "What if he has a gun?" Then she acted like a smart city girl. Instead of hauling out her own gun, or setting a dog on me, she ran to a security keypad embedded in the wall and pushed the panic button on her burglar alarm.

More lights. They blazed down from the roof and lit three acres, some flashing, while a siren began whooping loud enough to alert the next county. It was one of those *ah-whooo, ah-whooo* klaxons straight out of *The Hunt for Red October*, and I would not have been surprised to see Sean Connery submerge the Castle to a hundred fathoms. Nor would I doubt that the burglar alarm also sounded in the alarm company's New Milford office, where they would immediately dispatch a car, and alert Oliver Moody that someone was housebreaking on his turf. Oliver would respond first, armed and dangerous. I ran, tripped on a fallen limb, and fell face down, crunching my knee on a piece of granite ledge.

I have felt real pain twice in my life, but nothing like what I felt then. It was as if someone had driven a three-eighths drill through my kneecap, backed it out, and hammered in a rusty spike. I went blank for several seconds, dead to the world except for the siren, which grew faint. Then I started to vomit.

I held it down, ground my teeth, and dragged myself deeper into the shadows. The siren kept shrieking, throwing up walls of sound, and I thought I heard them arguing behind it. He wanted to come looking for me. She was saying no, hide. I worked at getting my breath back. And when I had, and my heart was slowing a little, I tried to bend my knee.

It moved. Not a lot, and not without considerable pain. But I'd be able to walk to my car—in a half hour or so—if I took it real easy and walked on the level road.

Inside the studio, Mrs. Long took charge again.

She strode first to the security keypad and punched in a code that stopped the siren abruptly, leaving an *ah-whoo, ah-whoo* echoing in my ears. Then she put on her blouse and went to the open window where her boyfriend was peering intently into the dark, and took his arm.

"Lock yourself in our room. I'll deal with the cops."

He protested.

She said, "I'll be fine. Here they come now. Go!"

I heard it too, across the hills the urgent scream of a state police siren. And on the low ends of the siren, the spectacular roar of a fullblown Plymouth Fury flat out.

Even if I ditched the camera and hid the tape, what possible explanation could I offer for trespassing in Mrs. Long's woods in the middle of the night? And even if Oliver didn't arrest me—fantasy, because he would find some charge, having waited twenty years for the opportunity—my name would be wrecked once again, and once and for all, in the town, which would put me out of business. You can't make money selling houses without listings. A number of straitlaced people had been very kind when I came home—kind perhaps to the memory of my father, kind nonetheless to give me their business. But two strikes and I was out. This stupid lark was about to finish me.

I stood up, took a step and fell down. It hurt like hell, but I knew nothing was broken. I just needed time. Oliver's siren got loud and his lights came bumping across the Longs' meadow as he careened into their driveway. I backed up the wooded slope, pulling myself along from tree trunk to tree trunk, getting nowhere fast. A wolf tree loomed, a huge, fat red oak, a sentinel standing alone, older than the second-growth stuff around it. Its lower limbs were dead, but enormous, barely clearing the ground that sloped up behind the tree. I got my hands around one, swung, and tugged myself up onto it. Then, clutching the main trunk, I climbed another and perched precariously on the backside of the tree, fifteen feet above the forest floor, some twenty or thirty feet in from the floodlit lawn. I peered around the trunk.

Oliver had gone in the front door and now he came out the back, wielding a five-cell Mag light, the brilliant halogen type about two feet long with instructions from the maker that it is not to be used as an "impact" instrument. "Stay inside!" he commanded Mrs. Long.

He started up the slope. He held the light in his left hand. His right hovered near his holstered gun.

4

Resident state troopers are a special breed, part Lone Ranger, part schoolyard bully. They rule the law-abiding in their vast territory by moral presence, and the lawbreakers by fear. Oliver Moody, who stood six-five and weighed two hundred and sixty pounds, came up the slope like an armored personnel carrier. He was ten years older than me, but I suspected that in a footrace up the hill, he'd be waiting for me on top with his impact instrument.

I sat tight and watched, shooting glances around my tree. He moved cautiously through the undergrowth, playing the flashlight on the shadows. To my relief, he was looking at man height, not tree height. Slowly, I forced the wounded knee to bend, wondering if I would ever straighten it out again.

Oliver stopped. He aimed his light at something on the ground. He studied it, picked it up, and pocketed it. I couldn't see what he had found. Then, with one last pass through the brush, he started back to the house.

Something yowled in the treetops, crashed through the leaf canopy, and landed, thrashing and crying on the end of the limb I was sitting on. When it caught its balance and turned toward me, I saw in the moonlight the masked face of a raccoon. Oliver came pounding up the slope.

I am not unaware of the comic nature of the preceding events, but I wasn't laughing. Raccoons don't fall out of trees unless something is wrong with them, and we were in the thick of a rabies epidemic. Rabies turns them lethally unpredictable—frightened in one instance, aggressive in another. When he saw Oliver's halogen beam darting between the tree trunks, he backed away, closer to me. Finally, he sensed me and growled. I pointed the camera at him. He retreated back from where he came only to get hit square in the face by the light.

He was a horrible sight; he had clawed his own stomach open in his agony. He bared his teeth and growled down at the state trooper, who had come to a halt a few feet below.

"Oh, you poor son of a bitch," said Oliver. "Now you just sit still. In a minute everything's going to be fine."

From the house, Mrs. Long called, "Are you all right, Officer?"

"Found your prowler," Oliver called over his shoulder. "Rabid raccoon. Go get a plastic garbage bag and stay inside until I call you."

I pressed like bark against the tree, praying he wouldn't see me and hoping he wouldn't splatter rabid raccoon all over me with the cannon he wore at his waist. Then Oliver, who was, for a mean, simple bully, one surprise after another, gave up another one. He glanced back, making sure Mrs. Long couldn't see him, and reached down and pulled a little Beretta .22 from an ankle holster concealed under his pants. In all the years I had known him, I never knew, and no one ever said, that he carried a backup weapon. You learn something every day.

It was the right gun for the raccoon. Holding his light in one hand and the gun in his other, Oliver caught the animal's attention by talking to it, telling it everything would work out fine, and shot him neatly through the head. It fell at his feet.

"Bring the bag," Oliver called.

Mrs. Long ran up her grassy slope; Oliver met her at the edge of the woods. Taking care not to touch the animal with his bare hands, he worked the bag around it and tied it shut. Then he sauntered down to the house, trailing the bag.

"What are you going to do with it?" asked Mrs. Long.

"Landfill." He walked around the house, slammed the Fury's door and drove off, as the burglar-alarm company's van raced up with a funny little blinking light on the roof.

There were lights in Town Hall, burning late as usual in the first selectman's office. As I drove past on deserted Main Street, the clock bonged eleven—amazingly early, considering my night so far.

My answering machine was blinking.

I went straight to the bourbon. Then I put the tape in the VCR and ran it on RECORD to erase it. I remembered Nixon and his missing eighteen minutes and wondered whether erased video recordings could be restored by computer enhancement. I played the tape on the TV: blizzards of snow. But what if Rose suspected I'd shot some footage before I got religion, and spent a bunch of Mr. Long's money on a rocket scientist hacker? What if the genius found Mrs. Long and her fella romping between the electrons?

I couldn't trash it. Recycling's very big up here, and a discarded video cartridge would be just the thing to catch the sanitation officer's eye. I was getting a little paranoid, but having decided not to participate in the Long divorce, I did not want to blow it by accident. If I had had a big fire burning in the hearth I could have burned it, I suppose, but it would have stunk to high heaven. So I hid it. Compared to a cell, a big old house has more stash holes than a maze.

I poured another drink and listened to my messages. No buyers had called, no brokers trolling Multiple Listings, not even an impatient New York detective. The only message was from Town Hall. Newbury's first selectman, a young woman named Vicky McLachlan, had phoned a reality reminder:

"A real estate broker who loses his driver's license for speeding is like a crow with one wing."

Vicky and I had been what were called in my Aunt Connie's day "dear friends."

We were two of the few single people in town in our age range and who liked each other's looks. Our mutual interest extended to my respect and admiration for her achievements and ambition and her slight awe of my multifaceted past. I think deep in her heart she regarded me as an interesting pet, the sort you'd keep in the barn. But her bio-clock was ticking and cast on me an unnatural glow, like the dark red blush from a bedside alarm that made me look better than I was.

I kept telling her that bright young politicians with a shot at the state legislature, and maybe governor by age forty, ought not to be seen hanging out with convicted felons, jailbirds, and other such riffraff. My noble sacrifice for the sake of good government had apparently had its effect. We hadn't seen each other in weeks.

But Mrs. Long and her happy fella had left me a little unsettled. In fact, I felt lonely, which was not usually my way. So I limped out of the house and up Main Street and stood outside Town Hall awhile, thinking, Well, maybe no harm in saying hello. Persuaded, I slipped in the unlocked side door, crossed the dark lobby, stuck my head in the first selectman's office, and rapped on the door frame.

"Got your message. Good to hear your voice."

Vicky looked up from her heaped desk. She was a small and angular fine-featured woman whose enormous, curliqued thicket of chestnut hair made her seem bigger than she was. It caught the light in many hues of gold and brown and stood her handsomely in photographs; nor did she ever go unnoticed on the campaign trail. Pinned to her bulletin board under a sign that read "About Time" was a newspaper photo of the president's wife lobbying three femininely dressed U.S. Representatives.

"You know darned well you can't afford to pay your ticket."

"Any chance of working it off with some community service?"

She said, "I'm too tired and hungry," but she said it with a smile. If Vicky's hair got her noticed, her smile won her votes. It was warm and quick and straight from the heart, a smile that seemed to promise each and every voter, I am hardworking and honest and the only difference between us is that you don't have the time to run the government, so I'll do it for you. A seductive smile.

"How about I cook you an omelet?"

"I don't want an omelet."

"Welsh rarebit and beer?"

I knew my woman. She practically rolled over and kicked her feet in the air.

"Come here. Let me look at you."

I did.

"You're limping," she said.

"Hurt my knee."

"You look like hell. You look like you've been sleeping in the woods. There's *pine needles* in your hair." She reached up and brushed them out. They fell on her desk.

She was good company when she wasn't too busy, but she was busy most of the time. And she was sexy in the easygoing way women get when they feel free to pick and choose with whom, where, and when. As for where, she was happier at her place, a tiny cottage secreted behind the Congregational Church. It had a kind of a kitchen-living room about the size of a Chevy Blazer, and a somewhat bigger bedroom, which the word *boudoir* would have described perfectly, if the down and lace coverlet weren't usually buried under paperwork.

"I'll just straighten up while you cook."

We had stopped at my place for beer and ingredients. I opened a couple of St. Pauli Girls and started melting cheese on the stove.

"So how'd you hurt your knee?"

"Keep a secret?"

She came out, wide-eyed. "Sure. What'd you do?"

"This goes no further. No kidding."

"I swear on the souls of my unborn children. Come on, Ben. What's going on?"

"A detective hired me to videotape a couple committing adultery." She looked puzzled.

"It's a divorce case."

"You took *dirty* pictures?"

"I didn't. I was supposed to. I mean I agreed to. But I didn't."

"You're weird, Ben."

"It seemed like a good idea at the time. Turned out it wasn't. I couldn't do it."

"I should hope not."

I told her about Alex Rose, and Alison Mealy's braces, and how the evening had gone downhill from there, leaving out the precise reason I had stopped filming. The raccoon sent her into stitches, until I told her how Oliver had shot him. She got misty-eyed.

"Had to put him out of his misery."

"I know, I know. It's just that it's so sad, they're just living their lives and along comes this disease they've no defense against and we shoot them."

Vicky had grown up in a big Irish-Catholic family in a close-in suburb and hadn't acquired the sterner eye you get when you farm at the edge of the forest. I said, "Why don't you tell Sally to look into oral vaccines? I read they're experimenting in Belgium."

Sally Butler was the dogcatcher. Rabies vaccine seemed a good way to steer Vicky McLachlan away from the adultery-taping subject, which I saw still troubled her. And later that night, in the dark, she asked, "Why'd you do it?"

"Alison—"

"Don't blame the teeth."

I told her my theory of 'Eighties dealmaking, wherein running the deal became far more important than the results.

"No," she said, "you're always trying to walk on the edge. It's the only thing that excites you."

"I got kind of excited a minute ago. Remember?"

"That wasn't me. You were remembering what you saw through her window."

As I formulated a reply, Vicky rolled over and said she was going to sleep. I moved spoonlike behind her, the way she liked, and kissed her back. It took me too long to realize she was crying.

Newbury celebrates Labor Day the third weekend in September, partly because the bigger towns have huge parades that siphon off the crowd we need to buy tickets to our fire department cookout, and partly because summer shouldn't end on the first Monday of the month. Weatherwise, it's a little risky, as we occasionally celebrate in a sleet storm, but the morning after my exploits at the Longs' dawned warm and sunny as August.

Vicky sent me packing early; she had a speech to rehearse.

I limped home. My machine was blinking. Alex Rose.

I got *his* machine.

He called back.

"So how'd it go?"

"Lousy."

"Yeah?"

"Yeah."

"How lousy? You get caught or something?"

For all I knew he had tapped the Longs' phone lines, in which case he would know the alarm had gone off. I told him the truth, in general terms. "I've decided against a rematch. I'll mail you your camera."

"Hold on."

"And your money," I said, and hung up. The bank was open till noon on Saturday, as was the post office. I bought a blank videotape, went home, wrote Rose a check for his five thousand dollars, packed the camera in its bag in a box some books had come in, stuffed the empty spaces with crumpled newspaper and the spare tapes, and walked the whole thing down to the post office, where I mailed it and insured it for five hundred bucks. Then I went home and cleaned my grill and my long-handled tongs and spatula, and took them to the lawn behind Town Hall.

They'd wheeled out the fire engines for the kids to climb on and hung a banner that read NEWBURY ENGINE COMPANY NO. 1, FOUNDED 1879. Doug Schmidle, the Town Hall custodian, was hammering together a viewing stand. Gary Nello was setting up a soda machine lent by the Yankee Drover. Mildred Gill had rigged a forty-gallon corn boiler, and the ladies of the Newbury Engine Auxiliary were spreading paper plates, ketchup, relish, and mustard on folding tables.

We arranged the cooking grills in order of splendor. First was Rick Bowland's gas-fired volcano-stone, hooded monster that had enough instrument dials and gauges to monitor a public utility. We put him downwind, because he didn't know any better. In the middle was Scooter MacKay at his thirty-six-inch charcoal-burning Weber. Last, and upwind, was mine. I stuck in the extra legs, which raised it to waist height. Rick Bowland nudged Scooter. "What in hell is that thing Ben's got?"

Scooter was not about to take guff from anyone who cooked on bottled gas. He had a big voice. "You know what gets me?" he boomed. "Used to be a man would apologize for buying a gas grill; now the sorry 'suckers don't even understand they weenied out."

"What?"

"You're a lost generation," said Scooter. "Benighted mall babies."

Rick tried to weasel out of it by ragging me. "Yeah, okay, but what is that you got there, Ben?"

"This is a triple-length charcoal grill for cooking meat, chicken, and vegetables out of doors. It's based on a hibachi design. I bought it on sale at Caldor's down in Danbury for nine dollars, and I fully expect old friends to toast marshmallows on it beside my grave."

"Nine dollars?"

I said, "We need a plan. Rick, I'll bet you've got real control of your heat with that baby."

"Believe it."

"Why don't you toast rolls and cook the dogs. Scooter and me'll do the burgers."

"Hey, this thing's great on burgers."

"We'll do the burgers," said Scooter. He's an excellent newspaper publisher, but too free with the Weber's dome, so I said, "I'll do rare, you do medium and well."

At noon Vicky mounted the new pumper to give her speech. Quite a crowd had gathered by then, and the first selectman didn't disappoint. She lionized our brave volunteer firefighters and suggested that when we make our contribution we compare the ease of check writing to the discomforts of waking up in the middle of the night to fight a neighbor's fire. She got a beautiful swipe in at her Republican opposition, likening their control of the state budget to the rabies epidemic, and wound up with a fierce call to every schoolgirl on the lawn that one of them had darned well better become president of the United States.

She ended it on "Let's eat," which swelled the drift toward the grills to a floodtide.

The next hour was a blur of hands thrusting open buns in my direction. I was just holding my own, rare but not raw, with the lines in order. Beside me, Scooter was smoking them medium, raising his dome with billowy flourishes to general applause. Poor Rick started some sort of grease fire that brought the firemen running with a high-pressure hose. Then I had a little fire, which I was knocking down with a water spray bottle, when I heard a harried Scooter say, "Rare? See my colleague at the nine-dollar grill."

I heard Pinkerton Chevalley, Renny's big brother, snicker, "She can have mine rare anytime," and I looked up into the smiling face of Rita Long, who said, "They tell me you're a rare man."

5

Hard to tell how long I stood staring at her.

She asked, "Wha'd I say?" and the fire I'd just put out flared up between us, prompting shouts from Scooter and Rick—who were still downwind—and a threatening advance by the high-pressure hose men, who had apparently found some beer someplace.

"Rare," I said, spatula-ing my best burger onto her bun with my left hand while extending my right to introduce myself. "Ben Abbott. I don't believe we've met."

She had a diet Pepsi in her other hand, but she extended an elbow with a grin, saying, "Rita Long. We're new in town."

"Oh, yes. Fred Gleason found your property."

"Are you a realtor, too? Right, right. I've seen your sign. You have that lovely Georgian house near the flagpole."

I like newcomers. They don't say hello thinking, Bertram Abbott's kid. The one who . . . She just took me as the guy who lived in the Georgian house near the flagpole. God, she was beautiful, lovely as I had seen last night, but now—dressed in pleated khaki pants and a faded workshirt—very much the married lady, friendly, but not flirting. Had I met her this way for the first time I'd have thought, Gorgeous, pleasant, and totally unavailable. Knowing what I did know, I thought, Loyal to her boyfriend, gorgeous, pleasant, and totally unavailable, a woman not about to run around on more than one man.

She asked, "Do you do appraisals?"

"Same as Fred. We're not bank appraisers, but we can certainly recommend a price range. Do you have a friend looking?"

Before she could answer, a greasy hand thrust a hamburger bun between us—Pinkerton Chevalley, availing himself of thirds, and a look down Mrs. Long's shirt. I dripped hot grease on his thumb, but it apparently didn't penetrate the calluses. Mrs. Long had backed away, and now she wandered toward the ketchup table. Pink demolished his third and reached for fourths.

I saw Rita Long look across the lawn with a secret smile, followed her gaze, and there was the boyfriend, munching a hot dog. He flashed a grin and circled through the crowd, pausing to investigate the new pumper, glancing repeatedly in her direction as she moseyed about. I decided they were recent lovers, deep in the eros stage, where every utterance was eloquent, and every motion erotic. And, just as last night, I admired their fun. They must have laughed themselves silly in bed.

He looked maybe a little older than he had in the buff. He wore chinos and a pinstriped shirt with the sleeves rolled up and had an air of being very much in charge of something. He reminded me of a type I'd met when I was working the Street—guys who started a medium-sized business and were looking to raise money to expand; or hotshot managers working a buyout. Only this one was smiling, like he'd already closed his deal. Once when he looked across the lawn at her she was watching some kids, and his face practically melted. In fact a video of his expression would have doomed them worse than last night's. He was nuts for the woman, which I found understandable. She seemed nuts for him too, which meant they had problems. I wondered if they had any inkling that her husband knew.

Mrs. Long came back.

"Another?"

"No thanks, that was great. Listen, do you have time to come out and give me an appraisal?"

"*Your* house?"

She glanced to either side. "Would you?"

I had more time than a retiree, but fair was fair and friends were friends. "Well, Fred Gleason is—"

"I'd like a private opinion."

"Ah."

"Ah?"

I decided that the only way to talk to this woman was to talk as if I had not seen her making love to her boyfriend the night before. Which meant I had to be my totally nonjudgmental realtor self. What was a private opinion? Well, it was not the first time I'd been asked by one side of a marriage to appraise the honeymoon cottage.

I said, "You know, of course, this is a hard time to sell, even a unique house like yours."

"But I would still like an appraisal. I'll pay the going rate."

"No, no, no. I don't work that way. I'll come out and have a look."

"How about after the cookout?"

"I can make it out there by five."

"Perfect. I have to run down to the mall. I'll make it back by five. After you look, it'll be time for a drink."

As I've said, there was nothing flirtatious about Rita Long. Even so, I felt that drinks at the Castle was the best offer I'd had in a week. Vicky McLachlan approached while I was packing up my grill: A bunch were drifting over to the Yankee Drover for post-picnic beers. I said maybe later, but I had to work. I got a look, and a question: "Who's the lady with the black hair?"

"Mrs. Long. She and her husband built the Castle."

That got me another look, and "Nice work if you can get it"—a reminder, not that I needed one, that the future governor of Connecticut had not been elected first selectman at age twenty-six on chestnut curls and smile alone.

I showered the smoke out of my hair and put on my uniform, tweed jacket over my arm in the warm afternoon. I was about to get into the Oldsmobile when I thought, What the hell, last warm day for a while. I stashed the Olds in the barn and pulled the cover off the Fiat. It was a '79 Spyder 2000 roadster, British racing green, that my father had bought new for my mother's sixtieth birthday. It had less than twenty thousand miles on it because my mother felt it was too flashy, no matter how often the old man told her how pretty she looked in it. She did, in fact; but when she moved back to Frenchtown she left it for me.

By daylight the grounds of the Long Castle were something to behold. The driveway paralleled a serpentine pond, complete with snowy egret, which would have done Regent Park proud. The hardscape surrounding the house was splendidly conceived and brilliantly executed.

"Hardscape" isn't in Webster's. It's a word coined by landscape designers to distinguish elements constructed from those that are grown—masonry from nursery, cobblestones from coreopsis. (The designers are divided on the corresponding use of "softscape" for gardens, grass, and trees. The better ones I've known would cross a swamp at night to avoid even hearing the word.) Hardscape is what you see in winter when the flowers are dead and branches bare. It forms the character of a house, like the bones behind a face.

I had heard that the Castle's granite walls and flagstone terraces, the cobblestone motor court, the sweeping drives and the paths that meandered among the as-yet-unplanted garden beds had been built by Italian stonemasons, who usually worked down in Greenwich and Cos Cob. It showed. We've got a few good local masons around Newbury, but there was a finished polish to this work rarely seen north of Long Island Sound. Walls that looked like dry stone had been cemented by an artful hidden-mortar technique; while I could not have slipped my business card between the slates of the front walk.

"I love your car," Rita Long greeted me. She had changed out of her workshirt into a snug cotton sweater. "What is it?"

I told her how I'd gotten it from my mother, and complimented her landscaping and the quality of the stonework. She explained that they had owned a big place in Greenwich. "When we decided to build here, Jack said we should use the workmen we knew. I felt a little funny cutting out the local guys."

"Tough call," I agreed. "Plenty of good mechanics up here, but it's nice to go with people you like. Who's the architect?"

"It was Jack's plan. I drew it, and then we paid an architect to work out the structural details."

"Nice. Who did the outside?"

"I did."

"Really?" I looked again. I don't care how talented an artist is, or how stylish an interior decorator, only one in a million retain their sense of scale outdoors. The sky is simply not a ceiling. I see magnificent houses every day with dinky steps, postage-stamp terraces, misplaced swimming pools, and tennis courts fenced like zoos.

She hurried to explain. "I had wonderful help. The masons saved me from a million mistakes."

I had no trouble imagining a mason making an extra effort for Rita Long. Her smile, the breeze in her hair: "Move this wall? No problem, *Signora*, it is only granite. Guido, *per favore*, the jackhammer."

I glanced up at the turret. The archers' slits were authentically narrow. A few sturdy yeomen could hold off anything up to tanks. "There's a rumor around town that you shoot deer from your turret."

"Oh, God. Jack did. Once last year, during hunting season. I told him I'd shoot *him* if he did it again."

"So the deer are safe."

"From Jack," she laughed. "Guaranteed. Are you ready to see the inside?"

We went in and wandered the many rooms, most of which were still unfurnished. A central staircase lit by skylights was magnificently paneled in rosewood. "Who's the cabinetmaker?"

"It's old. When Jack's mother died, we ransacked her apartment. She had it done in the Nineteen-Twenties or 'Thirties. It was so gloomy there, but here the light makes it work, doesn't it?"

"Sure does."

The kitchen was the sort you find in houses owned by people with endless bucks—the latest everything, the air vibrating with the ceaseless hum of electric motors. It was spotless, with takeout menus from Church Hill Road Shanghai Cafe and our matchless Lorenzo's Pizza Palace on the refrigerator.

The house did not have quite the rumored thirty-seven rooms, but there were three beautiful guest-room suites upstairs and a spectacular master bedroom with a fireplace and his and her bathrooms and his and her walk-in closets and a little attached sitting room-television room also with a fireplace. The bed was magnificent, with French-Canadian antique ironwork at the head and foot, and it would have taken a better man than I not to imagine the matchless Mrs. Long sprawled upon it, smiling through a veil of raven hair.

I could not resist asking, "What's down that hall?"

"Just my studio."

"Do you want me to look at it?"

She hesitated. "Sure. Just a second." She ran ahead, and when she called, "Okay, now," I walked into the white studio and saw she had draped the smaller easel as well as the big one.

"Works in progress?"

"Progressing slowly . . . So? What do you think?"

"I think you have a lovely house. And I'm sure I'm not telling you anything you don't know when I say there are a limited number of buyers for such a place."

"If you were handling the sale, what price would you ask?"

"Well, I'm not handling the sale, but if I were . . . four million."

"And what would you advise me to take?"

I hesitated. Then I asked, "Are you in business? Or are you a painter?"

"I'm not a painter."

"This looks like a painter's studio," I said.

"I play when I get time. No—to answer your question—I work closely with Jack. I know about business."

"So I'm not talking to a babe in the woods."

She still didn't flirt, but she did smile. "That depends on whose woods."

"We're just talking—just us—but you ought to know that the lowest number you allow to be mentioned in a conversation with your realtor is very likely the number he'll bring you in the end."

"Okay."

"I wouldn't take a penny under three million. And I'd fight like hell for three-five."

"Even in this climate?"

"Especially in this climate. You'll get some sharpy out here figuring to pin you to the wall—but he'll have the bucks, and if his wife gets a load of this place he'll pay you three-five or she'll stop sleeping with the louse."

Mrs. Long laughed. "I get it. Thanks. Come on, we'll have that drink."

We got down to the kitchen and she said, "Any objections to champagne?"

"None." I smiled back, thinking I couldn't imagine a lovelier end of the day, or beginning of the evening.

She filled a silver icebucket and dunked the bottle. Then she got a pair of flutes and said, "Grab that, if you don't mind. We've got a great place to drink it." She led me down a hall through a massive oak door to the foot of a narrow spiral stair that led up into the turret.

I smelled gunsmoke.

I said, "Your husband been shooting deer again?"

"No, he set up some targets last weekend. Deer size and shape but only paper."

It smelled more recent, to me.

I followed her pretty bottom up the stairs, flirting with a fantasy that she had broken up with her boyfriend after Trooper Moody and the burglar people left, sent him back to New York, and now felt the need of being consoled. This fantasy worked best when I ignored the fact that they had been playing hide and seek at the Newbury Cookout four hours ago.

Up and up we went, round and round, our footsteps on the metal steps echoing off the stone walls. Higher and higher, until right under the conical roof we came to a little round platform just big enough for a couple of small chairs and a table for our glasses. I put the bucket on the floor and sat down when she did.

"Would you open it?" she asked.

I peeled the foil and the muzzle, freed the cork with a modest pop, and filled our glasses. She touched hers to mine and met my eye. Her expression was clear, open and content. "Isn't this great?" she asked, and I knew in that moment that she was simply happy to have me as a guest in her house.

Directly in front of us was an opening wider than the bowmen's windows. Through it we could see for miles, a view like a Dutch or Hudson River School landscape, hills and trees and meadows, all in the fading light of a September evening.

That part of me that won't let things be asked, "How could you sell it?"

She drank deep, and I regretted asking, because quite suddenly she was not content. The idiot she had treated so hospitably had just reminded her of a conflict tearing her life apart. At least that's how I interpreted the pain that shadowed her eyes. She looked down, stared into her glass, and said, "Everything's a tradeoff."

It occurred to me that the Longs might have gone broke. The Castle wouldn't be the first great house to mask its owners' private desperation. But knowing more about her than I had any right to, I figured she was more likely considering leaving the husband, and the money, for the boyfriend.

I wanted to warn her that her husband knew. The question was what loyalty—or discretion, at least—did I owe Alex Rose. I had, after all, accepted his job and his money. Did quitting absolve me?

I looked at her, and she looked away and stood up and moved to the opening in the wall. She stared out. I drank champagne. Suddenly her whole body stiffened. She thrust her head and shoulders through the opening in the stone, straining to see.

"What's that?"

I stood up beside her and looked where she was pointing. The sun had deserted a meadow but for the eastern edge along the woods, and there in the last rays something gleamed white. It was quite a distance away, and yet I could sense it shiver when the wind riled the grass around it.

"I don't know," I said. "Looks a little like a deer's white tail, but they don't lie down in the open, and certainly not at this hour. It's feeding time. You've never seen it there before? . . . Maybe your husband shot another one."

"No," she said impatiently. "He's away." She turned to the stairs, worried, and said loudly, "I have to see what it is."

She started down the metal steps, fast. I left my glass and followed. Down the steps, my hurt knee locking, through the big door, down a hall, and into the kitchen and out the back door. On the lawn she broke into a run. I limped after her, to the edge of the meadow. She plunged into the higher grass before I could warn her about the deer ticks. I stopped to pull my socks over my pants and trotted after her. She could shower off later. I could dry her back.

She crossed the meadow, exactly where I had trod last night, and up the slope to the woods. Suddenly she slowed, then stopped, rigid, and put her hand to her mouth. I caught up. The white thing blowing in the wind, gleaming in the sun, was hair. Blond hair. Her boyfriend was sprawled on his back, with a brick-size bloody exit wound where his muscular chest had been.

6

There's truth in the cliché that people seem to shrink when they die. My father's body had looked hollow at Butler's Funeral Home; by the time we got him to the churchyard he was almost transparent. A prisoner I saw shanked—a big man—fell like laundry. Mrs. Long's boyfriend was different—robust—drinking in the sky with wide-eyed wonder. I remember thinking that the last innocent had escaped the planet, and those of us still stuck here were the dead ones.

His name was Ron; she kept calling him Ron as she knelt beside him and took his body in her arms. I reached to comfort her and lead her away, until I thought, Wait, this isn't television, let the poor woman grieve. I backed off, and stood guard, or something, at a distance.

It could have been a hunting accident. Some damned fool poaching out of season, spotting the white flash of Ron's hair, mistaking him for a whitetail deer. It happens, both in season and out, though most often when they issue doe licenses, because then the hunter doesn't even have to try to confirm he sees the buck's antlers. Just spot a white tail and blast away—Oh, my God, it was my kid; or my father; or my cousin. Or my wife. (Sometimes called a country divorce.) High-powered weapons, low IQs, and plenty of booze; little wonder we have too many deer.

I wished I hadn't smelled the gunsmoke in the turret.

It would be dark soon. I really should call Oliver. But Mrs. Long—Rita—she just wasn't going to be Mrs. Long for me any more, or anyone else, when it was established Ron was on the property—Rita was still holding him, still whispering in his dead ear.

Poachers tend not to have hunting accidents. They are, in their way, professionals. A woody who puts deer meat on his table, or earns some spending money selling to butchers, usually treats guns with the respect they deserve. I'm not saying that a Chevalley boy—or one of the Jervis clan—would never have an accident poaching, but it's less likely. Still, Oliver Moody and the state police investigators would be combing the woods for evidence. As soon as I called them.

I went back to Rita and said, "Mrs. Long, I'd better call the police. Are you all right here, or do you want to come with me?"

"I can't leave him here."

"I'll come back with a blanket."

"No. I can't leave him here."

I misinterpreted her to mean that Ron's body should not be found on her property, which struck me as both unrealistic and surprisingly cold. I said, "We shouldn't move him. The police have to investigate."

"He's dead. It doesn't make any difference. Help me get him inside."

"Inside?"

She took my heart again.

"There'll be animals at night. It's getting dark. I don't want him hurt any more."

I wished to God I could make things right for her. "I'll call the police and I'll come right back with a blanket and flashlights and we'll stay with him until they come."

Halfway to the house I looked back. She was dragging him through the grass. "Christ!"

I ran to her. The damage was done. She'd gotten her hands under his arms and had somehow moved him ten feet from where the bullet had killed him. She was breathing hard, gasping with each step.

The expression of total concentration on her face said there wasn't a thing she wanted to do other than get her man indoors.

I took one shoulder and arm, she the other, and we pulled him through the grass, his heels beating a path, the blood trailing down his pinstriped shirt and spilling under his belt. On the mowed lawn, I knelt, worked both arms under him, and carried him, cradled. Rita held his hand, letting it go only to open the front door. At her direction, I laid him down on a couch in the living room. It was upholstered with a silk brocade, but I knew enough not to suggest a towel. She arranged his arms and legs, and when she had him lying there as if he'd dropped off for a nap, she knelt on the Persian carpet, put her head on his shoulder, and wept.

I went into the kitchen and telephoned Oliver.

"What do you want?"

"A guy's been shot at the Long place."

"Dead?"

"Yes."

"Who shot him?"

"I have no idea."

"Who's there, now?"

"Just me and Mrs. Long."

"Don't touch a thing."

Angry, Ollie looked even bigger. "I told you not to touch anything." He stood close, muscles gathered, ready to throw a punch.

"You told me too late."

"You moved the goddamned body. You're impeding an investigation."

"It's done."

"Done, hell. I'll charge you."

"You want me to show you where we found him, while there's still light enough to see?"

He did. We walked across the lawn and through the meadow, Oliver fuming at the track we'd scored in the high grass. "Jesus, Ben, you've pulled some dumb stunts in your life, but this one takes the cake."

"We found him there."

"Stand back."

He strung yellow crime-scene tape in a fifty-foot circle around Ron's blood. It had looked to me when I first saw the body that Ron had fallen dead and hadn't moved an inch; now, who knew? Rita and I had flattened the grass. Oliver stayed outside the tape, and scanned the dark woods.

"What were you doing out here?"

"Appraising the house."

He took off his mirrored glasses and fixed me with his pale gray eyes. I had always preferred him in sunglasses. His eyes were reptilian: cold, and stupid. Komodo dragons are stupid, too, but they eat mammals.

"Appraising the house or appraising the wife?"

"Appraising the house."

"Did you know the guy?"

"No."

"Did she?"

"She didn't say."

"So why's she bawling?"

"She didn't tell me."

I supposed I'd be wise to cover myself in advance by relating last night's fiasco—bring it up before they back-tracked to Alex Rose through Mr. Long, Rose saying, Oh, yeah, I paid a local bumpkin to film them screwing. Ask him—he'll confirm they were lovers—but that reeked of snitch. I was caught in the middle. I couldn't cover myself by snitching and I couldn't lie; I never was a liar. So dancing Trooper Moody in circles was really a dress rehearsal for the state police major crime unit, which the cops themselves, I noticed, called the major case squad.

They arrived at last, a young, cleancut couple in plainclothes who looked like poster children for the FBI, Sergeant Arnold Bender and Trooper Marian Boyce. They listened to Oliver's report, then ordered him to rig lights at the death site. The woman, Boyce, went into Rita's house; Bender came to me.

"Why'd you move the body?"

"It was getting dark."

"So what?"

"Animals would eat it."

"Are you trying to be funny?"

"We've got raccoons, crows, turkey buzzards, weasels, rats, and mice." I was winging the weasels; I had no idea if they ate dead meat, but everything else did, which I wanted to establish before this moving-the-body thing got out of hand and led to charges. I sensed blood in the air; money, sex, and beauty demanded arrests.

"You shouldn't have moved the body."

"I found a dead raccoon the other day. By the time I got a garbage bag so the health department could test it for rabies, crows had eaten everything but the fur."

Bender sighed like a man who missed street corners. "Do you remember how the body looked? Before you moved it?"

"I saw a huge hole in the guy's chest. His eyes were open. He was staring at the sky."

"Was he on his back?"

"Yes."

"Curled up? Spread out?"

"Spread out. Like he'd laid down to look at the sky."

We walked to the site. Bender shook his head at the crushed grass. "Try to remember, Mr. Abbott, did it look to you like he crawled there, wounded? Had he come far?"

As he'd fallen on his back, even though he'd been shot from behind, I assumed he had probably staggered, caught his balance, then collapsed backwards. But that was Bender's department, so all I said was, "No. I got the impression he hit the deck, dead."

"Which way was he lying?"

"Head up toward the woods. Feet facing where we are now."

"Did you hear shots?"

"No."

"How'd you happen to find him then?"

I turned around and pointed at the tower. "We were in the top of the turret, looking out that window. See that square opening? We saw his hair."

"His hair?"

"It was shining in the sun. We went to investigate."

"Why?"

"It's Mrs. Long's property. She saw something out of place. I thought it was a deer lying dead."

"Why dead?"

"They don't lie down in the evening. It looked like a white tail. So I figured it was dead."

"You some kind of hunter?"

"My uncles were hunters. They taught me how to get along in the woods."

"What were you doing in the tower?"

"Drinking champagne."

"You got a thing going with the lady?"

"No."

"Trooper Moody tells me you're covering for her."

"Trooper Moody should stick to speeding tickets."

Sergeant Bender was half Moody's size, but he had the state police stare, which he gave me full force. "Trooper Moody informs me you did time."

"I served my time. I'm not on parole. You are way out of line."

"I got a dead man, apparently shot. You moved him. When my lieutenant reads my report he's going to ask, Why didn't you bring the jailbird in?"

"My false-arrest suit will be based on two facts: First, I was charged with a white-collar crime; second, when whatever happened to that poor guy happened, I was grilling burgers for three hundred people at Town Hall."

"You got some kind of problem with Trooper Moody?"

"Oliver has a problem with me."

"Why?"

"Ask him sometime. If you want a good laugh."

"Does Mrs. Long know the dead man?"

I had deliberately not asked her, so all I had to do was answer, "She called him Ron."

An elderly diesel Mercedes chugged into the drive, decanting Dr. Steve Greenan, who served as one of the part-time assistant medical examiners for the county. Largely retired, he was a tall, white-haired, handsome man whose big shoulders had begun to slump with age. He trudged our way, seeing the yellow tape; Sergeant Bender ran to intercept. I followed, passing Oliver, who was stringing extension cords from the house.

"Ben," Greenan called.

"How you doing, Steve?"

"Wonderful. I was busting my back planting bulbs for Mildred. This call saved me. Okay, Sonny," he said to Sergeant Bender, "where is it?"

No one stopped me, so I followed them into the house. Yellow tape cordoned off the living room. Ron lay there alone. Someone had closed his eyes—Rita, I supposed—and he seemed to be getting smaller.

"Jesus," said Steve. "That's it for this couch." He stepped under the tape.

The cops had a private word, after which Bender headed upstairs, where his partner had left Rita with a female officer. Trooper Boyce took me into the dining room, a vast, high-ceilinged echoing hall that the Longs hadn't yet furnished, except for a grim American Empire sideboard.

She was a nice-looking woman, wearing a knee-length skirt, running shoes, and a crisp white blouse under an unlined beige blazer. She had short hair, a wide, friendly mouth, and a take-charge manner, a little like an eager schoolteacher except for her trooper eyes, which were gray and wise, and warier than her open face. She had big hands. She played it soft at first.

"I'm going to ask you many of the same questions Sergeant Bender asked, just so we can gather as much information as you and Mrs. Long can recall. Okay, Ben?"

"Sure."

She indeed asked every question Bender had, including the jailbird jibes, couched in the careful manner of a graduate research fellow polishing her thesis: "I understand you served time in prison."

Her partner's "jailbird" had rankled more than I should have let it. Before she could stick it to me again, I said, "I was rehabilitated."

She got un-nice very quickly. "Are you trying to be funny? We've got a dead man here."

"*You* have a dead man here. I didn't kill him. I didn't know him. I just found him. If you want me to say I'm sorry he's dead, I will."

In truth, I felt very sorry he was dead. In an odd way I felt more for him than many people I'd known my whole life. So I calmed down and said, gently as I could to Trooper Boyce, "I was quite moved when I found him. He looked like a really decent person—very innocent. So I guess in that way he's all of our loss. If I sounded like I was wisecracking, it was because I'm irritated that you and your partner are wasting time on my past while whoever shot the poor man is probably in the next state by now."

"What makes you think he was shot?"

"Something came out of his chest with great force. Unless you think they're filming *Alien IV,* I'd guess he was shot in the back. Probably with a twelve-gauge deer slug. I'm sure Steve will fill you in."

"Steve?"

"Dr. Greenan. The assistant M.E."

"He's your doctor?"

"He delivered me."

Trooper Boyce frowned at her notes.

I asked, "Is Mrs. Long all right?"

"She's very upset. How well do you know her?"

"Met her this afternoon."

"At the cookout?"

"She wanted a burger. Then she wanted her house appraised."

"Just like that?"

"Happens all the time. People at a party ask Steve about their allergies. They ask me what their houses are worth. I'll bet they ask you how many miles over the speed limit they can get away with. Right?"

I got a smile at last, a pretty smile to mask a lightning jab: "So why'd you move the body?"

"I've been through this with Sergeant Bender."

"Go through it with me." No smile.

"We thought it best to move the body indoors before dark."

"We?"

"Mrs. Long and me."

"What if I told you Mrs. Long said you suggested moving the body?"

I didn't believe her. I said, "You've already reminded me I did time. Don't pull that chickenshit stuff on me. Mrs. Long didn't say anything of the sort."

"Sure about that?"

"Trooper, at worst we made an error in judgment. Are you investigating how the man got killed, or are you building a case against me and Mrs. Long for screwing up the evidence?"

"How the man died could explain who killed him. You may be an expert on prison life, Ben. I'm an expert on homicide."

She had me there. Not that I admitted it to her.

I said, "I'm beginning to understand that instead of good cop, bad cop, you and Bender play smart cop, stupid cop. You're the smart one, am I right?"

"You're working hard at making me your enemy," said Marian Boyce. "That's not a good idea."

"I guess I'll need a lawyer," I said, thinking of Tim Hall and wondering how the hell I could pay him. Alex Rose's five grand would have come in handy just then. Of course, if Rose hadn't sought me out, I wouldn't be standing in an empty dining room with an angry state police investigator.

She said, "I can't decide if you're a wiseguy or you're really hiding something."

I inventoried what I was hiding: Rose and the videotape; the gunsmoke I'd smelled in the turret topped the list. But I could not believe for one second that the joyous woman I had seen last night had shot her man.

"Are you sticking to some sort of inmate code not to rat?"

"We never liked the term 'inmate.' It made us sound like psychos."

"Oh, I'm so sorry. What did you prefer, 'criminal'?"

"I always thought 'prisoner' described the situation accurately."

"So are you obeying some sort of prisoner code not to rat?"

"I learned two things as a kid: not to snitch and not to lie. Served me fine, inside, and out."

"So you won't help?"

"I didn't *see* anything. The only 'help' I can offer is speculation, and I've already done that. Looks to me like a hunting accident."

One of her big hands kept slipping under her jacket, where I caught a glimpse of shiny handcuffs on her belt. She was reaching back again, when Doctor Steve barged in, saying, "I'd look for a deer slug in the grass if I were you. Probably what did him. Right in and *boom* out the other side."

"What range?"

"Close as you'd get to a deer. Fifty, sixty yards."

I let loose an internal sigh. If that were the case, Ron hadn't been shot from the tower. His body had fallen more like eighty yards from the tower. Whatever I had smelled up there had nothing to do with it. It was probably a hunting accident, in which case either some hunter didn't know he'd shot him, or did and was running like hell, with nightfall on his side. Now all Bender and Boyce had to do was find the slug, match it to a gun, and make a charge. Of course, who- ever was running had his gun with him, and it was one in a thou- sand the troopers would ever find it. In fact, if he was smart —which ruled out all the Chevalley boys and most of the Jervis clan—he'd toss it in the river.

Sergeant Bender walked in, calling, "Hey, Doc. You want to give Mrs. Long a shot or something? She's getting hysterical."

Steve Greenan didn't answer. He, like me and Marian Boyce, was staring at the shotgun Bender was carrying by a wire hanger through the trigger guard. The homicide sergeant said, "Marian. Get the kit and take a powder analysis on Mrs. Long's fingers after the doc calms her down."

"Where'd you find that?" I asked.

"Do one on the jailbird too, just in case."

"Where'd you find that?" Steve asked.

Bender smiled, pleased as punch. "In the gun rack in the turret. Been fired recently."

Steve hurried out with his bag to help Mrs. Long. Trooper Moody came in, holding a flashlight in one hand and a little plastic Ziploc bag in the other. "Found a slug," he announced.

I had one friend in the house, and that was Steve. Bender and Boyce got distracted when more cops arrived, and I took advantage of the interruption to buttonhole the doctor. As a medical examiner he was in charge of the crime scene, the boss until he ordered the body removed to the morgue.

"Can I see her?"

"I don't think they want you to."

"I know that."

Steve Greenan cracked a little smile. I knew for a fact he didn't love the state police. Now and then they got too rough and needed a medical opinion that an injured prisoner had fallen down the stairs. He'd told me once over a couple of cold ones that he dealt with that problem on a case-by-case basis: If the injured party was a violent son of a bitch Steve would blame the stairs; if he perceived brutality, he would tell them to find another doctor. Either way, he didn't appreciate being judge and jury.

"She's in a guest room. First right at the top of the kitchen stairs. I'll go have another look at the body and make some pronouncements."

"Thanks."

"You got something going with her?"

"No such luck."

Steve bustled back to the living room, calling loudly for help in turning the body. I cut through the kitchen and up the back stairs. I was afraid they'd hear if I knocked, so I opened the first door on the right and shut it behind me.

The room was big for a guest bedroom, bigger than the master in most houses. Rita lay on an elaborately stitched down quilt. She was on her side, staring into the cold fireplace, curled up like a question mark. Her splendid black hair shone in the light from the night table. When I was a child my mother's hair had been almost as long and black; nights, sometimes, she'd let me help brush its hundred strokes.

I moved around the bed into Rita's vision. She looked confused, and seemed to be fighting Steve's tranquilizer. The drug had strung a veil of high cirrus clouds over her blue eyes.

"Who are you? Oh, you. Guess I won't have to sell the house now." She was slurring.

"Can I do anything for you?" I asked.

She shook her head. Tears trickled down her cheek into the corner of her mouth. She licked them. I backed up. She said, "He was so wonderful."

"Ron?"

"Just wonderful . . . *We* were wonderful."

"I'm really sorry," I said, adding lamely, "You poor thing."

"Yeah, I'm a poor thing, all right. A real poor thing . . . Poor Jack . . . It's so goddamned *fucking* ironic. We tried so hard not to hurt him. Keep it from him, while we tried to figure out what to do. And now—now—he's going to know."

I had to tell her that her husband knew already, but it would keep till morning.

"Why did they keep asking me why we took him inside?" She sat up and swung her feet to the floor. "I told them it was my idea, by the way. I said you only helped, which was true. Why did they keep asking?"

"It has to do with their investigation. We didn't follow their procedure, so they're upset. Don't worry about it."

"Why did they test my hand?"

"They found a gun in the turret that had been fired."

"Is that what that test was?" Her eyes flashed. "Idiots. Jack and I were shooting last week."

"And they found a deer slug in the grass."

"Must have been a poacher. We caught one last month. And last night there was someone in the woods."

"Did you tell the cops?"

"They came out here. Shot a raccoon and said that was the prowler. . . ."

"Do the police know who he is?"

"Of course. I told them. What's to hide? It's all going to come out. There's no way Jack's going to believe Ron was here for any other reason than the very obvious."

"You can't tough it out?"

"When you stop sleeping with your husband and one day his former partner turns up at your house while your husband's in Washington, he's going to get the picture." She flopped back on the bed and covered her face with her hands.

"Former partner?" I echoed, surprised that Alex Rose, P.I., had neglected to mention this startling leg of their love triangle.

"Jack bought him out," she muttered through her hands.

As I recalled, Rose had admitted to me only that the Longs knew Ron well. Putting myself in his shoes, I thought, No, I probably wouldn't have mentioned it either to anybody jerk enough to sneak videos of lovers making love.

Rita was trembling. I said, "Would you like me to call anyone for you? A friend or someone?"

"Ron was my friend. He was my best friend. I told him everything. If I had a good day in my studio I'd call him up to tell him. If I had a lousy day in my studio I'd tell him. If Jack was driving me crazy I'd tell him. If I met someone nice, I'd call him up and tell him. . . . I was going to tell him I'd met you. . . ." She removed her hands from her eyes and seemed startled to see me. "What are you doing here?" Steve's dope was really cooking now.

"Just wanted to see if you were . . . if I could do anything."

"Thanks, no. Nothing."

"Some tea? Coffee?"

"No . . . Tea. Yeah, tea might be a good idea. The doctor gave me this pill. My head is like oatmeal."

"I'll make tea. Want to come with me?"

She sat up, abruptly. "I'm going to call him." She snatched up the phone, saw me staring, and said, as she dialed, "I'll get Ron's answering machine. His voice."

7

Cigarette smoke hung thick downstairs. There were cops everywhere, in uniform and plainclothes, gawking at the skylit wood paneling, the furniture in the roped-off living room, and the lavish kitchen, which had clearly cost more to build than any public servant's home. Country troopers tend to be the second sons of hardworking farmers, and I could only guess what was going through the minds of any who wandered into Rita's studio and undraped her drawing of Ron naked with skull.

"Excuse me." I shouldered between two giants with their hats on, filled a kettle, and set it to boil on the eight-burner Garland range. There were matching Sub-Zero refrigerator-freezers. The first held beer and wine. I found milk in the second, along with some Saran-wrapped pizza wedges, an open champagne bottle with a spoon in the neck, and a beautifully decorated plate of shrimp circling red and white sauces. Only a few shrimp were gone, as if Rita and Ron had adjourned hastily from hors d'oeuvres to bed. At least that's how I read it.

I found the tea in an airtight cabinet, chose Constant Comment. Sugar was where it should be, and a teapot was nearby.

Trooper Boyce was watching from the mudroom door. "Know your way around pretty well, don't you?"

"I sell houses for a living." I ran hot water into the teapot to warm the thick china. "You want some tea?"

"No."

I had not liked the look on her partner's face when he found the gun. And just in case the slug Oliver had found in the grass matched it, I decided to polish my manners and make a friend at the cops. "Mrs. Long would like some tea. You sure you won't have some too? Why don't you come up with me?"

"Who let you see Mrs. Long?"

"I hope I didn't do anything wrong. I'm sorry if I did. But I figured you were through with us, and she seemed so upset. Is that a problem?"

Marian Boyce regarded me warily. "I'll take some tea, here. I'll leave her in your capable hands."

"Milk and sugar?"

Upstairs in the guest room, Rita had dozed off. I put her cup on the night table and covered it with a paperback Patrick O'Brian novel. I sat in an easy chair and sipped and studied the room. They'd had a fire in the fireplace last night—it had to be "their" room—and candles on the mantel had burned to the stubs. There was a vase of asters, and in the bathroom a pair of empty wineglasses, rinsed to be taken down to the dishwasher in the morning. Two terry robes, hung on the door hooks, blue as Rita's eyes. And Ron's eyes. Terrific couple, I thought again. But it was funny how casual they were about "their" room. If they were as careful about not getting caught as Rita claimed, why had they left all this night-of-love evidence around? I would have thought they'd have scoured the place before Ron left.

Maybe he hadn't left. Long was away. Maybe Ron had just driven down to New York to get his mail or something and was coming back tonight. A long round trip, but do-able. Then it dawned on me: In order to get shot he had to have left the cookout ahead of Rita and come back here before driving to New York.

I heard a car door slam. I got up and looked out the window at the floodlit lawn. A Newbury volunteer ambulance was pulling down the driveway, flashers off and siren silent, doing double duty as a morgue wagon. I sat awhile longer, watching Rita sleep. Suddenly a whole slew of car doors slammed. I looked out again, this time on a scene out of Keystone Kops. State troopers were streaming from the house, running full tilt to their cars. Sirens whooped and gravel flew. Lights flashing, a caravan raced down the driveway.

Rita stirred but did not wake. I went down to the kitchen. Steve was on the telephone, hurriedly explaining to Mildred that he was going to be late and didn't know how late. He told her he loved her, and ran for the front door with his black bag. It was heavy and he was not young, so I grabbed it and ran alongside. We passed a rookie state trooper at the door, who looked put out that he'd been left behind.

"What's going on?"

"Plane crash," said Steve, climbing into his car. "You coming? Hop in."

I looked back at the house. Rita wasn't likely to wake up and the young trooper had it secured, so I got in. A shooting and a plane crash in a single day was more action than we'd seen since the Hawleyville Tavern burned down.

"What's the big deal—why'd the plainclothes go?"

"They found the plane at the end of Al Bell's strip."

"So?" There were a half-dozen private airstrips in the area—quarter mile cow pastures on the high plateaus.

"So when Al drove up to see if the pilot was okay, the cockpit looked like a snowstorm."

"Huh?"

"The troopers suspect it's not baking powder."

"Oh." Our isolated, privileged hunk of America is still America. You don't see crack and heroin peddled on Main Street, and addicts don't break into farmhouses, but that doesn't mean we don't have citizens who prefer illegal drugs to honest alcohol. Knowing the back country like I do, I could lead the DEA to several marijuana patches. A while back they busted an estate house outside Norfolk, which had a crack lab run by types from Boston. But by and large, even though we're not that far as the crow flies from gang-infested small cities like Waterbury, we don't get all that much dope action in Newbury. So little wonder that every state trooper at Rita Long's house was howling through the night in the direction of Al's private airstrip.

Careers were in the making. Suspicious death on a rich man's estate offered promise, but the big headlines would have to wait for a juicy trial, where the lawyers would hog them. While a plane full of coke crashing into northwest Connecticut's exclusive hills guaranteed a media feeding frenzy, with sound bites and on-camera back-grounders for all.

"What a day," said Steve, who was hunched over the wheel as he peered into an old man's night-blind gloom.

Without Trooper Moody to lead the way, it would have taken the state police all night to find Bell's airstrip. We climbed Morris Mountain on a switchback dirt road, took a number of unmarked turnoffs, then ran through a deep wood, which opened suddenly on two thousand feet of mowed pasture. Steve's headlights caught a drooping windsock. At the far end the police cars had clustered. We bounced across the grass. They'd aimed their rooflight at the plane, a little white Cessna, which had smacked its nose into a tree and bent its propeller into half a swastika. Out came the yellow tape again. A trooper hurried over and asked Steve to have a look at the pilot. I went with him, carrying his bag. Oliver Moody was guarding the entrance to the cordon. He saw me and said, "Get outta here."

I gave Steve his bag and went back to the car.

The doctor returned shortly, looking grave. "Ben, I'm sorry."

"What's wrong?"

"It's Renny Chevalley."

8

My cousin Renny was the only Chevalley boy ever to fly.

Chevalley women did all right, but the men just didn't fit in. It was a rare Christmas when one wasn't locked up somewhere for some misdemeanor or another. They tended to tumble out of the school system around eighth grade with enough reading skills to get a driver's license. It took flush times for them to prosper: They were great with a chainsaw, but you couldn't get one to work with a shovel for love or money; they were born to the seat of a bull-dozer, but hadn't the entrepreneurial skills to acquire their own machines, so only when the construction business boomed did they get hired. They made good truckers, until they drank too much, and when they drank they fought. And when they fought, normal people called the cops. They got better as they got older: My mother's brothers made wonderful uncles.

Renny stayed in school. In seventh grade Mr. Tyler, the shop teacher, taught him how to turn metal on a lathe. When the rest of us brought home our little wooden water pump lamps, Renny gave his mom a gleaming ship's helm lamp made entirely of polished aluminum. When I started prep school, Renny rebuilt a Pontiac GTO which his big brother Pinkerton raced to victory on dirt tracks as far away as Maine. When I got accepted at Annapolis, Renny cracked up the GTO on 361. It was the night before he was to go to Hartford to receive first prize in a statewide shop-project contest for a chrome version of the ship's helm lamp, and he nearly died. When he could walk again, he rebuilt a wrecked Piper Cub and learned to fly.

I thought then there'd be no stopping him, a hope confirmed when he was accepted into the Air Force. But though his scores were high, and reportedly no one could outfly him on a simulator or a trainer, the cold north slopes and swamps of Frenchtown exerted their strange pull, and Renny was quite suddenly discharged. He wouldn't talk about it, even when we went drinking. Years later, after I got out of prison, he told me he had quite simply gotten homesick. Air Force boot camp and flight school were the first time he'd ever slept farther from his bed than my house on Main Street. But he still wanted to fly, so he started working his way toward the Holy Grail of a four-engine jet license, which would allow him to pilot "Sevenfours," as he called them, for the airlines.

Acquiring flight time and skills was a long, slow process without Air Force backing, and very expensive. He had worked as a flight instructor, an occasional charter pilot, and, for the last several years, as a "freight dog." Freight dogs fly at night, shuttling between small airports to deliver bank checks to central clearinghouses. I rode along with him now and then; it was magnificent droning through a dark sky peppered with stars over astonishingly dark ground between clumps of light that marked the cities. We'd go to Hartford, Teterboro, Wilmington, Philly, and back to Hartford all before dawn, touching down just long enough to heave the bags aboard.

Gradually, he had given up the dream to be an airline pilot. Some of it had to do with one of the Butler girls, whom he married on her eighteenth birthday. Along came a baby, and a second. His father decided to retire, and the logical thing was to take over his Frenchtown garage—a dank, greasy establishment with a surly dog on a chain that scared most customers off to Jiffy-Lube. Renny discovered a flair for business. He cleaned up the garage, invested in some modern tools, initiated a free towing service for his startled customers, and turned it into a going enterprise.

I told Steve I had to see him.

———

"Coming through," growled Steve Greenan, gripping his medical bag in one hand and my arm in the other. He walked me past a grimly smiling Oliver Moody and right up to the plane. "You okay?" he asked me.

"I don't know." We climbed up the bumper and onto the hood of a police car they'd driven close to use for steps. Its roof lights illuminated the cockpit. The windshield was shattered. Renny sat buckled into his seat. Blood had trickled down his face and dried, marring his dark, lean good looks. I noticed, for the first time, a wisp of gray in his temples. He was wearing a leather bomber jacket. It was open, and it and his shirtfront were dusted heavily in white powder.

"I don't believe this," I said.

"I'm real sorry," said Steve.

"Is that coke?"

"Tastes like it to me."

"Renny wouldn't fly dope."

The doctor's silence said that he, like most of Newbury, wouldn't put anything past a Chevalley boy.

"Come on, Steve. He didn't need this. He had his business. Right?"

Steve said, "I'm just telling you it tastes like coke."

"Well, it's not his."

"That might have been the problem," Steve muttered.

"What do you mean?"

"Look at him."

I looked and saw what I hadn't noticed earlier. The cockpit was intact but for the shattered windshield, and the plane was barely scratched other than the bent prop. Renny's seatbelt had held, and it looked to me like he hadn't even hit the glass. Nor was there that much blood on his face.

"What killed him?"

"He's been shot."

"Shot?"

"The cops are creaming in their pants— Hold it!"

I had reached to touch Renny's face. Steve stopped me with a gnarled hand. "You don't want to see the back of his head. . . . Come on now. Let's get out of here. I told the cops I needed you for a positive ID. . . . Come on, Ben, I'll drive you home."

I walked from the plane in a daze, barely aware of anything but the smile on Oliver Moody's face. From his point of view, dead and injured Chevalleys and Jervises represented little victories. And in general I can't say I blamed him; he was the guy who had to break up bar brawls and pull violent men off their women. But it wasn't fair to Renny and I would never forgive that smile. It was some relief to feel angry.

"You want your car?" Steve asked when we got to 361.

"No, I'll leave it— Damn, I left the top down. I better get it. I'm sorry, Steve."

"Don't worry about it."

The Longs' floodlights were all blazing, and the young trooper was still guarding the door.

I put the top up and led Steve back to Newbury, where I lit a fire and had a couple of JDs. I thought of driving over to see Renny's wife. But I knew the whole huge clan would be there looking after her, which meant she'd be closeted with the women while the men drank, and I was much more in a mood for drinking alone.

The third bourbon sent me reeling. I staggered upstairs, swallowed a handful of Vitamin B for the morning, got into bed, and tried to sleep. I lay awake a long time, thinking slowly, trying to come up with a plausible reason why a thirty-five-year-old businessman with two babies would fly cocaine.

I had no doubt he owed plenty on his business. Turning a rathole of a small-town fix-it shop into a seven-bay wonder of computer diagnostics costs plenty. He was into me for a few grand, part of which he had paid down by shoehorning the Caddy engine into my dad's old Olds. I assumed he was carrying other personal loans, though the bulk of his money would have come from banks willing to take a chance on an upstart. Peebles Bank, I guessed, as their lending policies in the late 'Eighties were of the drunken sailor standard, and maybe Circle Bank, lately taken over by the government.

On the other hand, his business was booming. (Chevalley Enterprises, he had named it, a blunt stick in the eye of the old families that were accustomed to controlling commercial endeavor in our neck of the woods.) His timing had been impeccable. Nothing like a recession to convince people they could eke a few more years out of the family cars instead of trading them in on new ones. So once the extended warranties ran out on their shiny '88 Buick or '87 Toyota, they turned to Chevalley Enterprises, which treated them better than the dealers, fixed it right, and kept it reasonable. The last time I'd been in for an oil change, all seven bays were working and Renny'd been talking about adding two more, if he could get the financing.

Oliver Moody's smile floated before my eyes as the bourbon washed over me. My last thought was that I'd misread him. The trooper's pleasure in Renny's death was not general. He hated two people in the world. Renny and me. His smile had said, One down, one to go.

9

The telephone woke me. I should have let the machine take it, but I snapped it on the first ring and it was already in my hand before I was aware. I croaked a dry-mouthed, bourbon-fouled Hello, and the voice of my great-aunt Connie said, "I hope I didn't wake you."

"No, no, no, Connie. Just sitting here . . ." I found the clock. Seven.

She mistook my sleepy confusion for hesitation and asked, "You have heard about Renny, haven't you?"

"Last night."

She was on the "Fish Line," a telephone circuit used by older people who called each other in the morning to check that no one had fallen and needed help. It helped those alone to stay in their own homes rather than move to retirement communities, and it spread news faster than CNN.

"I'm sorry, for you. I know you liked him. At any rate, I must call on the Butler girl. Would you like to come with me?"

Connie was a forthright ninety, but, having been born very few years after the century, her manner of speech required decoding. "The Butler girl" was Renny's wife. Everyone else called her Betty Chevalley, but Aunt Connie tended to remember the rest of us as the children we had been; also, she had no truck with Chevalleys. As a good Christian, however, she must call on anyone in need. "Would you like to come with me?" was her way of asking if I would drive her. She would drive herself—the sight of her peering under the rim of the steering wheel would scatter the few who hadn't already taken cover at the first glimpse of her black Lincoln—but if I were to oblige she would take the sensible course. But she would not ask.

I said, "I'd like very much to go with you, thank you. It'll be easier seeing her together."

"Which car shall we take?"

"Why don't we take yours, Connie? I'll drive if you'll let me."

"Half an hour?"

"It's early, Connie. Maybe we'll give them a little time. I'll come over at nine."

I walked across the street to Connie's. Her house is a Federal-era mansion, by far the grandest in town. She's bequeathed it to the Historical Society, and if she ever dies—which doesn't seem likely to those who know her—Newbury will possess one of the most lavish museum houses in New England, chockablock with pre-Revolutionary antiques, Persian carpets, and Chinese art, porcelain, and vases. Hers is the wealthy side of the Abbotts, and the fruits of some three hundred years of enterprise and ingenuity have funneled down to this one last old lady, who will leave it all to charity. I went around the back. She was waiting at the kitchen door with her coat, gloves, and hat already on. She was lean and trim. Good posture and a thick crown of curly white hair fooled strangers into thinking she was only eighty.

"I've started the car to warm it," she informed me, adding tartly as I offered her my arm down the steps, "If we don't get there soon the poor thing will be obliged to offer us lunch."

"We're on our way."

"We will not stay for lunch."

"Of course not."

"We will go to church at eleven." Sunday. I'd forgotten my tie.

The stable was choked with fumes. The sun spilled in on a 1960 four-door sedan, black as midnight and bright with chrome. "Connie, please remember, don't start the car before you open the door."

"Let's go!"

She barreled in, waving the fumes with her pocketbook. I helped her with her seatbelt and drove out of the stable, stopped to close the door—no electronic door-openers in this house, thank you very much—went down the drive and on to Main Street.

Driving her old Lincoln Continental is to return to those decades we've come to call The American Century. Big as a full-size pickup truck, it has a powerful V-8 engine unencumbered by air-pollution controls, capable of propelling its several tons of steel, sheet glass, and chrome to velocities that might surprise Oliver Moody's hopped-up Fury.

"What happened?" she asked.

"To Renny?"

"Yes, Renny. Why did he do it?"

My question exactly. When I didn't answer immediately, Connie said, "You are aware he was smuggling cocaine?"

"I don't believe it."

"Why not? They said the airplane was crammed full."

"I saw."

"You were there?" She looked at me sharply, her bony face and snow-white curls frozen in sudden astonishment and—I was shocked to see—fear. For one second I could see her thinking, Oh, Lord, Ben was in on it.

"Steve Greenan took me to identify the body."

"What the devil for? He's known Renny since he was born."

"He knew I wanted to see him."

Connie nodded, relaxing back in the seat. "Stevie Greenan was always a very thoughtful boy. So you saw. Is it true he'd been shot?"

"Yes."

"So why don't you believe?"

"Connie, it doesn't make any sense. Renny's not a criminal. He was a businessman."

"Businessman? A Chevalley? Come on, Ben. I know you liked him, but really."

"Did he fix your car?"

"He was an excellent mechanic. And he picked up and delivered the car. I never had to go down there, thank God."

"Connie, he had seven mechanics working for him, two tow-truck drivers, and a secretary. He became a businessman."

Connie was no fool. "It takes a lot of money to hire seven mechanics, two tow drivers, and a secretary, not to mention purchasing the tools, the trucks, and the office. Where did it come from?"

"Banks."

"Perhaps he was having difficulty paying them back."

"Maybe. But I just don't see him doing that. Some people are naturally honest."

"Some people are brought up properly."

"Some people were lucky that way," I reminded her, remembering the time when I was fifteen and she, seventy, drove me down to Danbury, to the movies, to see *The Man Who Would Be King*. Vaster than television ever could be, it was the best thing I had ever seen. When it ended I just slumped in my seat, dreading the daylight outside. "Would you like to see it again?" she asked.

"Could we?"

"Certainly. Come along." Puzzled, I followed her down the aisle. I thought she'd said we could see it again, but here we were walking out as the people for the next show filed in. We hurried to the box office and Connie asked to buy two more tickets. The kid selling tickets looked at her like she was a visitation from *The Exorcist* and the manager came running to see what was the trouble. Connie set him straight. She paid for two more tickets and we went back in and saw it again. She had always been easy to talk to, and I asked her why she'd paid again when we could have just sat there for free.

She said, "We honor the objects of our desire by paying for them. And we honor the people who created them."

She had never approved of Renny as my friend. She was behind my father and mother's decision to send me to the Newbury School and, when she feared I was getting a little too wild, off to Stonybrook Military. She had interceded personally to get my senatorial appointment to Annapolis. And she'd attended every day of my trial, taking up residence at the Carlyle Hotel.

"Do you suppose," she asked as we drove down Church Hill, "that there is a connection?"

"Between what and what, Aunt Connie?"

"Between the two killings."

"Oh. You heard about the man at the Long place."

"I heard he was where he shouldn't be."

"How so?"

"*Mr.* Long was away. *Mrs.* Long was entertaining."

Connie glanced sidelong at me. Most of the elderly blue-eyed people I know around here get watery-eyed as they get older. Not Connie. Hers were dark and sharp enough to cut.

"You're a connection."

"Me?"

"Well, I hear you found the poor man's body. And now you tell me you and Stevie found Renny."

"Al Bell found Renny."

"Ben, should I be worried about you?"

"No, Connie. It's just a lousy coincidence. I'm sorry if you have to hear more embarrassing gossip."

"Ha!" She laughed, a little reminder that when it came to Society in this corner of New England, Connie Abbott set the standards and made the rules. "Now what am I going to say to that poor girl?"

We descended the long slope to Frenchtown—fantastic on a bike, hell walking it home—past Chevalley Enterprises, which was shut for Sunday. The twenty-four-hour wrecker stood outside, draped with black crepe from the firehouse.

If I thought that her rhetorical question about comforting Betty Chevalley meant she was done questioning me, I was wrong.

"Did you know Mrs. Long?"

"Very slightly."

"If she's the girl I saw chatting you up at the cookout, she's a great beauty."

"From you that's a compliment."

"Shut up, Ben."

"Yes, Rita Long is a great beauty."

"I was reminded of your mother."

"The hair."

"And that woman who testified against you."

"Same thing," I answered sharply. "Her hair."

"I always thought you were a fool for women."

"Not *all* women, Connie."

"Too bad. You'd grow out of it faster. . . ."

Ahead lay Renny's neat little ranch, built down the road from his parents' ramshackle farmhouse. Trailers up the hillside housed brothers and sisters. The drive and the lawn were scattered with pickup trucks parked at urgent-looking angles. A gang of men with caps pulled over their long hair were hanging around the front door, sipping coffee from containers and morning Buds from cans. Aunt Connie asked, as I parked on the road, "Are you still seeing Victoria McLachlan?"

"We're just friends."

"Too bad. There's a woman going places. She could use a good man around the house."

Caps flew and the gang at the door melted with a mumbled chorus of "Good morning, Miss Abbott." She greeted each by name. There wasn't a man among them who hadn't raked leaves for her at some point in his boyhood. I got my usual allotment of "Hey Ben"s and a few consoling "Sorry about Renny"s. Pinkerton Chevalley stood off under a tree, looking like he would kill someone if he could only figure out who. I gave him a nod and a clenched fist, and he fisted back.

Inside were women, coffee, and cakes. Renny's mom—my Aunt Frances, a grandmother many times over at fifty-five—hugged me and shook hands with Connie, whom she called "Miss Abbott." Aunt Frances was a Jervis, with just enough Butler and Trudeau blood to bring her indoors. She had cut a fabled swath through the young men of the town in her middle-school days before settling on Renny's dad, my mother's quiet older brother, who was nowhere in sight. Still a looker with her taut French cheeks, dark hair, and meet-me-in-the-hayloft eyes, she wore this morning the rigid smile of a woman who did not yet believe that she had lost her son. Any minute, she was telling herself, Renny would come walking in the door with a good story for his absence.

Aunt Connie took her hand in both of hers. "I'm sorry, Frances." She had a gift for making the simple phrase "I'm sorry" sound as if she grieved for Renny's mom from the bottom of her heart. Because she'd never been married and had no children of her own, people accorded her a priestlike understanding of human loss and failure. Her presence was balm, her words wisdom.

"May we see the widow?" she asked after a proper interval.

Frances, obviously glad of a job, ran ahead to alert Betty Butler Chevalley. I trailed Connie into the bedroom, where Betty was sitting with a bunch of her sisters, all as redheaded and round (and ordinarily jolly) as she. They were stabbing out cigarettes and rising nervously for Connie, who trundled in waving them down with her pocketbook. She went right to Betty and took her hands and spoke quietly and urgently for a moment.

Betty, who was twenty-three, looked like a child who had lost her pet. She'd been crying. Her fair skin was blotched, her eyes swollen slits. She turned to me when Connie let go of her hands.

"You saw," she said. "Did they hurt him?"

"He couldn't have felt a thing."

"That's what Dr. Greenan said."

"I'm sure he's right."

"Renny didn't do anything."

"I know."

"But the cops searched here. They searched, here with the kids. They handcuffed Pink. They scared my kids. And Oliver Moody said they'll be back. They're going to search the garage."

"I'll call Tim Hall. Keep 'em away from the kids, at least."

Renny's mom came in and asked if Connie would like some coffee. She started to say No thank you, but noticed the gaggle of Butler girls eyeing her like the grande dame from their favorite soap opera and said, "Yes, thank you. Would it be possible for me to sit down here?" Girls leapt. A chair was offered and they gathered around.

I went out and joined the guys. Joey Meadows got a cold one from his truck and pressed it into my hand. I said, "Here's to Renny," and drained half of it in a bourbon-sluicing swallow.

"Anybody know was that his plane?" I asked.

Gary Nello said, "I hear it was rented."

"You saw him?" Pete Stock asked me.

"Yeah. He never felt a thing."

"So how'd he crash?"

"I don't know. I don't really think he could have tried to fly. Doc said the whole back of his head was gone."

"So he crashed and then he got shot."

"Unless the guy who shot him crashed it."

"Yeah, maybe that's what happened. Guy shoots Renny, tries to take off, and blows it."

"Why didn't he just dump Renny?"

"Maybe he was going to ditch the body in the water."

I said, "There was coke all over everything. Like a bag broke. . . .Who would bring coke by plane?"

Several men looked off at the woods.

Freddy Butler gave me a hard stare. He was a weaselly little guy who hung around some of the Jervises. He drove a new four-wheel-drive Ford pickup with a show bar and flame decals, though he hadn't had a job since the lumberyard went bust.

Someone else mumbled, "I hear they drive the stuff in same as grass."

"Who up here would buy that much?" I asked.

"Maybe there's some more spics with a factory."

"They wouldn't need Renny," Joe Charney scoffed. "What do you think, Renny flew it from Colombia in that little plane?"

"I don't think Renny flew it from anywhere," I said, a pronouncement met with silence. We batted it around awhile. Few thought smuggling cocaine was the end of the world, though most, but not all, agreed it was pretty stupid, especially since you could get murdered doing it. Pink wandered over from his tree, fished a fresh Bud out of his truck, and stood shaking his head. "This whole damned thing don't make no sense. Somebody's bangin' us."

"Did you know he was flying again?"

"Told me he was flying some charter jobs. Taking rich people out to Block Island."

"Where'd he get the time?"

"Made the time. The bucks were good. Needed the bucks."

"Was he doing it a lot?"

"Once, twice a week most of the summer."

"Where'd he get the plane?"

"I don't know."

"I mean what airport did he drive to? He didn't fly out of Al's field, did he?"

"I don't know. Maybe he drove down to Oxford. They got an airport. Maybe he flew out of somebody else's field right here."

"But where'd he get the plane?"

"I don't know."

I slipped a hand around Pink's thigh-sized bicep and walked him back to his tree. "Pink. Do you think he was flying dope?"

"I don't know."

"Pink, for crissake, it's me. Was he flying dope?"

"I know it's you. I don't know. I ain't his nurse."

"Would Betty know?"

Renny's big brother regarded women as flawed food-and-sex machines. "If Betty found coke she'd powder the baby's ass with it."

"So who would know?"

"I don't know," said Pink, looking away.

"Come on."

"I don't know."

"Pink, give me a break."

"Maybe Gwen Jervis."

"*What?*" I was astonished. Between my real estate business and my far-flung family, there wasn't a whole hell of a lot going on in Newbury that I didn't know about. "Gwen Jervis?"

"Hey, you give women a couple of babies, they don't want to do it any more. Renny's normal. Guy's gotta get his ashes hauled. Right?"

"Gwen?"

"You got a problem with that?" Pink, never far from looking dangerous, began to look very dangerous.

"Well, she's his cousin and—"

"They're not making babies, they're just doin' it."

"Okay. I'm just a little surprised. I thought things were great with Betty."

"Long as Renny had Gwen, things were great with Betty," said Pink. "You don't know shit about life, do you?"

I went back to the others and asked bluntly whether anyone had heard any talk at all about my cousin flying coke. I got some shrugs and some "No"s and "No way"s, while a concerted shuffling of boots and battered running shoes separated me and the group. All but Freddy Butler, who draped one elbow on his flame-covered hood and gave me another hard look.

"You're going to piss some people off if you don't shut up."

In school Freddy had been the little kid who made friends with the bully, so I didn't take him very seriously.

"What people, Freddy?"

"I'm just saying you don't want to step in the middle of something."

"Because for a second there it sounded like you were threatening me."

"Not me, Ben."

There are four corners on Main Street at the flagpole and three churches. The fourth corner is the Yankee Drover Inn, in whose cellar bar I would ordinarily be reading the Sunday *Times* with a Bloody Mary. Instead, I was across the street sitting next to Aunt Connie in the front pew of the Episcopal church, listening to a hastily written sermon on the subject of the Sixth Commandment. Ordinarily, Reverend Owen would have dusted off his regular Autumn Sermon—"To everything a time, a time for sleep and death"—but while our two killings had occurred too late for the morning papers, he'd risen to the occasion. There wasn't much he could say about Ron without getting heavily into the Seventh Commandment, and besides, nobody knew him. But Renny was local, and to give Landon his due, he never once credited the cocaine story. He just stuck to the fact that Renny had been murdered.

He asked the congregation to join hearts with our neighbors in the Catholic church across the street—Renny's church—whose parishioners would be mourning one of their own. This was no small thing, considering that there were many old people in our congregation who had been raised to believe that Catholics kept guns in their churches for the day the Pope would order war on the Protestants.

As we shuffled out after the benediction, on line to shake Reverend Owen's hand, Connie asked, "Where was your mother? I thought we'd see her there."

"Aunt Frances told me she had just left."

"Well, sometime this week it would be nice if you would drive over there with me. I've not seen her in some time, and I heard she's a little low. . . . You do see her regularly, don't you?"

"I go for dinner."

"How often?"

"I'll call her. Maybe we could drive over Wednesday."

"Landon," she said as she pumped the minister's hand. "That was an excellent sermon."

"Sad days," he said. He was young and, I knew, wavering in his faith. He'd told me one night sitting on the lawn in front of the church that he felt useless when his parishioners' lives got twisted. He was thinking about going back to school to study psychology. It seemed a practical thing to do, but the decision to leave the church was tearing him up.

Oliver Moody was directing traffic as the Catholic, Congregationalist, and Episcopal parking lots emptied simultaneously. He held everything up for Connie to cross the street. Whatever he held for me in his gaze was hidden behind his sunglasses. I walked her home, offered her lunch at the Yankee Drover. She said she was ready for a nap. I wandered back across, without Oliver's help this time, into my office to check my silent answering machine, left a note on the door where I could be found, then walked to the General Store for a paper, and finally into the cellar bar of the Yankee Drover, where I ordered a Bloody Mary and a burger and settled into the cool dark. The place was nearly empty, as it would remain until the regular parishioners drove their wives and mothers home. Tony Franco, the owner, who tends his own bar on Sundays, set down my spicy, straight-up Bloody and said, "There's a guy in the booth asking for you."

I watched in the back bar mirror as he emerged from the shadows. He had exchanged his "country" clothes for a "Sunday best" suit, neatly tailored for his ample frame.

"Home at last?" said Alex Rose. He looked smug as a CNN correspondent in the middle of a brand new war.

I said, "Your camera's in the mail."

He said, "They're gonna arrest Mrs. Long for murder."

10

Renny held a monopoly on my emotions, and at first the strongest feeling I could rouse for Rose's news was surprise that the New York P.I. knew his way around my town better than I.

"Where'd you hear that?"

"I bought a friend in the Plainfield state trooper barracks. Tipped me off in time to get Mr. Long up to the house with a limo load of lawyers."

"Shouldn't you be holding their coats or something?"

Rose's beefy face got hard at the edges. "You got a problem with me?"

"I got a problem with everybody at the moment. I just lost a friend. If you don't mind I'd rather drink alone. Even if you do mind."

"Your cousin Renny. I'm sorry, fella. I didn't know you were close."

I turned back to the political cartoons in the "Week in Review" section of the Sunday *Times* and stared at a gag line I'd already read three times.

Rose said, "Rita's innocent."

"I know that."

"She didn't shoot him."

"You don't have to convince me."

"I want to know exactly what you saw when you found the bastard. They're basing the case on the M.E.'s opinion of the angle of entry."

"He wasn't a bastard. He seemed like a decent guy."

"Screwing his friend and partner's wife."

"She chose well. So did he."

"That why you didn't do the tape? You fell for them, didn't you? You liked them as a couple. I'm not surprised. I had a witness in New York, a gay waiter, raving on about how romantic they were."

I raised the paper and tried to read Anna Quindlen, who was pulling hard for another Pulitzer with a piece about forty-year-old male dropouts and the families they left behind. No problem; I had a few years to go, and no one to desert when I got there.

Rose said, "Let's get back to when you found the body."

"Why are they charging Rita Long?"

"Her shotgun. Her fingerprints."

"Powder test?" I asked through the paper.

"Passed it. But she could have scrubbed. Or she could have worn a glove."

"Anyone suggesting a motive?"

"Lovers' quarrel."

"Bull."

"Old reliable. Juries do love the lovers' quarrel."

"Long's standing by her?" I asked.

"One hundred percent."

"Why? I thought he wanted a divorce." I lowered the paper. Guys were coming in to the bar, discussing whether the Boston Red Sox would disappoint us in the playoffs. The optimists were betting they'd wait to disappoint us in the World Series. This occasioned some shouting.

Rose raised his voice to be heard. "Why? Hey, just because he's rich doesn't mean he's smart. Maybe he loves her. Maybe he figures with Ron out of the way, he's got a clear field with his wife again. Catch her on the rebound."

"Who was Ron?"

Rose looked surprised. "You don't know?"

"Nobody told me. How should I know? I just know she called him Ron and he used to be Long's partner, a fact you neglected to mention."

Rose did not apologize. "Ronald Pearlman," he said. "Sold his father's furrier chain before the fur market crashed. Bought a Hong Kong chip factory and merged with LTS."

"LTS? What is that, Long Techno-Something?"

"Long Technical Systems. I thought you knew all this from your M&A days."

"I worked my miracles in the Rustbelt— Rita told me Long bought Ron out."

"He hates partners. Ron had brought him excellent manufacturing capability, but once he had those offshore factories, it galled him that Ron would split the profits."

"Did they fight?"

"Over what? Ron goes from let's say ten million bucks from his father's business to two hundred and fifty million bucks for his Hong Kong operation. The guy's thirty-eight with enough money to buy Rhode Island. He's got it all."

"Except his own wife."

"Some guys are greedy."

I wondered why, if Rita wanted to run off with Ron, she had wanted to sell the Castle when he had a quarter billion bucks in the bank.

"How'd he parlay ten million into two-fifty?"

"First you answer my questions. Then I'll answer yours. What did you see when you found the body?"

I asked Franco for a refill. Rose ordered a beer. Then I told him everything I'd told the state police. Rose asked some intelligent questions, and when we had hashed it out he asked, "So you still think he was shot from the woods?"

"Hey, I didn't do the autopsy. I heard Steve guess it was close range. The woods were about fifty yards off."

"How far was the tower?"

"Eighty yards."

"Long shot with a deer slug."

"That's what I thought."

"They think she shot him from the tower."

"That will be a tough one to prove."

"They don't seem worried."

"So how'd Ron Pearlman multiply ten million dollars into two hundred and fifty million?"

"He was well connected in Hong Kong from his old man's fur coat factories. The government gave him grants to expand. Hot operation. The chip factory had some new process. A bunch of different American outfits wanted to control it for their own exclusive supply. They got in a bidding war. LTS won."

"Connected, smart, and lucky."

"Great combination," Rose agreed. "I'd be envious, if he weren't dead."

"I don't buy the lovers' quarrel."

"I was hoping you'd say that."

"Why?"

"We'll expect you to tell it to the jury."

"What?"

"If it comes to a trial—and that's certainly what the state's attorney has in mind—we'd like you to appear as a sort of character witness."

"I'm not sure I'm following you," I said, though I had a bad feeling I was.

"You saw them together, right?"

"Briefly. Like I told you on the phone."

"Well it's too bad you blew the taping, but at least you saw them together. No one else has. They were really careful in New York. I got a shot of them getting into a cab, and some waiters who'll testify they had lunch together. But in you I've got a well-connected local guy who can persuade the jury that Ron and Rita were deeply—nonviolently—in love. *Nonviolently* being the operative word here."

"Wait a minute—"

"I know you don't want to stand up in court and admit you were sneaking around the woods taking pictures."

"You're right about that."

"But you were. And Mrs. Long's freedom lies in the balance."

"You're forgetting my rep. The prosecutor will eat me for breakfast. He'll discredit me to discredit my testimony."

"I don't think so."

"He will."

"Oh he'll try to destroy you. No avoiding that. But he can't discredit your testimony. I don't care how much of a sleaze he reveals you to be, the jury will get that those two people adored each other."

"I don't want to be destroyed here. This is my home."

"Sorry, fella. You want that woman to sit in jail for the rest of her life for something she probably didn't do?"

"Probably?"

Rose shrugged. "Whether she blew him away is not the question. The question is Will she serve time for it? Now Mr. Long is up there with four of the top lawyers in New York to answer No. And I'm out hustling witnesses, to answer No."

I started to protest. Rose cut me off. "This is not debatable. We'll subpoena you. You'll testify for the defense. And then you'll duke it out with the prosecutor. No one's asking if you *want* to do this. You're doing it."

"And if I refuse to testify?"

"Look what happened last time."

I would have decked him right there in the cellar of the Yankee Drover, but whether I wanted to testify wasn't the issue, because I'd seen something at the Castle that Rose had not. Rita's spooky drawing would steamroller any sympathy I could build for the loving couple.

So instead of knocking him off his barstool, I said, "I'm sure she didn't do it. I'll do what I can to help her. But I'll tell you right now, anything I say won't help one damned bit the second the jury gets a load of one of Mrs. Long's drawings in the studio."

"Which one?"

I described the figure of Ron, naked with skull. "Like I say, I'm sure she didn't kill him, but if you let them get her as far as a trial, they'll show that picture. Any twelve northwest Connecticut jurors will take one look and say, Yup, a woman who'd draw a picture like that would shoot a man as soon as look at him. They'll make me testify I saw her draw it and it'll hang her."

Rose took a leather-bound notepad from his jacket and opened it to the first page. "Bear with me just a minute. . . . Just checking their warrants. . . . No. There's no such picture."

"It's on the smaller easel. The cops must have seen it. Ask your friend at the barracks."

"No, I was just up there. The big one was a landscape—the view from the turret, as a matter of fact—"

"The little one. On the smaller easel."

"No. That was a landscape, too. A pond and a fence. I don't know what you saw, but it wasn't there now and there's no mention of it in the warrants."

"You took it."

"No. You said the cops would have seen it yesterday. I wasn't there yesterday. Just you and her and Ron." He closed his book and pocketed it with a satisfied smile.

I said, "There was someone else."

"Who's that?"

"The shooter."

"Right," said Rose. "The shooter."

"You think she killed him, don't you?"

"The jury won't give a rat's ass what I think."

"But you think she did it."

"I don't *care* if she did it. My job's to help get her off. Wake up, fella. Mr. Long's paying for a program here: top criminal lawyers in court; me backing them up on the street. The man who's paying says his wife will not go to jail."

"Does he believe his wife killed her lover?"

"The state's attorney has a pretty thin case so far. Mr. Long's strategy is to scare off an indictment. Trouble is, you got a small-town prosecutor here who sees a chance to get famous trying a rich, beautiful defendant. So if it comes to a trial, you're on, my friend."

"I asked you if Long believes his wife killed her lover."

"He doesn't confide in the help." Rose got up from his stool. I put my hand on his elbow. He gave it a get-out-of-my-face look. I curled my fingers until I had his full attention.

"If I testify, I have to testify I saw her drawing."

He tried to pull away. "I thought you said she's innocent."

"She is, but I can't lie for her."

I let go. Rose flexed his arm, muttering, "With a friend like you, she won't need enemies."

I switched to bourbon old-fashioneds. I'd had enough tomato juice, and felt like something sweet.

11

Sunday didn't get any better.

Around dark Franco cut me off, suggesting I appoint a designated walker to get me home. I was dimly aware he gave the sports crowd watching the TV a nod, and my walker appeared in the form of an agitated Vicky McLachlan, whom I had earlier sent away, saying I had no desire to talk about Renny, thank you.

"You don't drink like this," she noted, which was true, by and large. By the time I came up with a smart reply, we were already out the door, where I promptly forgot what I was going to say. The way home was a mismatch. Vicky is simply too short to steer a drunk and too lightly built to keep one from falling.

"Are you okay?"

I was in Scooter MacKay's hedge. "Fine. I'm fine."

Vicky turned away from a car full of staring voters. I collected my thoughts. "I'm sorry you never got to know Renny."

"I didn't know you knew him that well."

"Oh, I did."

"But you didn't hang out with him."

"He was busy. And I was . . . busy."

"Get out of the bushes."

I climbed out, with her help. "Do you feel guilty?" she asked.

"Why should I?"

"I've never seen you so upset. You weren't like this when your father died."

"You hardly knew me when my father died." He had gone suddenly, heart attack in the ambulance. I got home just in time for the funeral. She spoke well at the church.

"You were cool as ice."

"Then, I felt guilty. . . ."

At my front door, I invited her in. Vicky bit her lip. "I'll put you to bed."

"I'm not sure I'm up—"

"I'll be the judge of that."

Lying in Scooter's hedge, I had known that I had lost every inhibition and was about to renege again on my promise to myself to get out of Vicky's life before I did serious damage. I groped her on the stairs—artfully, I thought. But Monday morning I awoke to every indication that I had spent the night alone.

My mind was clear, despite a ferocious headache. Two hangovers in a row were one too many, and I had no intention of chasing this one with beer and Bloody Marys; I had coffee in my office, paid a couple of bills, balanced my checkbook. August is always a slow month. This year September looked worse. At nine-thirty, I telephoned Trooper Boyce.

"I was just about to call you," she answered the phone. "Wondering if your memory has improved at all."

"Would you like to have lunch with me?" I asked.

I believe she was so surprised that she said Yes before she could say No. I suggested the Hopkins Inn, overlooking Lake Waramaug. We agreed on twelve-thirty.

I telephoned the *New York Times* and booked another ad for the Richardson place. One of these days it was going to sell—you can't buy that kind of privacy easily—and I intended to be there at the closing. Then I walked over to the General Store and bought a *Times,* and the Danbury daily, to see what the papers had on Renny and Rita and Ron.

The *Danbury News-Times* gave what they called "The Death

Plane" front-page treatment, with an equal-size headline for Rita's arrest. She was described as a "wealthy weekender from New York City." Bail hearings were scheduled for this morning, which meant the poor woman had spent the night in jail despite her hotshot attorneys.

The *Times* had twelve lines in the Metro section about Renny and his plane but not a word about Rita's arrest. As I understand these things, the edition we get trucked up here leaves the printing plant about nine P.M. I wondered if they'd had time to print a story, or if Long's lawyers had hired a publicist to sit on it.

We're too far north to receive News Radio 88 from New York, and the local news tends to be of the canned national variety or the momentous public-broadcasting type. So what it came down to was that Rita's arrest was being downplayed and nobody but a few locals cared about Renny. I had, of course, missed the TV news Sunday night but assumed that the Hartford stations, at least, had included interviews with major case squadders Bender and Boyce.

The latter arrived at the Hopkins Inn looking flatteringly flustered. I had the definite feeling that some small female-kid part of her wanted lunch to be a date, so *I* was flattered. She looked kind of cute in a brown suit, with a handbag big enough for an automatic, and her hair all fluffy. She had on more makeup than on Saturday. Eyeliner, mostly, and some shadow that turned her gray gaze silver.

"Sorry I'm late," she greeted me.

"Bail hearing?"

"Denied." She studied my reaction. I was surprised. I had figured Long's legal muscle could spring Rita on bail. Of course, local courts don't always cotton to $400-an-hour outside attorneys throwing their weight around.

Trooper Boyce said, "Should we order a drink or should I open my notebook?"

"Coffee for me. What would you like? And you're going to need two notebooks."

She spread her big hands on the table. "Two?"

"I want to talk to you about Rita Long and I want to talk to you about Renny Chevalley. Renny first."

"I'm going to read you your rights."

"No need."

She read them anyway, in a low voice, by heart, while holding a menu. A prosperous-looking couple at the next table exchanged the little smile lovers do when they see another couple sharing a special moment.

"Are you ready?" I said.

"Do you understand your rights?"

"Yes, goddammit. This isn't a confession."

"But your memory has improved."

"Renny first."

"Go."

"Renny Chevalley would not fly coke into Newbury."

"How come?"

I told her all about my cousin. She listened, taking notes. When I was done, she said, "Your opinion is noted. It's now part of our investigation."

"No. You don't get it. What everyone thinks happened up there didn't happen. It's something else."

"What?"

"I have racked my brain. I can't think, but it's not what you see. If he was flying dope he was tricked into it. Maybe he discovered it and tried to stop them. Maybe that's why they shot him."

"We've considered that."

"And?"

"We're considering various possibilities. The problem with this theory is Why did they leave the coke behind?"

"The bag broke."

"Maybe. But it would have been worth the trouble to stuff it in their pockets. Thousands of dollars. Dope smugglers usually do it for the money." She saw my disappointment. "Tell you what I'll do: I'll follow up each of the facts you've laid out about your cousin's life, his business. We'll see what his financial situation was. Keep in mind, whatever he did, *someone* shot him, and that's murder."

I still hadn't conveyed how absurd it was. "Saturday night I got the impression that the police think one smuggler killing another isn't the crime of the century."

Marian Boyce said, "I just told you, I'm investigating a murder. Two murders, actually. What did you recall about Mrs. Long?"

"Where did the plane come from?"

"Your cousin rented it in Danbury. What did you recall about Mrs. Long?"

"She didn't do it."

Marian Boyce gestured for me to continue.

"She didn't do it," I repeated.

"Who did?"

"I still think it was a hunting accident."

"The coroner doesn't agree. He was shot in the back from the turret. The slug struck him at a high angle."

"The woods slope up sharply. It could have come from the woods. Thirty yards inside the trees, a hunter would be standing as high as the top of the tower."

"We found no sign of a hunter."

"Mrs. Long told me they had a prowler the night before."

"Turned out to be a raccoon. Trooper Moody shot it."

"What if the raccoon didn't do it?"

"Huh?"

"What if there was a prowler and the raccoon happened to be the wrong raccoon in the wrong place at the wrong time?" I was not unaware that *I* had been the prowler; I was merely trying to get the detective's attention. It wasn't working. She inspected her nail polish.

I said, "You've probably figured out by now that they were lovers."

"No shit, Sherlock."

"Has it occurred to you that her husband might have shot Ron?"

"Mr. Long was in the Rose Garden of the White House, having his picture taken with the President of the United States. . . . Do you have any more information?"

I had no information, and, with Jack Long off the hook, only one theory. "If I find a hunter—a poacher—who shot him by accident, can I come straight to you?"

"Fast as you can dial 911."

"I'm trying to tell you she didn't do it."

"You've got the same problem with your cousin: You're not telling me why."

"I just know it. I know she could not have killed Ron."

"Why?"

"She loved him too much."

"Wait a minute. You said you met her at the cookout. And you went to appraise her house. Then you drank a glass of champagne in her turret. If that was your total contact with the woman, how do you *know* she loved her boyfriend too much to kill him?"

I was close to telling her about the video and the couple I saw they were. But I was afraid it would lead to more misery for Rita Long rather than less, so I said, "By the way she held his body."

"I hope the food here is worth the drive." She put away her notebook. "So tell me, what's it like to grow up a rich kid?"

"I wasn't a rich kid."

"Trooper Moody said your father was mayor. Mine pounded a beat in New Haven. To me, you're a rich kid."

"Well, in that case, it was very pleasant growing up in Newbury. A little boring, but we made our own fun."

"I heard the guys at the barracks laughing about some fun you made with Trooper Moody."

I couldn't stop the grin that jumped on my face. "The next time you see Ollie, watch how he always walks behind his car before he gets in."

"Wha'd you do? They wouldn't tell me."

"Why not?"

"One thousand state police. Fifty women."

She spoke matter-of-factly, but I got the impression that being tough enough to handle bigotry didn't mean she didn't get lonely. So I said, "Renny helped."

"Is that supposed to be a character reference?"

"Yes, as a matter of fact, because he was backing me up. Trooper Moody had done something pretty awful to me."

"What?"

"A cop thing. . . . I was a teenager. It seemed like a big deal at the time."

"Did he humiliate you in front of your friends?"

"How'd you guess?"

"I'm a cop. So wha'd you do?—Don't worry, as long as you didn't murder somebody the statute of limitations is up. Besides, I don't kiss and tell." She flashed her pretty smile. I told my story, the least I owed her for the information, which hadn't made the newspapers, that Renny had rented his plane at Danbury Airport.

"There was a dance that night at the grange hall. Out on the edge of town? So Renny and I sneaked a double-barrel twelve-gauge out of my father's gun case and hid it in the field behind the grange hall. Then we borrowed a hundred-foot logging chain from Renny's brother Pink—by the way, handcuffing Pink the other night was not your finest community-relations effort."

"Judgment call," Marian shrugged. "The man's big enough to do a lot of damage. So what happened?"

"Well, we wheelbarrowed the chain to the Church Hill Diner. And when Ollie drove up and went inside for his coffee break, we tied one end around that huge maple out front and the other around his rear axle."

"You're kidding."

"Bunched the slack under the car. Renny was afraid of getting caught, which was fine by me because I wanted to watch, so he ran back behind the grange hall to fire the shotgun in the air. Both barrels. *Kabooooooom!* You can imagine how it echoed on a still summer night, and just to make sure, he re-loaded and let off two more.

"Ollie came out of the diner like someone had fired him from a cannon, leaped into his cruiser, hit lights, siren, and ignition all at once and floored the beast. He was driving a big, fast Ford that year—"

Marian was starting to laugh. "The LTD. Four-barrel carbs."

"That's the one. It took off, *screaming* up Church Hill, smoking, burning rubber. He hit forty before the chain fetched up. All of a sudden—Bang!—rear wheels, axle, and differential were bouncing at the end of the chain, but Ollie kept going. He slid a hundred yards in this huge spray of sparks and smoke before he finally scrunched to a stop in the middle of Church Hill Road. Scooter McKay took a picture, but his father wouldn't print it."

"Rotten kids."

"Long time ago. . . . Marian—May I call you Marian?"

"Yes, Ben. Of course, call me Marian."

"We were both 'rotten kids.' Me worse than him. But he was never a kid to smuggle coke. He just wasn't. You gotta know that."

"And Rita Long's not a woman to shoot her lover. You know something? You're a romantic guy, Ben. Got a girl?"

"Nothing that's going anywhere. Which is fine with me. How about you? Got a fella?"

"Two at the moment," she answered, volunteering nothing more about her love life as she picked up the menu. "What do you recommend?"

"The view."

She perused the menu, noticed me frowning, and leaned over the table. "Hey."

"What?"

"You're kind of pent up about your cousin, right now. Why don't you just give yourself a couple of days to rethink all this?"

"I knew Rita Long didn't kill her boyfriend before I found out about Renny."

Trooper Boyce sighed. "I checked you out, Ben. I know your background. Put yourself in my place. Remember what you thought of hunches when you were in Naval Intelligence?"

"I remember 'Naval Intelligence' sometimes seemed like a contradiction of terms."

She smiled her pretty smile. "Hunches are nice. Facts are better. Remember? Suppose a cute little midshipwoman reported her C.O. grabbed her ass behind the anchor. Did you look her over and think, Sweet young thing—she'd never lie. Let's courtmartial the louse? Or did you take a report, interview witnesses, and marshal your facts?"

"I remember hunches that led me to facts."

"Fine. Call me when you get some facts. We've set up temporary headquarters at the Plainfield barracks."

"911?"

She took a card from her bag and scribbled with a smile. "Try this number first."

We had trout. It was great. As for the *purpose* of lunch, it was a disaster. I still wondered if I should confess about the video, but instinct still said it wouldn't help. After coffee Marian signaled for the check.

"No, my treat," I protested.

"You get the next one—when it's not business. Call me. Anytime."

I headed back to Newbury with the distinct impression that neither of Trooper Boyce's fellas were in for the long haul. Or was she humoring me?

I drove straight on through Newbury, on toward Danbury.

12

Two propeller planes droned around Danbury Airport. One flew for the highway patrol, hoping to ambush the last speeder on the planet unaware that white crosses painted on the shoulder marked an aerial speed trap. The other plane, painted Chinese red, belonged to Sky Rentals. The owner was practicing approaches, apparently, touching down on the runway, skipping away, touching down again, and wobbling back up. I waited beside a hangar. At the end of the runway sprawled the gigantic Danbury Fair Mall, former site of Danbury's fairgrounds where we used to watch Pinkerton Chevalley race Renny's GTO on the stock car track.

The airport is a dinky little thing by comparison to the shopping mall. The megalith Macy's, Sears, and Lord & Taylor dwarf the hangars. The runway looks smaller than its parking lots.

At last, the red plane came down and trundled up to where I was sitting. An angry man in golfing togs stormed off to a BMW and sped away. His companion climbed out of the plane whitefaced and shaking.

"You waiting for me?"

"If you're the Roy Chernowsky who rents planes."

"Sorry I took so long. I was checking out a renter."

"I gather he didn't pass."

"No, he didn't. What can I do for you? Looking to rent?"

"I'm Ben Abbott. Renny Chevalley's cousin."

"Renny's your cousin?" Chernowsky glanced around, frightened, as if I were the coke crew's executioner.

"Relax," I said. "I'm just trying to figure out what happened. I don't believe he was flying coke."

"Then who shot him?"

"You tell me. Who was he flying with?"

"Just the cat."

"What cat?"

"You don't know about the cat? The cat's the kind of thing I thought he would have told you about."

"No, no, no. We didn't work together. I rode along freight dogging a couple of times, but this whole thing just makes no sense to me. What cat?"

"The cat belongs to this rich doctor, right? The doc's got a house on Block Island. She goes out for a week at a time. The other day, she couldn't find the cat, so she went without it. Then her housekeeper finds the cat. The doc says, Great. Box it and tell Renny to fly it out here."

"The doctor knows Renny?"

"Sure. Renny runs her out regular. So the housekeeper gets hold of Renny, who hires my plane and flies the cat out to Block."

"So how does this turn into coke?"

"You tell me, cousin. He's supposed to be back here by one in the afternoon. Instead he telephones and says he's keeping the plane late. I say how late, he says home by dark. Fine with me. I'm paid by the hour, and nobody else had booked it. Comes dark, no Renny. No plane. No calls. Till around ten, when a trooper shows up waving a search warrant, takes my books, informs me they're impounding my plane, and tells *me* not to leave town. Like yeah, where am I going minus a plane that ain't paid for?"

"Who's the doctor?"

"Zelda Schwartz."

"Got her number?"

"She's still out there. Hey, you want me to fly you to Block Island?"

"I doubt I could afford it. But I would appreciate her number."

"I think it's private."

"Never mind, I'll call her office. . . . Tell me something: How far could Renny go in that plane?"

"Far as he wanted."

"How far? I mean, could he fly to Boston?"

"Sure."

"Chicago?"

"He'd have to refuel."

"Let's say after he left Block Island, how far could he have gone until they found him?"

"I'm not following you."

"What time did he call you from Block Island?"

"Cops wanted to know the same thing. About eleven."

"So from eleven to dark, let's say, how far could he have flown? Obviously farther than Block Island to Newbury."

"You're talking about nine or ten hours flying time—that's a fast plane—nearly two thousand miles, minus fueling time."

"Chicago and back?"

"Guess so. Toronto, Montreal, Washington, Philly, Atlantic City. Anyplace east of the Mississippi. Of course, he would have been one whipped puppy flying that distance alone."

"Did the plane have autopilot?"

"Yeah, but still it's not like he could put his feet up and go to sleep."

"Didn't he have to file a flight plan?"

"Didn't have to. He could stay out of the patterns—which of course he'd want to do if he were smuggling coke."

"*Did* he file any flight plan?"

"The way I heard it, he flew from Block to LaGuardia."

"Where'd he go from there?"

"No one knows. He filed for Teterboro. Flying at the unrestricted eight hundred feet, he could have gone anywhere."

"Wouldn't Teterboro notice he was missing?"

"Not if he radioed a course change. Could have said he was going to Atlantic City instead. You could ask the state police about this if you want. They've probably checked him out with the FAA already."

"Thanks."

"Listen, if you talk to the state troopers or anybody, would you ask about my plane? I hope to hell I don't have to hire a lawyer to get it back."

"That could get expensive."

"I'm afraid they'll keep it. They've got some kind of law about taking vehicles used in dope deals. You ever hear of that?"

"I don't see how they can take your private property."

"They've done it so far. Sure I can't fly you anywhere?"

"Positive." I found a pay phone, lost a quarter, and decided to bite the bullet and finally buy a car phone. I had had one, of course, back in the 'Eighties, when they ran two grand. Now, the price was down to about a hundred bucks if you went with a carrier doing a promo. I found a discount electronics outlet in the mall, paid a hundred bucks I'd have to subtract from my Yankee Drover bar budget, and rejoined the late Twentieth Century.

Dr. Schwartz's nurse agreed to ask the vacationing doctor to call me. I was nearly home when my new phone buzzed and a gravelly voiced woman asked for Ben Abbott.

"Dr. Schwartz?"

"My nurse said you're Renny's cousin."

"I am. My mother is his father's sister."

"Well, I'm sorry about your cousin, Mr. Abbott. How can I help?"

"I don't believe Renny was smuggling cocaine, Doctor, and I wonder—"

"I don't believe it either, but I don't know any facts to the contrary. He was a pleasant, shy man, punctual, a confident pilot, and polite—none of which would prevent him from doing what the police say he was doing."

"When did he leave Block Island?"

"He was still at the airport when my caretaker picked me up."

"Didn't you see him take off?"

"No. It's not that small an island. And there are plenty of planes on the weekend."

"So you have no idea if he stayed for five minutes or five hours?"

"As I told the police, Mr. Abbott, all I know is that my caretaker gave him the telephone message and he said that he would see me next week to fly me home."

"Someone left a message for him?"

"It sounded like another flying job: 'Pick up Mr. Smith at two-thirty.' "

"Smith? Where?"

"Just the name and the time. Anything else, Mr. Abbott?"

"Thanks for calling back."

"Pick up Mr. Smith at two-thirty" said nothing. Renny had filed a flight plan to LaGuardia from Block Island. He could have stopped anywhere along the way. Or he could have picked up Mr. Smith at LaGuardia and flown him damned near anywhere in eastern America. Or "Mr. Smith" could be code for a bag of coke. I had a feeling the cops hadn't learned anything that would change their original take on Renny's death. At least not from Roy Chernowsky and Dr. Schwartz.

Coming home to Newbury from the suburbs and cities south of Interstate 84 is like passing through a mirror. Behind, a world of crowds and too many automobiles; ahead, open space that people usually go on long vacations to find. By nightfall I was sitting in the deep silence of my "library," an old thick-walled room in the back of the house—the oldest part of the house—watching apple wood burn orange in the fireplace. I was thinking about having a drink but didn't really want to get high.

There was something supremely humbling about seeking information from people whom the cops had already questioned. The cops were team players; when they got a new piece of information they enlisted all sorts of colleagues to follow up leads, check stories, float theories. Alone, I was in the position of trying to re-invent the wheel without the benefit of an axle and spokes. All I really had going for me was a strong conviction—which was being sorely tested—that Renny would not commit such a crime. What had Marian Boyce called me? A romantic without the facts. Yet maybe their facts just *seemed* like facts. It *looked* as if Renny had had a falling out with a partner while smuggling coke. He had cracked up in Al Bell's field. There was cocaine in the plane. Renny was shot. And Renny had had plenty of time to pick up a partner and dope somewhere between Block Island and Al's landing strip. There was no way that I alone was going to find out where else my cousin had touched down.

I needed a partner. A professional who could work his contacts in and out of the law. A sleaze in an S-class Mercedes. I didn't like Alex Rose. But at least I could afford him. I found his card. I hadn't really looked at it before. It had a neat little rose embossed on the lower left corner. His collected-sounding receptionist answered the telephone. I asked if the boss was still in.

She remembered my name and told me Mr. Rose would call right back. My phone rang as I was tossing another log on the fire.

"What's up?"

I said, "I want to deal."

"What deal?"

"Testimony in support of Mrs. Long."

"There's no deal. You got to testify."

"I'll be a friendly witness."

"I don't care if you're friendly or unfriendly."

"You will do better if the jury likes me."

"True," Alex Rose conceded. "On the other hand, the prosecution's going to ask whether you've been paid to testify."

"I don't want money."

"Oh yeah?"

"Two things. Alison's teeth. The orthodontist."

"No problem there. I'd like to see the state's attorney bitch about that to a jury of loving parents. What else?"

"Help me find the guy who murdered my cousin."

"Whoa!"

"What's wrong?"

"Tall order."

"Long can afford it. Put it down as a consulting fee or something."

"Why don't you just wait for the cops to find out?"

"They're looking at it as a drug fight."

"From what I hear they're looking at it correctly."

"They're not trying as hard as if he were an ordinary businessman, which he is. They just don't see him that way."

"You're wrong there. I spoke with Trooper Boyce. She's hungry.

Bender gets the credit for Mrs. Long. Boyce'll kill to find her own murderer."

"Boyce is starting from a prejudice."

Rose was silent for a while. I could hear music in the background. Cocktail bar piano; the kind of "I Did It My Way" joint you drop into at six to see who wants to get laid for dinner.

I said, "I know it looks bad."

"That's for sure." Rose was quiet again, then he said, "You're coming from some kind of family faith. You got to tell me more—find some fact that'll help me believe before I get involved."

"Like what?"

"Somebody believable who has reason to believe that Renny Chevalley had no intention of landing dope in that hayfield."

"If I find that, I can take it to the cops."

"To the cops it'll be hearsay. Self-serving hearsay. To me, it just might convince me that your cousin wasn't the two-faced son of a bitch dope smuggler the cops say he was."

"He was just a businessman."

"Do you have any idea how many 'businessmen' play both sides of the street? Goes with the territory. They get ripped off by their employees and raped by the government. When they see a chance to even the score, lots take it."

"Renny wasn't like that."

"Did he give discounts for cash?"

"Sometimes, I suppose."

"Did he pay taxes on the cash?"

"Hold on. Skimming cash isn't the same as running dope."

"Would you run dope?"

"Of course not."

"Neither would I. Would you skim cash?"

"No."

"I might," Rose said.

"That doesn't make Renny a drug runner."

"Prove it."

"That's what I'm asking you to do."

"In exchange for fudging evidence?"

"I didn't say I'd lie for her. But I will describe the loving couple I saw. And hope to hell the state's attorney hasn't found that picture."

"Why don't we start with the kid's teeth?" Rose replied.

The way I read him, he was having second thoughts about my testimony but was keeping his options open.

I was glad I had asked Vicky McLachlan to come over and help work out the logistics of the orthodontist's deal. We sat around the kitchen table—Vicky, Alison, Janet Mealy, and me—and it soon developed that things weren't going at all the way I thought they would.

Alison's mother listened, wringing her bony hands. Finally she whispered that braces weren't possible. She couldn't afford them.

Alison said she didn't want them anyway.

"All paid for, by my friend Mr. Rose."

"It's not right. We've taken too much already."

"But it's not costing me anything. It's a trade for something I did for him." I glanced at Vicky for support and chose my words carefully. "Mrs. Mealy, this is the sort of thing that can make a real difference in later life. I'm just glad the opportunity has come the child's way."

Alison's big eyes narrowed with wary bewilderment. "Why do you want me to wear braces, Ben?"

When I hesitated, bubbly tears pooled and dribbled down her cheeks, and her mouth started to quiver. Her mother reached to comfort her. But Alison's jaw set and she squirmed away, up and out of her chair, glaring across the table, demanding an explanation.

"I don't get it, Ben. What are you doing?"

"Hush," her mother cautioned.

"No, Mom. He has to tell me."

I turned imploringly to Vicky, who asked, "Sweetheart, why are you crying?"

"I'm not crying." Alison slapped impatiently at her tears, blinked them away.

"Then why are you mad at Ben?"

"He hates me."

"Hate you? No I don't. I like you, very much."

"He thinks I'm ugly."

"No I don't. As a matter of fact, I think you're a real cutie pie."

"No you don't!"

I was flabbergasted. Considering the number of orthodontists who keep polo ponies in the area, I had assumed that braces were as American as apple pie. Plenty of Alison's school friends wore them, I knew. But if I had forgotten that she wasn't a Main Street girl, her mother remembered.

She put a finger to her lips, counseling silence.

But Alison turned away. "I thought you liked me."

"What's going on here?" I said. "I *do* like you. Come on, hon, you know I do."

"No you don't," she cried, and this time the little girl dissolved sobbing into her mother's arms.

I thought I knew her and I thought she trusted me. She had tagged after me all summer, playing in the garden, borrowing my tools and books. And when her bum of a father suddenly showed up drunk, it was to me she'd come, to talk it out. Maybe that was why I'd made the mistake of thinking she was wiser than her years. Solid as she was, I'd cracked her armor for sure.

Mrs. Mealy stared at the table top, shaking her head, and asked in a small voice, "Why?"

As it was clear from whom Alison had inherited her teeth, I doubted Kissinger himself could have finessed an answer. At that moment, a kind God made the phone ring.

"It's Rita Long," came her soft, low voice. "I have to talk to you."

"What's the number? I'll call you right back."

"I'm home."

"You're *home?*"

"Bail. Can you come over?"

"I'll be there as soon as I can."

I hung up the phone and faced the kitchen table. "Alison, no one says you're not pretty already. Braces are just a way of becoming prettier. Right, Vicky?"

Vicky was staring at the phone.

"A girl can't be too pretty, right, Vicky?"

Vicky looked at me as if I had just urinated on the steps of Town

Hall. She reached for Alison, got her arms around her shoulders, and left the lower half of her on her mother's lap.

"Sweetheart," she said cozily, "here, let me hold you. . . . I'll explain. Ben's heart is in the right place, sometimes. But mostly, he's a jerk. He's very shallow. You know what I mean, shallow?"

Alison, held between the two women like a roll of carpet, glowered at me through her tears and said, "Yeah."

"Pretty isn't important," Vicky went on gently. "Women are much, much, *much* more than their looks. And when you look good inside—when you like the way you look—then you look great."

Janet Mealy studied a burnt spot on the table and worried a button on her sweater.

"Ben thinks I'm ugly," said Alison.

"Hey," said Vicky, shaking her hard, "Ben's so shallow he wouldn't be your friend if he didn't think you were pretty. Do you think he'd be *my* friend if he didn't think I was pretty?"

"Now hold on—"

"*Would* you?" she rounded on me.

"We're friends. Who notices—"

"You do," she shot back. Her face got red. And then *she* started crying.

"He treats women like dolls," Vicky sobbed. "Every time he looks at me I think there's something wrong with my hair."

Alison squirmed around and combed her fingers through Vicky's curls. "I love your hair. I want hair like your hair."

Vicky sniffled.

Alison hugged her hard in her skinny little arms. "I know just how you feel. Ben's always trying to change us."

"That's right."

"He does it to me too."

"How did I ever try to change you, Alison?"

"You make me pick spinach."

"You *like* picking spinach."

"Don't you intimidate her," said Vicky.

"*You* thought braces were a good idea."

"I'm rethinking it. You're forcing a little girl onto a treadmill of vanity."

"He's always bugging me about potatoes," muttered Mrs. Mealy.

"*Treadmill of vanity?* That ought to be in one of your speeches."

"It should," sobbed Alison. "It should."

"She's pretty enough," said an emboldened Mrs. Mealy. "*I* never had braces."

"I wish I didn't," said Vicky, though her grimace revealed a bite that would have done a Bechstein proud. "They hurt."

"They hurt?" asked Alison. "Ben never said they hurt."

"Ben never said a lot of things."

"It's for health, dammit. I spoke with the doctor this morning and he assured me that braces are vital for healthy gums."

"Ben, go for a walk or something. Look what you've done to this child."

I backed out of my kitchen. Slinking by a few minutes later with my wallet, coat, and car keys, I heard Vicky promise to set Alison's hair in curlers.

I called Rita Long on my new car phone and told her I was coming out. She sounded lower than I was. I asked if I could bring anything. "Milk," she said. "I just got home. There's nothing here."

"Have you eaten?"

"They let me out before dinner."

"What would you like?"

"Nothing."

"You'll be hungry later. What would you like?"

"You decide."

Wondering where the hell her husband was—and all the high-priced lawyers—I turned around and drove back to the Grand Union, shopped, and arrived at the Castle with two bags of groceries, the day's papers, and a bottle of wine, though presumably somewhere in the Castle's dungeons was a stocked cellar. I saw her sitting on the front steps as I drove up. They, like everything else in the house, were oversized, and she looked like Lily Tomlin's little girl on a giant set. She had her hair pulled back in a sleek ponytail and was wearing jeans and sneaks and a thick Irish sweater. Her makeup was exquisite. Her hand was freezing.

"Getting cold?" I said.

"You have no idea what it's like to be outdoors after being locked up."

"I remember," I said. "I brought some basic eats. There's a bottle of wine here. Like a sip?"

"I'm afraid of crashing to pieces."

"Some tea?"

She hesitated. I saw her gaze sweep the lawns. The daylight would linger another hour. I said, "Stay here. I'll make the tea and bring it out."

"Thank you. You have wine, if you like. There's a champagne in the fridge, I think."

I made two teas and while the water was boiling I unpacked chicken breasts, chopped veal, linguini, broccoli, greens and carrots, breakfast cereal, a loaf of bread, a couple of quarts of milk, some orange juice, and some local apples. I found her where I had left her on the front steps, drinking in the sunlight on the lawn, which was striped in long shadows. She wrapped her hands around the mug.

"Heaven," she said after a moment. "Thank you."

"You're welcome."

"You brought me tea the other day, didn't you? I found it by the bed."

"Dr. Greenan slipped you a mickey."

"When I got home today I stood in the shower until I ran out of hot water."

"I'll bet."

"Alex Rose said I should call you."

"Why?"

"He's my husband's detective."

"I know."

"He said you could explain a few things."

"I doubt that."

"He said you could help me."

"Did he say how?"

"He said you'd explain. What's going on?"

I stood up and walked down the steps and kicked the gravel in the motor court.

Rita said, "I don't understand your connection. It was just coincidence you were here when we . . . found Ron."

"It was," I agreed. "Sheer coincidence." In actual fact, I had to admit I had been wondering how much coincidence it was. She had invited me out. She had invited me to drink champagne in the turret. She had spotted Ron. She had moved him. She could have established me as a sort of witness to the discovery, and a sort of accomplice in moving the body. But she had invited me *before* Ron was shot. Had she set the whole thing up? Coldbloodedly decided to kill him and coldbloodedly planned our discovery? No way, I thought.

"He said you'd explain." She was insistent.

I kicked some more gravel. It was the small size, rolled into an oil layer atop only the best driveways. Money stone. Damned little of it kicked loose.

"Well?"

"You're not going to like this."

"I haven't liked anything since last Saturday." She had a bleak look in her eyes, a wary expression, and now, a hard edge in her voice.

"Your husband knew about you and Ron."

She blinked, stood up, stammered, "What do you mean?" She didn't have a clue. I wondered what sort of talking they had done with all the lawyers and jail guards listening. "Oh, my God."

"Didn't Jack tell you?"

Rita sank to the steps again and put her head in her hands. "We left it unspoken that Ron was here for the obvious reason. Jack was very forgiving, very supportive. He said it was his fault for being too busy to stay close with me. He *knew?*"

"A lot's been going down," I said. "Where is he now?"

"New York. He drove me home and left. He said he needed time to think. He'll be back to sit in on the next meeting with the lawyers, whenever that is. I'm not allowed to leave Plainfield County."

"How much was bail?"

"A million and a half and my passport. What's your connection?"

"You're not going to like this."

"Tell me." She was getting angry now, jerked around by too many people, and now another jerk was dancing on her driveway.

"Alex Rose is the connection. Your husband ordered him to collect evidence of your affair with Ron Pearlman. He followed you around New York."

"We didn't do anything in New York."

"I know. He got a picture of the two of you in a taxi and some talk from waiters who served you lunch."

"That skeeze. That slimy fat skeeze. There's something so disgusting about Alex Rose. He took *pictures?*"

"And talked to waiters."

"I'm not allowed to have lunch with a friend? That's all it was, just lunch."

"The waiters thought you were a lovely couple."

"Jesus! So where do you fit in?"

"I was the raccoon."

"You lost me." But not for long. She jumped to her feet, dropping her tea mug, which cracked. "You were in my woods?"

"Yes."

"Spying on me?"

"Yes."

"Why?"

"Rose hired me to shoot a video of you and Ron for the divorce lawyers."

"You're kidding."

I didn't know if she meant I was kidding about divorce lawyers or kidding about taking the video. She cleared that up. She meant both. "Divorce lawyers? Jack was going to *divorce* me?"

"Rose thought so."

"Beat me to the draw? I was going to divorce him."

"Were you?"

"I don't know. I didn't want to hurt him— You had a camera?"

"Rose gave me a camcorder."

Standing a couple of steps up, Rita Long looked down at me like a snake that had just slithered off the lawn and was heading for the warmth of her house. "You took our picture. A video. You disgusting—"

"I erased it."

"You saw me and Ron—where?"

"In your studio."

"Oh, Jesus." Her eyes cast back to that night. "Oh, no."

"You were fully clothed."

She cast back again. "No. I took off my—"

"I never saw your body."

"I took off my blouse."

"All I saw was your face."

"You saw me kiss—"

"No. I only saw your face when you turned to the window. I stopped the camera. I threw away the tape. It fell on the lawn and I ran out to get it. That's when you heard me. When I got home I erased the tape and hid it. All I gave Rose was his camera and a blank cassette."

"Get off my property."

"Could we talk?"

"Get out of here."

"It wasn't like that. *I'm* not like that. It was a stupid thing to take Rose's job, but it just seemed sort of funny when I didn't know you, so I took it."

"And now you *know* me," she echoed scornfully.

"I knew you that night. That's why I stopped filming."

"What did you know?"

"I knew you were happy."

Rita Long stared, her mouth hard, until her eyes filled with tears.

I said, "I knew the two of you better than I knew anybody in the world. I was happy for you both. And I was head over heels in love with you."

"Through a window?"

"I never felt so close to anybody in my life."

Still crying, she said, "My god, what did you think at the cookout the next day?"

"I almost grilled my arm."

She shook her hair and gave a baffled groan. "What kind of game is Rose playing?"

"I don't think he's playing a game. Or at least he doesn't think he's playing one. He thinks that if there's a trial it will help your defense if I testify that you and Ron appeared to be a gentle, loving couple.

That's what he wants you to talk to me about. The lawyers intend to challenge the prosecutor's lovers' quarrel motivation."

"They want to indict me."

"So I hear. It's a thin case though."

"It's unbelievable. . . .Would you go now?"

"Would you answer a question first?"

"Just go. I hate what you did to us."

"Where's the drawing you drew that night? The picture of Ron?"

"You saw that— Of course you did. Get out of here."

"Where did it go?"

"It didn't go anyplace. It's in my studio."

"Have you seen it there since Ron was killed?"

"No."

"Would you check?"

"What for?"

"Rose says it's not there and that the cops didn't take it. Would you check?"

"All right."

"May I come with you?"

"No."

She ran up the steps and banged the door behind her. I heard her pound up the central staircase to the second floor. She came back, looking wary. "It's not there."

"Was it there when I came to appraise the house?"

"I don't know."

"But you ran ahead into the studio to cover it."

"No. I always cover my work. I just went to make sure I hadn't left my panties lying around."

"So the easel was covered when you ran ahead?"

"Yes."

"But now you found a landscape of a pond and a fence?"

"How'd you know?"

"Rose told me. So where's your picture of Ron?"

"I don't know."

"Somebody took it. Who could get into the house? When you were at the cookout maybe."

"Just Ron, when he came back."

"What about your husband?"

"He was in Washington."

"No one else has a key?"

"We changed the locks when construction was done."

That was common practice, when a homeowner had allowed keys to the subcontractors. "What about a housekeeper?"

"I don't have one yet."

"Rita? Can I ask why you drew the skull?"

"What do you mean?"

"I mean, that picture could give jurors in a trial an impression of . . . strangeness."

"For chrissake, it's a foundation technique. You start with the bones and add muscle and flesh and skin. No big deal."

"I see."

"Any art teacher could explain it," she added impatiently, as if the skull was the least of her problems. Perhaps it was, but I couldn't help feeling that jurors might wonder, like I did, what else was in her head the night before her boyfriend was murdered.

"When I came over to appraise the house, where did you think Ron was?"

"He said he was going to drive to New York and come back late. But when I got home from the mall the Jag was in the garage. He would use my Jag, which I don't usually drive up here. I had the Land Rover." I had seen her get into it at the cookout—a genuine British Land Rover, roughneck daddy to the wimpified Range Rover.

"So where did you think Ron was?"

"I couldn't find him in the house. I supposed he had gone running, and I knew that if he came back and saw your car he would come quietly. It's a big house."

"And that's what you told the police?"

"Would you please go away now?"

"I'm sorry for what I did."

"You've got to live with it," she said. "I've got my own problems."

"Would you answer one more question?"

"I'm going in." She turned and headed up the steps.

"But they don't believe you," I called after her. She kept going.

When she reached the door I ran up behind her. "Could your husband have killed Ron?"

"Jack was in Washington."

"I know. But if he weren't, could he?"

I thought she was going to tell me to hit the road again. Instead, she answered reflectively. "I asked myself that a thousand times, sitting in that cell."

"And?"

"Could he pull the trigger? I don't know."

"Or have hired a killer to shoot Ron?"

"I don't even know the answer to that. I ask these questions and I wonder how well do you know somebody if you can't answer such a question."

"How long were you married?"

She stood on the door sill, looking down on me, shaking her head. "Nine years. I still can't answer the question."

"Did your lawyers pose it to the cops?"

"They're Jack's lawyers too."

"And Rose is his detective."

"Jack told me he wants to work things out."

"How do you feel about that?"

"I am numb, Ben. I feel nothing."

It struck me as a dangerous mood in her position. Before I could voice that caution, however, Rita mused, "The thing I can't understand is, I always had a funny feeling that Jack . . ." She looked at me and said, "Why am I telling you this? Good night. Goodbye—Oh, and you can take your testimony and shove it."

She plunged inside, slamming the door.

I walked down to my car and called her on the phone. On the fourth ring the machine picked up. I said, "It's Ben Abbott."

She broke in. "What?"

"What were you saying a minute ago? The thing you couldn't understand? A funny feeling that Jack . . . something?"

"I was just thinking about how Ron and I met."

"How'd you meet?"

I figured she'd hang up on me. Instead she groaned, aloud, then sighed. "Do you want some more tea?"

"Thanks."

I walked back to the house.

"This has got to be the weirdest relationship," she said. "Voyeur and object."

"I'm not a voyeur. You are not an object. And this is not a relationship."

I followed her into her beautiful kitchen. She looked around like a stranger. "Are you hungry, by any chance?" I asked.

"Suddenly. Maybe there's some cheese."

I opened the refrigerator. She gaped at the interior, bright with greens and meat packages. "What's this?"

"Groceries. They sell them in the Grand Union. The receipt is on the counter."

She picked it up and read the printout.

"What about the wine?"

"On me. How about a veal burger?"

I had noticed the day Ron was shot that someone—possibly her architect—had installed a splendid spice rack beside the refrigerator. I worked tarragon, anise, caraway, parsley, and a little salt, pepper, and garlic into the ground veal, formed patties, and let them sit while I washed the arugula, cross-cut the endive, and threw some garlic into a lean oil-and-vinegar mix.

"Exhaust fan?"

Rita turned it on. It had the fan outside the house, silent but powerful enough to vent a burning oil well. I had seen the switch myself, but I wanted her involved. I heated the smallest pan I could find— just big enough for the two thick patties—salted the bottom, and tossed them in.

"Don't you want oil?" she asked.

"The salt keeps them from sticking."

I seared both sides, turned the heat down, and let them cook a moment longer. Rita wanted to know how I had learned to cook. "Living alone, it was that or starve."

I opened the wine and we sat on stools across the kitchen worktable and ate. "God, that's good," she said.

"Compared to the Plainfield County hoosegow?"

"Compared to anything. You just buy veal and do that?"

"Your spice rack gets the credit."

"Thanks."

"You can do something similar with the chicken breast I left you. Just lightly coat the pan with butter or oil first. "

"Yeah, right."

"You never cook?"

"We have a cook in New York. I just haven't decided if I want one living in the house up here. I was enjoying my privacy," she added with a thin smile.

"Did you have one in Greenwich?"

"Oh yes. We did a lot of entertaining. With Stamford and New York so close, we did business in Greenwich."

She finished her salad. I passed her the Grand Union French bread and refilled her wineglass. "How old are you?"

"Twenty-nine."

I was surprised. It wasn't that she looked older. It was just the way she handled herself. "You were twenty when you married Jack?"

"Yes. And I don't want to talk about it."

"Sorry. You were going to tell me how you met Ron."

"Yes, I was. Wasn't I? I was thinking about how Jack introduced us. Right after he made his deal to buy Ron's factory, I gave a celebration dinner. Small dinner party, just us and the lawyers and one accountant from each side. Anyway, that afternoon, before the dinner, I was just finishing with the cook and housekeeper, and I was about to do the placecards. I always do them myself. As far as I'm concerned the food can suck, but if you put people in the right seat they'll remember a good time."

I suddenly felt sympathy for Jack Long. She might have married him at twenty, but she had grown up fast. She'd smooth his hard edges and make up for his busy-businessman bad manners and stroke the people he dealt with.

"Anyway, Jack called from New York. He said Ron had just flown in from Hong Kong and was wiped, so he was sending him on ahead. Could I set up a guest room? A few minutes later the limo arrived. He'd fallen asleep in the car and he got out all woozy, looking about fourteen. I thought, Oh, God, gorgeous . . . You gotta know,

Ben, I did not play around. Ever. But here's this guy who really . . . Well, you know. Anyway, I knew trouble when I saw it. I sent him upstairs with the housekeeper. And an hour before the guests were to arrive, I told her to bring him some coffee. Ron came down all fresh and clean in a great-looking suit and we just sat and talked."

"You were already dressed for dinner?" I asked.

"I dressed early. By the time Jack got home, Ron and I were friends. It was a great party. Everyone was pleased with the deal and all." She fell silent.

"Then what happened?"

"Jack went to Washington. When he left, he invited Ron to stay at the house."

"When was this?"

"Just last year."

"You already had this place?"

"We were finishing it. We stayed in the Greenwich house until this was done."

I nodded. Most of the people I sell houses to are pretty well fixed, but few can afford three places at once. In fact, I see quite a few sales fall through because the buyer can't unload his own house in time for a closing.

"So Ron stayed in Greenwich," Rita continued. "All very on the up and up. I took him to dinner at the club. And sailing with friends. Jack flew out to Hong Kong. Ron took polo lessons. Broke his hand. That seemed like a reason to stay longer. And one morning we ended up in bed."

"Morning?"

"I brought him coffee."

I looked away.

"What?" she asked.

"I'm sorry," I said. "Sounds like fun."

"As you saw," she answered with a bitter smile.

"I didn't see anything. I just imagined."

Rita reached for the wine bottle. I emptied it into our glasses. She sipped hers and said, "The thing is, looking back, I have the funniest feeling that Jack deliberately threw us together."

"Deliberately?"

"He made it very easy. Looking back, it was almost like he wanted us to have an affair."

"Were you getting along?"

"Oh, sure. We always got along. I mean, we didn't fight. We didn't love much either, but we didn't fight. My mother remarked once that we had an old-fashioned 1950s corporate marriage. You know, hubby at the office, wifey holding down the social fort. It worked. For eight years, anyway."

"Why would Jack throw you together?"

"I don't know. It's driving me crazy."

"Maybe he's having an affair?"

"I don't think so."

"Maybe he is and wanted you out of the way. Figured to ease you into an affair with Ron and file for divorce. Possible?"

"I don't think so."

"You told me you weren't sleeping together."

"I looked for signs. I didn't see him look suddenly younger or happier. You know what I'm saying?"

"Oh, yes."

"Maybe I should hire a detective too."

"But Jack's standing by you. He told you he wants to work things out."

"Maybe he felt he had to say that before they bailed me out. I mean, he's a decent man. How could he tell me he was divorcing me when I was locked up in a cell?"

"You wouldn't be the first prisoner to get a Dear Jane letter."

"Maybe so. But when I got out today he still said he was on my side."

"You said he went to New York to think. What's he thinking about?"

"I don't know."

"What do you want?

"I want Ron back alive." She started crying.

"I'm sorry."

"Thanks for cooking dinner. I'm tired. I want to go to bed. Thanks for coming over."

I said, "I will testify for you if you think it will help."

"I don't want to think about it now."

"No rush. Maybe you'll get lucky."

"How?"

"Maybe they won't indict."

"Maybe raccoons will fly."

I got up and headed for the door. "That's okay. I'll find my way."

She tagged along and opened the front door, a massive iron-strapped affair with hobnails. I'd seen a similar one once guarding Edinburgh Castle.

"I'm sorry about telling you to shove your testimony."

"I'm sorry I did what I did."

"I was really upset. I know you wouldn't have done it if you'd known me."

I wished her good luck. I almost bent to kiss her cheek, but she suddenly looked frail and tired and I didn't think it would help.

13

Early next morning, Wednesday, I took the remote phone out to my cutting garden and moseyed barefoot on the cedar mulch. Sheltered north and west from early frosts by the stone foundation of an old outhouse, the garden was still producing mums, roses, snaps, some weary cosmos, and even a late surge of balloon flowers. Aunt Connie telephoned at seven to remind me of our lunch date with my mother.

"Shall I drive?" asked Connie.

"Oh, I'll drive."

As we fox-trotted through that ritual, I held the phone in the crook of my neck and deadheaded the mums, which had exploded while I'd been chasing Renny's ghost.

"Well all right, if you prefer. . . . Would you like to drive my car?"

I told her that I'd be delighted, cautioning, "If you warm it first, Connie, please remember to open the stable doors."

"I'll remember. You told me that Sunday. I'm not an idiot, I'm just old. What are you bringing your mother?"

"White roses." They were her favorite John F. Kennedy hybrid teas. I had asked when she moved to Frenchtown if she wouldn't like to take her prized roses. "You can bring me flowers," had answered wise mother she.

"What are you bringing?" I asked Connie.

"There's a pie in the oven. My russets are almost ripe."

I suppressed a groan. Her Roxbury Russet apple trees were enormous, and the thought of her on a ladder . . . "I'll pick you up at eleven-thirty."

"Now listen to me," she said. "I'm told your mother is very upset about Renny Chevalley. This latest . . . 'event' will only make things worse."

"What event?"

"You know very well what event."

"I'm afraid I don't."

"It's all over town. You've been calling on the Long woman."

The Fish Line was bottom-trolling. I said, " 'Calling on' implies a connection that isn't there, Aunt Connie."

"People are talking."

"People should mind their own business."

"People should also obey the Ten Commandments, but they don't, so we accommodate reality. The point I am making, Ben, is that you ought to try and put your mother's mind at ease. She's a worrier. Let her see you at the top of your form."

I went back to my flowers.

"Morning, Ben." Scooter MacKay's big voice boomed across the fence.

I snipped three red American Promises and brought them over for Eleanor. Scooter was juggling a cup of coffee and his morning cigarette, which Eleanor does not allow him to smoke indoors. Come winter you'll see him smoking in the snow. I laid the roses atop the hedge. Eleanor knew to cut them again when she put them in water. Scooter gave me a broad wink. "I hear your friend's out on bail."

"Are you publishing that?"

"That she's your friend or that she's out on bail?"

"Publish that she's my friend and I'll sue you."

"Would you trammel a free press?"

"Cheerfully."

Scooter indulged me with a laugh. The *Clarion*'s crime column inclined toward moving-violation stories, spiced with colorful quotes from Trooper Moody in the mode of "cited for failure to keep left."

This week I anticipated a page-two item headed "Deaths Fail to Mar Cookout Weekend."

"Steve Greenan says she's a knockout."

"The doctor is right. She's also in love with the guy she's supposed to have shot."

"Do you think she did him?"

"No way."

"How come they arrested her?"

"She's rich and beautiful."

"I hear her fingerprints were on the gun."

"Scooter, could you hit a buck at eighty yards with a slug?"

"Sure, if he walked into it."

"It's long range, isn't it?"

In his youth, Scooter MacKay had been a legendary hunter. Even Chevalley boys would walk the woods with him. But like a lot of us brought up to hunt, he had lost the cold, blind eye. "Depends on the loads. And the gun, of course," he said. "But it's long."

"That's what I thought."

"Did you happen to notice the make of the gun?"

"Ithaca Deerslayer. Twelve-gauge."

"That's a fine shotgun," Scooter mused. "First shotgun specifically designed for deer slugs."

"But eighty yards is still long range."

"When they test-fired the Ithaca at a *hundred* yards they got a seven-inch vertical spread. Six horizontal."

"From a bench."

"But your friend nailed him at *eighty.*"

"She's not my 'friend.' And she didn't 'nail' him at any yards."

"That's fine shooting. Wonder who taught her."

I changed the subject.

"What's the word on the new medical examiner? Do you think his autopsy will stand up?" Steve and the other doctors who part-timed as assistant medical examiners did the field work. The M.E. conducted postmortems at the Plainfield morgue.

"Name's DeAngelo. He wrote the book. One of the top medical examiners in the country."

"What the hell's he doing in Plainfield?"

"He retired from Boston. His family had a summer place there."

"So he's pretty old. Maybe he's losing it."

Scooter smiled. "I met him at the animal shelter benefit up there. The man's pushing fifty, at least. He might be as old as fifty-two."

"Terrific."

Scooter took a last drag on his cigarette and announced in a voice that carried to the flagpole, "Your lawn looks like hell."

"I gave up the weed service."

"Bad move."

"I had second thoughts about putting all that poison in the ground."

"Notice you're spending less on ads too."

"They were drawing zip."

Scooter shrugged. He can afford to. He hires out the *Clarion*'s presses to print most of the other town weeklies in our section of the state. It's as lucrative as printing money, and less trouble.

Connie had started the Lincoln, backed it out of her stable, and closed the doors herself. She was sitting in the passenger seat at eleven-thirty, wearing a cardigan sweater over a summery dress and a Lilly Daché hat she had purchased when invited to launch a World War II battleship. Her pie sat on the back floor, swathed in tinfoil. I laid my roses on the back seat, their stems bound in wet paper towels and Saran. As I climbed behind the wheel, I lifted her veil and kissed her astonishingly soft cheek. Her jaw was rigid.

"You hurt?" I asked.

"No."

"Connie."

"Drive."

"Are you up to this?" She suffered from temporal arteritis, a relatively rare inflammation of an artery to the head, which created excruciating pain when it flared. There was an operation, but we'd been putting it off. Steve and the specialists down in New Haven were reluctant to put her through it. Only when the pain became unbearable would she take a pill, fearing addiction.

"You know, I could run out and get Mom and bring her to your house."

"Drive," she said.

I drove.

Just as Connie had always regarded my father as the son she never had, my mother was in some similar way the daughter. But whereas Dad made the perfect son in all his proper splendor, my mother was a Frenchtown girl. As much as she loved Connie, she could never feel comfortable in her presence. Typically, when we arrived at the farm, Mom was fluttering up the walls of her dining room, convinced that something must be wrong with the table setting. Bear in mind she was seventy-five herself, but this morning she was the eighteen-year-old that Bertram Abbott had brought home to a stunned Main Street. She was so distracted that she forgot to worry about me and kind of brushed my cheek hello as if I had just seen her for breakfast a couple of hours ago.

Connie, who had her blind sides, said, "Oh, let's eat in the kitchen. Dining rooms are so gloomy in the daylight."

I saw my mother start to die and intervened.

"Let's eat here. The table's set." My mother had probably set it the night before, reset it in the morning, and fiddled with it again as we came in the drive.

"Mom, can I help carry?" I asked as she headed for the kitchen.

"No, you talk to your Aunt Connie. I'll be all right."

"He already bored me in the car," said Connie. "Come sit with me, Margot. Let Ben serve."

It worked. My mother gambled that I was capable of shifting her chicken pot pie and salad to the dining room without dropping it and conjured a similar leap of faith regarding the lemonade pitcher and bread basket.

After lunch Connie sat with her in the kitchen while she washed up and I went out and wheelbarrowed some firewood from the shed to the kitchen porch. There was a nip in the air and no question fall was descending on Frenchtown, which was always colder than Newbury. Sometimes I wondered why my mother came back out here, and sometimes I had the feeling it was for reasons I hadn't guessed. But on a fall afternoon, there is no place like it. One woman's dank swamp is definitely another's teeming marsh. The water draws the migrating birds. The sumac and red maple that thrive on moisture turn red early. The air is thick, damp, and full of life.

My mother came out while I was fixing the woodshed door, which was losing a hinge. She's a tiny little thing, almost as small as Connie now, and blessed with those dark Chevalley eyes and hollow cheeks that age with dignity. I could see she was pleased that lunch had gone well. "Connie's napping," she said. "Are you warm enough?"

"I'm fine."

"Would you like something?"

"Love a coffee."

She hurried inside the house and came back with two mugs and a slice of Connie's pie for me. I sat on a stump, she in her favorite Adirondack chair, which I had carried down from the patio while she cautioned me not to hurt my back. Settled at last, the coffee still warm, we watched the birds on a feeder and talked about the weather.

"I missed you by five minutes at Renny's," I said, after a long silence and a hesitant smile said she wanted to talk.

"I couldn't stay. I was so upset. I thought, Oh my God, it could have been you."

"How so?" I asked carefully.

"He was your age. You used to be like two peas in a pod. His poor mother."

The generations were skewed here. My mother had been forty when I was born; Renny's, barely twenty. Sisters-in-law separated by more than twenty years, they had nevertheless become like sisters.

I said, "Don't believe the stories. He wasn't doing anything wrong."

"I'm sure he wasn't. If it were Pink or one of the others I'd say I wasn't surprised. But not Renny."

"I feel the same way."

"I'm sure there's an explanation for everything."

"Everything," I agreed.

"Even the money."

"What money?"

My mother looked distressed. "Frances called this morning. The police searched the garage."

"And?"

"They found forty thousand dollars in cash."

"*What?*"

"Forty thousand dollars. In a shopping bag."

"Where?"

"In back of a closet."

I was stunned. Where the hell would Renny get forty thousand in cash? And why would he hide it in a closet? . . . Even if he was skimming—à la Rose—no garage in this neck of the woods generated that kind of extra cash. . . . Why? I glanced at my mother. She was hanging in there for her family, but the look on her face forced me to admit that she too had lost faith.

She looked back at me, blinking rapidly. She dabbed her eyes with a Kleenex and folded her hands, her fingers working.

"Were you involved?" she asked coldly.

"With Renny? No."

"What about this woman who shot her boyfriend?"

"I was only there doing an appraisal."

"I couldn't bear for you to get in trouble again."

"I won't."

"Promise me."

"I promise."

"It killed your father, and this time it will kill me."

I took a deep breath, stood up, and walked rapidly down to the swamp, which started quite abruptly at the edge of the mown lawn. It spread for acres, spiked with the bleached gray trunks of dead trees. Mysteriously, the water table had risen when I was a kid, and suddenly the swamp was twice the size it had been and much closer to the house. I did not kill my father. But she thought I did, which was almost as bad.

I felt her eyes on me, and I imagined her stomach churning as she warred within, angry at me, and angrier at herself for showing she was angry at me. I took another deep breath, working hard at lightening up, and walked back to her, a light comment on my lips. "I swear the swamp's still rising. Gets any higher you'll have to swim back to Newbury."

"*Never,*" she cried, startling me with her vehemence. This was one time we would not let things slide in the interest of peace, though God knows I tried, laughing, or trying to.

"Well, at least you know you've got the option."

"I will never go back to Main Street. Ever. And when *I* die, don't you dare try to bury me up there."

"Mother—"

"I've put it in my will. I want to be cremated."

"Am I supposed to scatter your ashes on the swamp?"

"My brother will."

"Running the gears" at Leavenworth meant thrusting a sharp object into your enemy and jamming it around, slicing up organs, until they pulled you off the body. Well, Mom was running the gears on me at the moment. This was the first I had heard about cremation or scattering ashes. Clearly, she didn't trust me with the job.

"I don't ever want to see that house again." Her jaw was working and she was twisting her fingers like a nest of worms. I was terrified she would cry next.

"But you lived most of your life there. Your whole time with Dad."

"Fifty-five years."

"You weren't unhappy."

"I was very happy. It's a lovely house."

"It's your house."

"Not any more . . ." She gazed past me at the ugly little farmhouse she had grown up in. It was one small step up from a shack. Her father had attempted to improve it back in the 'Fifties with asphalt shingles. "Down here, people don't turn up their noses."

"Mother, you had dozens of friends on Main Street."

"Down here everyone's got someone in their family who's been to prison."

Stung again, I fired back, "That's just because they're easier to catch."

"It's not funny. All my so-called friends, I knew what they were thinking, they were thinking, Ben's Chevalley blood came out. My blood. Your father never would have had such a son if it weren't for Margot Chevalley."

"Oh, Mom—"

"You erased fifty years of slowly fitting in, slowly getting accepted."

"I didn't mean to."

"I don't mind," she said, fingers flying. "I never fit in. They knew it. I knew it."

"Dad loved you. Connie loves you."

"Connie is a Christian. Which is more than I can say for most of that crowd."

I stood there shaking my head, helpless to unravel the strands of hurt and imagined hurt. I thought that she had been living alone too long with no one to talk to. Telling her that wouldn't do anything to cut through her confusion, however. Nor, I had to admit, was it entirely confusion. There was a diamond-bright core of truth at the center of my mother's thinking. The women she had called her friends—the wives of my father's school chums and neighbors—were, by and large, prisoners of their neat, orderly lives and hostages to their belief that appearances on earth mirrored God's image of their souls. But they served a second master, a pagan garden-farm god, who both taunted and comforted them with daily evidence that, God-be-damned, good stock was all. Good seed will out. Bad blood will out. I was the tainted product. Proof that Margot Chevalley couldn't escape her fate.

No wonder she had suspected me of flying coke with Renny. The poor thing thought it was her fault.

"I'm sorry," I apologized again. It had not occurred to me, back when I was standing up for my own principles, that I wouldn't be the only one to pay. I had survived the public censure of the court, survived the fines that took every penny I had earned in the 'Eighties, survived prison. Now I felt like a commando who had penetrated enemy territory and lived to tell tales of far-off victory and dead friends. And to wonder if it was worth it.

"Your mother's a wreck," Connie said in the car. The afternoon sky had turned dark. It looked like rain.

"I know."

"What did you say to her?"

"Exactly what I told you."

"Don't get snippy with me, young man." Her nap had set her up, and she was rarin' to go.

"Sorry. I'm a little upset myself."

Connie sat silently until we were well out of Frenchtown. Then she said, "Would you entertain some advice from someone old enough to know better?"

"Right now I'd take advice from a three-year-old."

"Since you've come home—and it's been what, three years now?"

"Two years." Less time than I had served in prison.

"Since you've come home you've remained somewhat detached. You're here, but not here."

"That's not true. I'm running the office. I may not be getting rich at it, but in this climate survival's an achievement."

"Yes, yes, yes. But we're not discussing earning your living. You are earning your living, I suppose, and maintaining your family's business. That's all well and good. But you're living like a stranger in your own town."

"So?"

"Don't interrupt. . . . I'm trying to find the proper words to describe what's become of you. . . . It's as if your old friends have grown up normally, while you're still the boy who left . . . I know what it is! You're like a reformed drunk, missing part of your emotional past. . . . It's high time you got involved. Time to embrace something."

"Or someone?" I asked, scoping out where she was leading.

"You could do worse than the first selectman."

"Vicky doesn't need a felon in her career."

"Do you propose to spend the rest of your life getting over prison?"

"Now wait a minute, Connie."

"I have seen four generations come home from terrible wars. Most get over it and move on with their lives. Those who can't fell on the battlefield. They simply didn't know it. . . . Did you die in prison, Ben?"

"No."

Her eyes flashed at me through her Lilly Daché veil. "Then what are you waiting for?"

"I thought I was doing pretty well. That wasn't me in Renny's plane, despite my mother's worries. It was Renny. And it wasn't me who shot Ron Pearlman. It was God knows who. I'm not sure why all this is falling on my head."

"Because you seem susceptible," said my aunt. "Neither here nor there."

I cogitated that in sullen silence. The rain, which had been looming darkly, started all of a sudden. Four or five fat drops splashed on the windshield, and the next instant it sluiced the Lincoln like a firehose. I turned on lights and wipers and powered the driver's seat forward so I could lean into the glass. The road gleamed slick and black, coated in patches of yellow maple leaves.

"My poor delphiniums," moaned Connie. "They bloomed again, but the stems are weak."

"We'll be home in a few minutes. I'll stake them for you."

"No thank you. I imagine you've got your own to prop."

My delphiniums, in fact, were giving every indication of premature death, but I didn't say so, being too busy concentrating on the road, which was flowing like a river.

"Ben, look out! Where are you going?"

"I see him."

An idiot in a huge, windowless van was actually attempting to pass. Figuring he was drunk or suffering a genuine emergency, I veered toward the narrow shoulder to make room.

"Ben!"

Having given him much of the road and all of the shoulder, I had nowhere to go when he cut in on me. I blew the horn to wake him up, but suddenly he was alongside like a moving wall. I caught a glimpse of one of those little round tinted plastic bubble portholes in the sheet metal and, through that distorting lens, the gleam of an eager face urging on the driver, whom I couldn't see.

How did I know he was urging him on? Two clues. A maniacal, toothy grin, and the shockingly loud crash as the van and Connie's Lincoln smacked flanks.

"Ben!" Connie cried, frightened, and cried out again as her head cracked hard on her window.

He came at me again. To my right there was a stretch of old-fashioned guard wire—two strands affixed to wooden posts sufficiently sturdy to prevent a baby carriage tumbling into the deep ditch beside the road. I jerked the steering wheel left. The second crash was much louder. Glass shattered in the rear. Rain and road poured in, but the old car gave back as good as it took and bounced the van halfway across its lane. I floored the accelerator. Multi-barreled reserve carburetors, which hadn't breathed fire since they left the factory, cut in with a heartening roar. God bless Renny, who had kept them tuned. We took off, forging ahead.

Unfortunately, the road curved left. Nor did the shoulder get any wider. The van, too, had a splendid engine, and its driver was very, very good. Higher up, he spotted the end of the guard wire before I did. He couldn't overtake, but he could hit me hard near the rear end and he did, with such force that my rear tires broke loose from the slick road. Swerving wide left, he disappeared around the bend. The Lincoln fishtailed and skidded violently.

I like cars, but I've never been the world's greatest driver. I think I could have powered the front-wheel-drive Olds out of the skid, but in Connie's car I didn't have that option. Despite my best efforts with the power steering, the Lincoln spun hard against the wire, plowed up a hundred feet of posts, and slammed into the ditch, with its tail in the air at a forty-five-degree angle and its nose in the mud.

"Connie!"

We were hanging half upside-down in the car, Connie limp in her seatbelt, one leg covered in blood. I was bleeding too, from where the horn had broken and sliced a finger, which I discovered as I spread more blood trying to help her.

She had a terrible bump on her brow where she'd hit the window and a gash on her knee, which had come in contact with a chrome air vent. Her skin, so thin that it was translucent, had parted like paper, and there was blood everywhere.

"Connie?"

She looked frail, and tiny, and every one of her ninety years. She opened her eyes, glanced wildly about. I could see her hover on the edge of mind-emptying shock. In that endless moment, fear and confusion threatened to overwhelm her. I didn't know what to do. It was like watching a porcelain vase teeter on the shelf.

"Connie, I'll get help. Can you hear me?"

"What happened?"

"We ran off the road."

She blinked a couple of times. "Oh," she said. "Oh, look at my leg. . . ."

"Does it hurt?"

"Yes. . . . No. Yes. Not too much. . . ." She looked around at the steaming hood angled into the mud, at the tangled guard wire, the trees we'd wedged between, the pouring rain. Then, to my immense relief, her gaze steadied and she was suddenly Connie again. "Ben, you've gone and smashed my car. Help me out of this. I'm all tangled."

The volunteer ambulance arrived in ten minutes, by which time a dozen cars had stopped and people had helped Connie out of the ditch into a Pontiac. She greeted the nurse and driver by name. Under no circumstances, she informed them, was she going to the hospital. "Just send Stevie Greenan around when he has a moment."

The duty nurse was fighting a losing battle to take her blood pressure, after dressing the cut on her knee, and the driver kept pleading that the hospital should take X rays. I finally took him aside and explained that at her age Connie saw a visit to the hospital as a one-way ticket and got him to agree to just take her home and wait until Steve arrived. She wouldn't even do that, however, insisting that they might need the ambulance for someone else. She accepted a ride home in the Pontiac, while I stayed to answer surly questions put to me by Trooper Moody.

"How fast were you going?"

"Ten miles under the limit."

"Come on, you're a speeder. You'll always be a speeder."

"It was pouring."

"And you say you just lost control?"

"I told you, a couple of guys in a van forced me off the road."

"License number?"

"Yeah, right. Listen, Ollie, I didn't get a number, I didn't see the driver. But I know he was gunning for me."

"Any witnesses?"

"Connie saw a little. Not much."

"Did she get the number?"

"Number? She got her head smashed on the window."

"Well, I'm going to issue a citation for failure to maintain control of your vehicle."

"Ollie, I got run off the road."

"Now who would want to run you off the road?"

"I don't know."

"If Miss Abbott recalls the license number of this—what was it, a van?—you be sure to inform me right away. Until then, I've told you time and again to slow down. You drive like a maniac."

"Look at the car. You can see where he hit me."

The Lincoln was just emerging from the ditch at the end of a wrecker hook operated by Pinkerton Chevalley. I showed Ollie the broken rear-door window, a long scrape that scored both doors, and the rear bumper, which the van had ripped away from the fender on the driver's side. "There's where he hit me the last time—slewed the rear around, sent it skidding."

Ollie surveyed the damage, then hunkered down and touched the metal with his big fingers. "All I see is where you hit that big rock down there. See where you chipped it? Gee, Ben, that's town property. Vicky McLachlan gets a load of what you done to her rock, she'll sue you." He laughed, an unpleasant sound, and returned to fingering the scrape. "Here you can see where the guard wire ripped her up something fierce. Yup, you skidded, all right. Good thing you were wearing your seatbelts."

He fixed me with a hard stare. "You *were* wearing your seatbelts?"

"That rock didn't break this window and you know it."

Ollie pretended to inspect the shattered glass.

"I seen them pop like this all the time. You hit that safety glass just right and boom—gone." He stood up and shook his head. "Funny thing, your new cars, the trim's all plastic, just breaks up in little bits. Fine old automobile like this, though, look at that chrome, all bent to hell. And will you look at that—you rammed the grill right through the radiator— Hey Pink, how you going to find a new radiator for a thirty-year-old Lincoln?"

Pink looked at him. For a second I thought he was going to call Ollie out, gun, badge, and all. Then he seemed to remember that the stewardship of Chevalley Enterprises had fallen into his thoroughly incompetent hands and that the state trooper had considerable say in who got called for towing jobs.

"We'll find a junker somewhere," he said. "Don't you worry, Ollie."

Ollie laughed. "I'm not worried. I didn't crack up *my* rich aunt's car."

By the time Ollie got done harassing me and I caught a ride home to Main Street, Doctor Steve was waiting for me at Connie's. "She's okay. I put her to bed. But if she shows any disorientation—or especially any vomiting—then right in the hospital."

"I better stay here tonight."

"No. I already hired Betty Chevalley. I want a real nurse, just in case. How are you?"

"Fine, fine."

"You look all shook up."

I said I was upset about wrecking Connie's car. I could tell Steve thought I was overdoing the manly bit about not reacting to an automobile accident, but I didn't like going into the fact that some son of a bitch had deliberately run me off the road.

"What'd you do to your hand?"

"Cut it on the horn." I unwrapped the handkerchief I'd wrapped around it and let Steve clean it off and Band-Aid it. Then I went home and telephoned Alex Rose.

"The state police found forty thousand cash in Renny Chevalley's garage."

"I heard," said Rose.

"What do you think?"

"I think it looks like he was flying dope for a living."

"Have you found anything new?"

"I told you I'd look when you found some convincing reason to. Forty big ones in a shopping bag does not fall into that category."

"How are you doing with Rita Long?"

"Mr. Long's lawyers sprung her."

"I know."

"It's a start."

"That's it?"

"We found a ballistics expert who will testify that the shot could have come from the woods."

"Great! Is he a heavy hitter?"

"Yeah. He used to work for Robert DeAngelo."

"DeAngelo's the Plainfield M.E."

"My guy learned everything he knows from him."

"Is that good?"

"The lawyers ought to have fun with it."

I dropped in on Connie. She was still sleeping, so I went down to the drugstore to pick up a prescription Steve had called in and ran into Al Bell, who had found Renny on his airstrip. The old pilot was inquiring, loudly, if his batteries had come in on special order. They had, and I helped him load them into his hearing aids. He's a kid by Connie Abbott standards, and still an ace pilot, but of an age that his fingers are clumsy. Mine weren't much better, shaking at slow-motion replays of the van growing large in the Lincoln's windows. I braced my hands on the counter and finally got the batteries in their slots. Al screwed the little flesh-colored amplifiers into his ears, fiddled the volume knobs, and shouted, "Say something."

I said something and his face lit up. "Now you're talking."

Walking out to the cars, he explained that the only problem with his superior Japanese hearing aids was their odd battery size. "Been deaf for a week. They cut out together."

"How'd you happen to hear Renny's plane land?"

"Didn't. Car went by the house like a bat out of hell. Later, I got to thinking maybe some kids were messing around, so I drove up to check my plane."

"You saw a car? What kind of car?"

"Like I told the cops, all I saw was his dust through the privet hedge. . . . Sorry about Renny. Tough way to go, getting shot."

"Must have been a shock, finding him."

"I didn't realize he was shot. I thought he'd cracked his head on the windshield. Took his pulse. Dead as a rock. Poor kid. He was really making something of himself. . . . Say, heard you got mixed up with that lady who shot her fella."

"No, Al. I was just there appraising the house."

"Hell of a woman."

"You know her?"

"Sure. Had 'em up for drinks. They were supposed to come to dinner next week."

I shouldn't have been surprised. Alexander Bell, like his namesake great-great-great-uncle, had been a famous inventor in his day. Still was, actually, with a consultancy to the U.S. Air Force. He flew around the country in his old P-51 Mustang, which he had bought new, surplus, after World War Two, and, being of the family he was, he knew everyone who was anyone. If new people who sounded interesting like Jack and Rita Long moved into town they'd receive an invitation to come up to Bell Farm for cocktails. If they *proved* interesting, they'd get invited back to dinner, where the food was indifferent but the company sparkled. I'd attended dinner occasionally, on Connie's coattails, and once or twice when they needed an extra man who knew the correct direction to push a soup spoon. (Al couldn't have cared less whether I snorted it up a straw, but Babs was a stickler, and if a guest didn't possess some startling quality, he had damned well better know how to conduct himself at table.)

"Hell of a woman," Al repeated, his leathery face glowing at the memory. "How the hell she got hooked up with that cold fish of a husband, I couldn't understand. Babs knew something of his family, but good Christ, Ben, what a bore. All takeovers and mergers and— you know, that kind of crap you used to do—but not a goddamned thing to say on any subject worth talking about. There she sat all dark and mysterious and then *boom!* that big smile bright as a supernova. I thought, Oh Lord, to be seventy again."

"Terrific woman," I agreed.

"So how'd you get mixed up with her?"

"Are you sure those batteries are charged, Al? I just told you, I'm not mixed up with her."

"I'm sorry to hear that." Al had a reputation for chasing skirts. I don't know what he chased any more, but he seemed to assign to me some of his fantasies. Lowering his voice, conspiratorially, he glanced up Church Hill in the direction of Town Hall and asked, "How you making out with the government?"

"Friends."

"The best way." He nodded enigmatically, then climbed into his jeep and roared off.

I went home and telephoned Trooper Boyce. She was out and returned my call around five. "What's up, Ben?"

"Some son of a bitch ran me off the road. Almost killed my aunt and me."

"I heard," she said coolly. "Any witnesses? Get a license plate?"

"You've been talking to Trooper Moody."

"And *you've* been talking to the wrong people, bugging them about your cousin. That's a no-no, Ben."

"In other words, you don't buy Trooper Moody's story that I was speeding."

"In other words, get out of my face. It's my investigation, my job, not yours. . . . How's your aunt?"

"Sleeping it off."

"I hear she's very old."

"She ran away from boarding school to be a nurse in World War One."

"Really? Wow, I didn't think anybody was alive from then."

"What's the story on the cash you found in Renny's garage?"

Marian was silent for a while. Then she surprised me: "Take me to dinner. Maybe I'll fill you in."

"I'll bet if I asked Sergeant Bender, he wouldn't ask me to take him to dinner."

"You don't owe him a meal."

"Good point."

"Besides, he's working tonight, and even if he weren't, he'd hang up on you because it's none of your goddamned business."

"Why would you talk to me? Other than dinner?"

"Sergeant Bender and I have different standards and different agendas. Where shall we meet?"

"It's lobster night at the Yankee Drover."

"You're on. I can make it by six-thirty or so."

"I'll wait for you in the cellar bar. The door's right off the parking lot."

I got there early and suspected Marian would be late, so I ordered a glass of white wine. I was halfway through it when she arrived in blue jeans and a snug sweatshirt dressed up with a collar. "This is how I eat lobster down in New Haven. I hope I'm not too casual."

"Perfect." I looked her over, wondering where she'd stashed her gun. Her bag was too small and her clothes intriguingly snug. "Ankle holster," she said with a friendly smile. "Do I get a wine too?"

I told her the town was hers, which turned out to be prophetic.

14

Wine in the cellar bar. Lobster upstairs at the Wednesday-night all-you-can-eat $21.99 special. Not a bad life. Particularly in the company of an attractive, sure-of-herself brunette.

Marian Boyce had apparently concluded that a man who had had a life in New York City could be trusted to applaud her ambitions. Not that she needed applause, she just didn't want to be put down for them. (I was no stranger to this trust. When I taught the real estate workshop at the high school's career day, kids confided dreams that would curl the toenails of their dairy-farmer parents. I was proof that the shiny world television promised was out there, waiting for them.)

Marian's cop father, she told me, wanted her to hang up her gun and have babies, before she got shot like he had. But she was gunning for sergeant, master sergeant, lieutenant, captain, then major and a division command. That was just the beginning. She planned to retire from the state police after twenty-five years and, still in her early forties, graduate law school and hit the big time—get elected Hartford or New Haven state's attorney and then the Executive Mansion.

"I'll be governor at fifty. What do you think?" This all spewed out with happy abandon, and total confidence, and an unwavering grin.

"I have a friend you ought to meet."

"Told you, I have my hands full."

"This is a woman. Our first selectman, Vicky McLachlan."

"Yeah, I heard about her. The hair."

"You might end up running against that hair."

"I'll win in a walk. She won't have a chance against my law enforcement background. Maybe I'll let her be lieutenant governor. So what about you?" she asked, as we headed back for thirds. "What are you doing with your life?"

I started to answer, but when we sat down again she remembered a night course she was taking at WestConn—"History of Wall Street, 1920–1990." "You guys were a piece of work."

"We had our fun."

"Now the markets are booming again."

"Low interest rates are making a lot of players smart, same way junk bonds did when I was there."

"You miss it?"

I wasn't about to proclaim my innocence to a cop, even on her night off, so I said, "I'm banned, as you probably know, but even if I managed to clear my name, I doubt I'd go back. I'm happy in Newbury."

Marian went along with the change of subject, gracefully, I thought. "It's a beautiful town."

"Want to buy a house?"

"On my salary I was lucky to buy a little condo in Plainfield. Of course, in this market, if I sold tomorrow I'd still owe the bank." She snapped a claw with her fingers and popped the meat between her lips. "Can I ask you something? What's it like to make a ton of money and then go broke?"

I laughed and drank some wine. "It's been years now, but it still hasn't hit me. I know I have bills to pay I never used to worry about. And I have no plans to buy a new Jaguar. But I still don't *feel* broke, most of the time." After some more wine, I said, "When I see some poor homeless guy on the road, I know it could be me in a few bad years— I'll bet you never see that happening to you."

She looked briefly startled but recovered with a laugh. "I'm vested in a growth industry."

Todd Gierasch, the be-zitted kid bussing tables, hauled off her third gutted lobster tail. I asked if she would like more. "I'm ahead of you," she protested, with a glance at her watch. I went along and had a third while she had a fourth. They were small. Franco finds some miniature breed with a titanium shell for all-you-can-eat night.

"You were going to tell me about the forty thousand dollars cash they found in Renny's garage."

"Officially?"

"I'd like the official take and then your take."

"You look ferociously serious, Ben." *She* looked mildly flirtatious. Once again, I felt a little sorry for the two guys who thought they were getting somewhere with her. Adults, presumably, who could take care of themselves.

"Seriously, Marian."

"Okay." She pushed back her plate and said Yes when Todd darted over with coffee. Across the restaurant, Franco wiped his brow; the deal was, once coffee was poured, the lobsters were history. "Okay. Officially, you can use your imagination to see how it looks to our investigation. We got a garage mechanic murdered in a plane full of coke. We find major cash hidden on his premises. We conclude that he did not earn this money replacing ball joints."

"Does Sergeant Bender read it that way?"

"Yes."

"Do you?"

Marian hesitated. "Understand I can't discuss cases with civilians?"

"Not to mention felons."

"Felons I can relate to," she smiled. "At least they've been around some of the same blocks I have."

"Seriously," I prompted again.

"Don't quote me." She raised a finger in a very serious warning.

"I won't."

"It's too pat. . . ." I waited. She took her time. "I'll buy your cousin running coke. Why? Means: the plane. Need: heavy debt. Connections: felonious relatives—and I don't mean your kind of felonious,

I mean heavy hitters. I won't mention names. You know who I'm talking about."

I said, "Chevalleys aren't that heavy."

Marian gave me her thinnest smile. "I'm playing straight with you, Ben. You know damned well I'm not talking about Chevalleys."

"Just testing." I knew she meant Jervises.

"Ben, I'm good. If I were male I'd be Bender's boss. I will be anyway."

A paranoid question rattled my brain at that point. Was she pretending to be open with me to lull me into trusting her? Did she really think *I* was suspect in Renny's shooting?

"Sorry. I know the relatives you mean. So you think Renny had the means, the motives, and the connections to run coke. Where's the *but?*"

"But I walked through his garage. He could serve his own lobster night on the floor, the place is so clean. I go into his machine shop. It looks like diamond cutters work there. I check out his front office. Brain surgeons should be so orderly. This isn't a man who stashes forty thousand dollars in a shopping bag in the back of a closet—a closet, by the way, that contains neatly sealed boxes of tax records, clearly labeled, right down to the year they're supposed to be thrown away."

"Thank you," I said, sitting back and feeling better than I had since this whole mess started. "That's the Renny *I* know." The Renny who could turn Detroit iron into chrome. "So where did the money come from?"

"I don't know, Ben."

"But?"

"But what? What am I supposed to do with my marvelous intuition? Do I go to Bender and say somebody else stashed it?"

"Why not?"

"Because Bender asks, Who?"

"So you tell him, Somebody who wanted to frame Renny."

"Then Bender asks, Who? again, and, While we're at it, Silly Marian, why? And, incidentally, Where would somebody not in the drug trade get that sort of cash? You withdraw that amount from a bank and there's a record. And a report filed. What I'm saying, Ben, is my boss would laugh me and my intuition out of the barracks."

"When I played on the Street we always kept a safe full of cash. Slush fund, walking-around money, who knew? And I never heard of a hot outfit that didn't."

"*Forty thousand* in an office safe?"

"I don't know how much. We did not tip the sommelier with Visa."

Marian smiled gently. "Do you want me to tell Bender to round up the usual Wall Street suspects?"

"I'm not laughing, Marian."

"Lighten up. All I'm saying is I don't have a thing to go on, other than my impression that the man ran a clean garage. Maybe he was a compulsive neatness freak. Maybe he just tossed the money in there and rushed out the door, intending to stash it in his safety deposit when the bank opened."

"Did he have a box?"

She gave me her back-off look, warning me that she might share the occasional theory but never information. But I had the instant impression that she had searched Renny's box and found nothing but wills and insurance policies. I asked.

Before she could tell me aloud to mind my own business, little Alison Mealy came running into the restaurant, skidded past Franco, spotted me, dodged the owner's attempt to stop her, and pounded between the tables as only an eleven-year-old can pound in sneakers. "Ben!"

"Hello, Alison. What's up? Say hello to Trooper Boyce. Trooper Boyce, this is my neighbor Alison Mealy."

"Ben, there's a man sneaking around your house."

"What?"

"I went over to play the tape again and he's inside."

I jumped up. "Come on, Marian. Do you still do simple burglaries?"

"Sit down, Ben."

"What?"

"Sit down. If there's someone in your house, call the police."

"You're the police."

"I've had three glasses of wine. I can't even drive home, much less walk into your house with a badge in my hand."

"Well, excuse me. I'm going over to see who the hell is in my house. Alison, stay here."

"Sit down, Ben."

I ignored her. "Where's your mother?"

"In the barn."

"Okay, you stay here with Trooper Boyce. Have a coke and don't offer her any wine— Franco, Coca-Cola for the young lady. I'm going to find out who's in my house." I had matched Marian glass for glass and was only vaguely aware that the wine was talking now.

Marian said for the third or fourth time, "Sit down, Ben." She looked like she meant it. I figured it was my check and I'd sit when I felt like it. I headed for the door. Marian caught up in the foyer and took my arm.

"Don't. Use that phone. Call Trooper Moody."

"I just want to scare them off."

"What if they're armed?"

"Franco, can I use your phone?" He was staring openly from the reservations desk.

"Yes," said Marian. "Use his phone."

I dialed Oliver. "Somebody's burgling my house."

"Who's this?"

"Ben Abbott. You want to come over and do something?"

"On my way." He hung up.

"See?" said Marian. "Wasn't that more sensible?"

"I feel weird. My house is a hundred yards down the street and I'm standing here while somebody's invading it."

"How about dessert?"

"You order. I'll be back."

I caught her by surprise and was running down the sidewalk before she got out the door. I felt the blood pounding in my head. Some small cautious voice said, Look out, you'll get your head blown off. I was really surprised how angry I was; I hadn't realized how attached I had become to that house. Somebody was invading me and I wanted to kill the son of a bitch.

I stopped at the foot of my driveway. Oliver wasn't in sight. Nor did I hear his siren. I heard Marian running up behind me. A shadow moved across one of the lighted windows in my office.

"Goddammit!" I charged up the drive, and threw open the side door to my office. There were two men. One was deep in the closet. The other, rifling my father's desk, reached inside his windbreaker.

15

I slammed the closet door, kicked the visitor's chair in front of it, dove for the guy at the desk, and tried to pin his wrist. He was short, broad, and very fast. He chopped my jaw with his free hand. I slipped most of it over my shoulder and kneed him while I battled his other hand. He hit me again. I saw stars, kneed him again, and this time connected. He doubled over. I tore his hand out of the windbreaker. He held a badge on a leather case. "State police," he gasped, straightening up and straight-arming my chest. "Back off. Now!"

"What?"

Major Case Squad Sergeant Bender pushed out of the closet, waving a search warrant.

"What's going on?" I was utterly baffled, aware only that the other cop was circling behind me, looking to throw a kidney punch.

My telephone rang. Bender picked it up. "Thanks. He's already here."

Marian Boyce crashed through the door. "You horse's ass," she said to Bender. "What took you so long?"

"Jailbirds know how to hide stuff."

I looked from Bender to Marian. To her credit, she couldn't meet my eye. "What stuff? What the hell is this about?"

Bender handed me the warrant. I skimmed a blur of print. Blood and adrenaline were tearing around my head. I recognized my name and address. The warrant was signed by a county magistrate.

"What are you looking for?"

"Cash," said Bender. "In a shopping bag."

"What? What the—"

Alison hovered at the open door, her little jaw dropping. I took a deep breath and scanned the warrant a second time. It covered the house only, not the barn. She and her mother were safe. "Alison, may I introduce Sergeant Bender and—" I looked at the cop I had kneed. He was still holding his badge, but he didn't tell me his name. "This is Alison Mealy, my neighbor. Say hello to the nice police officer, Alison."

She looked as bewildered as I, but she stepped into the room and gave me a reassuring little grin. "Hello," she said to Bender.

"Don't offer your hand."

"I wasn't going to. Are you okay, Ben?"

"I'm okay. Go home, hon. Go on, everything's fine."

"Frisk him," Bender ordered.

I backed up a step. "Let the child go first. Marian, would you please walk Alison home? Go on home, hon. It's okay."

Alison didn't move.

I said, "Thanks for coming and getting me, Alison. I appreciate it."

"Come on, sweetie," said Marian, reaching for her hand. Alison ran like the wind.

"Spread 'em," said Bender.

Boy, did a patdown bring back a lot of memories. I felt myself losing it, calculating the optimum moment to throw the two of them through the windows. The patdown is a humiliating example of the guard's power and the prisoner's lack of it. Particularly if the guard is doing it just to show you he can, which is what Bender was doing, knowing full well I hadn't gone armed to dinner with Marian; nor did he think I had palmed a lobster cracker from the table. To my surprise, instead of losing it, I went cold, like I had learned inside, just stepped out of my body and let them think I was still there. Marian returned as they were finishing and I asked, "How about a strip-search?"

"Watch your mouth," said Bender's sidekick, backhanding my face. It was a stupid hit, opening his entire front from head to toe. I took full advantage.

There was a long, very ugly silence. Uniforms would have beaten me bloody with their nightsticks, but Bender, years out of uniform, did the right thing, saying to his partner as he helped him stand, "You asked for that," and to me, "Next time, you'll need an ambulance."

Marian's face was as unreadable as a Beijing street sign, though I didn't doubt that "next time" she would cheerfully hold their coats.

I sucked a knuckle where I'd opened up the cut I'd gotten from Connie's horn. "Up yours. You're in my house. Execute your warrant and get the hell out." To Marian, I said, "Bender forced you, didn't he? Threatened your career. You went along, hating yourself."

"No," said Marian. "Sergeant Bender would not have thought of it. He doesn't like working nights. What did you do, Arnie? Stop for supper?"

"We found guns upstairs. He's got an arsenal."

"All permitted," I said. "They were my father's."

"Gun permits for a convicted felon? Let's see 'em."

Having served more than a year and a day—three times more, in fact—I had had to apply for relief of civil disability to get my realtor's license. While I was at it, I had applied to renew my father's gun permits under my own name. His old desk was my physical connection with him, more than the guns, which he really never shared; but in the first months outside of prison, the right to keep them had seemed very important.

"Goddamned pussy courts," growled Bender, holding the permits to the light as if suspecting a forgery. "Look, the jailbird is licensed to carry! What'd you tell 'em, you sell houses for cash?"

"Only to cops and drug dealers."

For a white-collar felon, the gun permits had come easier than my realtor's license, as it allows me to hold money in escrow. Only after Connie had invited a Plainfield judge down for tea did I finally get the right to run the business.

"Marian," I asked, "why the charade? Why not just knock on the door with your warrant? I'd have let you in. Would have offered you coffee. Wine, even."

"You invited *me*," she said. "Remember? The warrant came through. And I took the opportunity to conduct a clandestine search. Sometimes it works better that way."

She was explaining but not apologizing. I said, "I presume you know by now you struck out."

"We're not done," growled Bender.

"If you want to stay up all night to make a stupid point, I can't stop you. I'll be in the library." I went in and closed the door behind him and sat with my books. I couldn't bear to see them pawing through the rooms. An hour later, Marian stuck her head in. "We're done."

"Close the door on your way out."

"I had a nice time at dinner," she said.

"We'll have to do it again."

"You might want to know I really did accept your invitation before the warrant was processed."

"Can I ask you something, Marian?"

"Sure."

"What if we'd had some more wine and you'd decided to accept my invitation to come home with me for brandy and dessert?"

"Might have happened."

"Yeah, what would you have done if we came back here and your partners were still here?"

"In that case, I might have gone for the strip-search." She smiled. I didn't. She said, "Good night." I didn't.

I got out the vacuum cleaner, started on the top floor, and worked my way down to the kitchen. Then I mopped the kitchen floor and cleaned the guest bathroom, which one of them had used.

They came back in the morning with a warrant for the barn.

"You sure I didn't move my shopping bag after you left?"

"We watched the house."

"Am I a suspect?"

"Renny Chevalley was shot late in the afternoon. You left the cookout at three-thirty and called on Mrs. Long at five."

"I took a shower."

"Plenty of time to drive up to the airstrip, shoot your cousin, before you called on Mrs. Long."

"That's ridiculous."

"But not impossible."

Alison had left for school. I took her terrified mother out for breakfast at the Church Hill Diner while they searched the barn, and tried to convince her that everything would be all right. Janet Mealy kept nodding her head, agreeing that the case had nothing to do with her, but the haunted look in her eye was still there when we got home to the empty barn. She asked to borrow my vacuum cleaner, and I went to see Tim Hall, my lawyer, who listened and assured me he wasn't worried.

"Can I sue for harassment?"

Lawyers are like Br'er Rabbit. Don't throw me in that briar patch, don't make me go to court. Tim said he didn't think a harassment suit was a good idea. The cops were just doing their job, pursuing an investigation. "I'm sure the warrants were good," he said. "Forget about it. They're just clearing up loose ends."

"They wouldn't do this if I hadn't been in prison."

Tim shrugged. He's young, with a big, broad, open face and a perpetually worried light deep in his eyes. He'd taken over his father's firm, as I had mine, picking up the old man's bank retainers and a client list comprised of the older families. He does their wills and their trust accounts for grandchildren's college and tries to defuse their occasional feuds, but real estate closings are his real bread and butter, so he was currently starving, like me. His father had been a force in the region; the jury was still out on whether he would be too. I suspected that in the long run—a couple of decades—he might, though if he did he would do it quietly.

He asked, quietly, "Is there anything you want to tell me?"

"Yes. I didn't do it. Neither did Renny."

"Would you like me to call Ira Roth?"

"What the hell for?" Ira Roth was *the* criminal lawyer in the county. Nobody could remember the last time he had lost a case.

"Well, you know," said Tim. "You've been in the real world longer than I have. When you have a problem you hire a specialist, right?"

"I can't afford Ira Roth, for one thing. I can barely afford you. For another, I don't think I have that sort of problem."

"Yet," said Tim.

I stood up.

"He might not be able to help, anyway," said Tim, walking me to the door. "I hear the Long attorneys have retained him to plead Mrs. Long's defense if they indict."

"That's sensible."

Tim agreed. The two-thousand-dollar suit crowd did not set well with local judges.

"What's the word? Do you think they'll indict?"

"Gossip is they don't have that much of a case against her. Seems to me the state's attorney will have to pull some additional rabbit out of his hat. What's he got? Her gun, which somebody else could have used. No witness. No priors. Lovers' quarrel is a dandy motive, but if they indict on that alone, Ira would probably win a motion to dismiss before they even seat a jury."

"Good. So he'll have time to bankrupt me. Good seeing you, Tim."

"How's Aunt Connie?"

"Sore. And mad as hell about her car."

"I saw it. Lucky you're both alive. . . . Can I ask you something?" He had followed me all the way to the landing outside the front door of his office, which he rents upstairs from the General Store. It used to be a storeroom and still smells sweetly of kerosene and grain, though no one's hitched a horse outside in a long, long time. In his father's day, farmers and businessmen trooped steadily up the outside wooden stairs, and it was said that no one ran for Congress from our side of the state before he paid a call.

"What's up?"

"What's with you and—I mean, are you—"

"Am I what?"

"Are you seeing Vicky McLachlan?"

"We're friends."

"Oh."

I looked at him. Tim wasn't yet thirty and a very young thirty at that. He seemed young now, young and confused. And, it dawned belatedly on me, crestfallen.

"Why do you ask?"

My attorney stammered.

Like any sensible country lawyer, he had worked for Vicky's election campaign as soon as he realized her chances of winning, so I knew he had seen her in action and had observed something of the forces that drove her. I laid a calming hand on his arm.

He said, "I'm just . . ." and ran short of words, again.

"Do you ever go out with her?" I asked, not so innocently.

"We had sandwiches in her office yesterday."

"That's Vicky."

"Well, I'll tell you, Ben. She's really something."

"Terrific woman," I agreed.

"But I've heard you two—"

"Friends," I said, "just friends," with a strange feeling that I was burning a bridge I would regret. Tim was a nice guy. Vicky could use a nice guy. I said, "She's got a big future. The only possible downside would be if it bothered you to play second fiddle to an ambitious woman."

"I don't care about that stuff," said Tim. "Seems to me if you love each other it's all shared anyhow."

"Don't let that talk get around, you'll be disbarred."

Tim laughed, light as a balloon. "Jeez, I'm glad we talked."

I descended the wooden stairs beside the General Store with mixed emotions: happy for Tim, provided he was reading her signals correctly; slightly relieved that I was no longer under the gun; and yet wondering if I would regret it. I also wondered if the honorable thing to do would be to go over and tell Vicky goodbye. Or should I just let things drift? I walked over to Town Hall and asked the clerk if the first selectman was in. She was.

She stood up behind her desk and offered a cheek, which I kissed.

"Hello, stranger."

"Hi." I hadn't seen her since the braces imbroglio.

"How's Connie?"

"Much better. . . . I was just up at Tim's."

"What's happening?"

I filled her in on the Renny thing and the police search. She commiserated and seconded Tim's advice to lay the groundwork at least for retaining Ira Roth.

"I'll call him, if you like," she offered. "Ira owes me a favor. You won't have to pay him unless you need him."

"I'll tell you if it comes to that. Thanks."

Vicky glanced at her watch. "To what do I owe the pleasure of this visit?"

"I was just talking to Tim and . . ."

"And?"

"He's got good taste in women."

She got it right away and turned neutral. "What are you saying?"

"He asked me about us."

"Us?"

In a rush of words, I said, "I told him we were friends."

"What is that supposed to mean?"

"It means it's okay for him to ask you out."

"Oh, good. I'm glad you've cleared that up. Ever since I moved to Newbury I could never find the proper authority to whom men are supposed to apply for permission to take me out. From now on I'll just direct all calls to you?"

"I didn't mean it that way."

"Do you have a deputy in case you're out showing a house and I'm really hot for somebody and can't wait?"

"Ha ha."

"Oh, I wouldn't be hot for somebody?"

"All I'm trying to say—"

"All you're trying to say is you're dumping me."

"Well—"

"You can dump me. That's your privilege. But goddammit, Ben, you cannot give men *permission* to go out with me."

"I was just assuring Tim the field was clear."

"So Tim can plough me. And seed me. Can he fertilize me too?"

"He was merely paying me a courtesy."

"*Tim has no right to pay that courtesy, you bastard. You have no right to receive it.*"

My next bright answer really angered her. I eventually left Town Hall, thoroughly confused and miserable in the knowledge that I had ended our friendship as well as our love affair, and had probably poisoned poor Tim Hall's dreams too. I sat in the sun at the table in front of the General Store and drank some coffee. I finally figured out what I was trying to say to Vicky, found a quarter, and telephoned her office.

"What I meant was Tim was screwing up his courage to ask you out. He wasn't asking my permission, he was asking for help."

"That's his problem. What's your excuse?" *Click.*

I returned to my coffee and brooded. One misery led to another: Vicky; poor Renny; the cops invading my house; my sinking business and my nonexistent earnings. Scooter MacKay lumbered by with a bundle of newspapers on his shoulder. The *Clarion* delivers by truck and by mail, of course, but Scooter maintains an old tradition of the publisher personally carrying the new issue to the General Store.

He tossed a *Clarion* on the table. "Hot off the press. Read all about it."

It was actually warm. Ink smeared my fingers. To my immense relief, there was no photograph of Connie's Lincoln on the front page. She would not have been pleased, having been raised back when only the crass published their wedding pictures.

Jack Long, however, looked very pleased, grin to grin with the President. The headline read: "Local Resident Joins Other Prominent Business Leaders for D.C. Lunch with President."

Scooter himself had the byline: "Morris Mountain weekender and Land Trust advocate Jack Long flew to Washington, D.C., Saturday for what White House media spokespersons described as a 'business lunch with the President at which meaningful views on the economy were exchanged in an atmosphere marked by its informal cordiality.' "

Scooter came out with a cup of coffee, sat beside me, and lit up.

I asked, "Don't you mean 'cordial informality'?"

"Can't you read? I'm quoting the rocket scientist who issued the press release. I'm being ironic."

"Oh, I get it."

I read on. Scooter had described Long as "a new resident of Newbury already active in local affairs."

"Local affairs?"

"You get it?"

"I get it."

After historical references to other Newburyians who'd lunched with the President—an Olympic gold medalist with Eisenhower and some school kids with Nixon—the story continued on page two. I turned to page two and found myself gaping at my picture—a file photo the *Clarion* had run when I came home and took over my father's office. The headline read: "Main Street Realtor's Office Searched by State Police."

I looked at Scooter. He took a deep drag on his cigarette. I couldn't tell whether he was embarrassed or secretly enjoying my discomfort.

"Was this necessary?"

"You're news, my friend. Raids, wrecks, what's next?"

"Scooter, I didn't need this. I got troubles enough. Christ, page two? Who the hell is going to list with me now?"

"My news editor wanted to run it on the front page. I prevailed. And note that I didn't embarrass your aunt. Probably would have won a Pulitzer with that photo."

"Thanks a hell of a lot. Connie would have had your balls for pea soup."

"Nobody reads page two. Besides, I'm not the only one. Have you read the dailies?"

"My customers don't read the Danbury papers. And the people around town selling old houses read yours. Goddammit, Scooter."

I had not exaggerated my financial situation to Tim. I was slipping under—taxes looming, car repairs, furnace oil with winter coming. If I had some big expense, like having to retain Ira Roth as a defense attorney, I was out of luck. I stood up, angrily.

Scooter said, "You look like hell, Ben. You look miserable."

"It's been a rotten week."

"It can only get better, right?"

I started to say, Wrong, but before I could a silver Jaguar pulled up. A tinted window slid down. And Rita Long called, "Hello, there."

Black hair swept into a ponytail, black sunglasses, onyx earrings, she looked as mysterious as the night, very beautiful, and suddenly vulnerable when she flashed a tentative smile.

I introduced Scooter. Rita took off her sunglasses and complimented the *Clarion*'s photography. Scooter preened. As he left, he muttered to me, "Told you it would get better."

I told him quietly to go to hell.

16

―――――

"Terrific-looking car."

"Come for a ride."

I got in. Sunk into delicious leather. It was the V-12 model—a deluxe rocket ship. At the controls, a super deluxe pilot.

"You look well."

"Thank you."

She looked rested and artfully made up, still in jeans, but topped today with a black cashmere sweater instead of her usual workshirt. Her hair shone like a seam of anthracite. She could have walked into any house in the county, announced, I'm here for the husband, and encountered no resistance.

She tooled out of town, along 7. Fall was coming in with a bang and the colors were exquisite, with red maples, birches, and ash leading the parade. We enjoyed it silently for a few miles. When we got to Academy Lane, I said, "Turn right."

Right again at Richardson Street, and down the sugar maple tunnel. I had been meaning all summer to come out with a chainsaw and cut up some of the fat, dead lower limbs which would make hard, dry firewood. Borrow Pink's truck and haul in a winter's worth. The Main Street house doesn't have a wood lot, of course;

about all the fuel the place provides is when something awful happens to a favorite tree, wood I reserve for fires on special occasions.

Frank LaFrance was haying the fields with his patched-up Leyland tractor. I waved, but he rode by, stiff-backed. At that distance all he could see was Rita's Jag, and Frank wasn't about to waste a wave on city people.

"Where are you taking me?" asked Rita.

"My favorite house."

She glanced over at me, over the tops of her sunglasses. "Is it for sale?"

"Perpetually."

"What's wrong with it?"

"I don't know. Ellie Richardson died four years ago. It's been on the market ever since. Wait till you see it. Most beautiful location, private, and reeking of old New England."

"Business is still that bad?"

"Mine is. There was a mini-boomlet for a while, but now people are fixing places up instead of moving."

"Sounds tough."

"That depends on what business you're in. The hardware store is going great. So's the paint store. The nurseries are booming. I wouldn't want to own a moving van, I can tell you."

"Or a real estate agency."

"Cycles. Everything goes in cycles."

"Like ice ages."

"It was always a swing business when I was growing up. For a while my dad would drive a new Olds. Then an old Olds. Hell, when I got out of the navy in '81, you couldn't sell a house to save your life. Twenty-one percent interest. But down on Wall Street, something was already cooking. . . . The driveway's right up ahead. . . . There. Watch the potholes." The low-slung Jaguar bucked and bounced and scraped its tail, and then we were past the worst of them and within the yard.

"Oh, it's lovely," said Rita. But, to my disappointment, she gave the neglected grounds a cursory glance and returned to our conversation, saying, "How long can you wait out the market?"

I was feasting on the steep gables that spiked the sky. "Adlai Stevenson visited his mistress here."

Rita looked puzzled.

"Ran for president," I explained. "Twice. Back in the 'Fifties."

"Before we were born."

"Yes. A whole gang of famous people used to visit here. When I was a kid I'd bike over and watch from the woods. My Aunt Connie had told me about the parties. I was too late. They'd all gone. Around the other side are beautiful walks and rose gardens. Clay tennis court. I'll bet you've never seen one of those."

"What did you think you would see?" Rita asked.

"Beautiful cars. Women in long dresses."

Rita still looked puzzled. "It was a long time ago," I explained. "Before 'Masterpiece Theater.' "

She smiled. "And now you're hoping for a buyer who'll restore it."

"Somebody's going to fall in love with this place." I laughed, a little nervously; I was regretting talking too much. "Your friend Alex Rose pretended to be house-hunting, so I drove him out here. He didn't get it."

"He's not my friend."

"Well, he's on your side."

"How long can you wait?"

"For what?"

"To start selling houses again."

"Financially? Who knows?"

"Are you carrying a mortgage on your house?"

This seemed like a pretty forward question, even from someone who I knew in some strange ways. I said so.

"I'm asking for a reason. Do you have big expenses?"

"It's not really my house. It belongs to my mother. I pay the taxes and whatever upkeep I can afford. If I can't afford it, I try to fix it myself. I kept promising to paint it this summer, but I spent the time pointing the cellar walls. Next year on the paint. God willing the furnace will make it through the winter. Why are you asking me this?"

"I'd like to offer you a job."

I laughed again. "What is it about this place? Last time I was here, Rose offered me a job. Now you offer me a job."

"Rose works for my husband. I'm second on his list. I'm afraid the state's attorney will indict me. I would feel better if I had someone on whose list I was first."

"Well, I hear you're hiring Ira Roth for your defense. You'll be number one on his list."

"My husband is hiring Ira Roth."

"Don't worry, all Ira cares about is winning."

"I want you to help me."

"I'm not a lawyer."

"I want you to be my Alex Rose."

"I'm not a detective."

"You were an investigator with Naval Intelligence."

"Rose tell you that?"

"He told Jack."

"Well, he was just trying to sell me to Jack."

"I checked you out. I know it's true."

"So you know I was seconded to Naval Investigative Services. Sounds bigger than it was."

"With Admiral Denny."

I didn't cover my surprise. "How the hell did you get to him?"

Rita looked at me over her glasses and gave me one of her prettier slow smiles. "I remembered an assistant secretary of the Navy who had a nice time at one of our parties. Nice enough to check you out and ask Admiral Denny to talk to me."

"Denny wasn't an admiral when I knew him. . . . What did he say about me?"

"A few things I promised I wouldn't repeat. But he did say you weren't as dumb as you sometimes act."

"The man was always lavish with praise."

"I intend to hire my own 'friend.' I'd like him to be you."

"To do what? Your lawyers won't talk to me. Ira will hire his own investigator if it comes to that."

"Don't let it come to that."

"What do you mean?"

"Find out who killed Ron."

"Rita, I did one murder investigation in the navy. It was a race thing—they were rioting on the ships in the late 'Seventies. I ran a bunch of harassment investigations. And we engaged in a little spy-hunting."

"Catch any?"

"Why don't you ask your highly placed friends?" She started to interrupt with an impatient gesture, but I went on. "It was years ago. I was twenty-two years old. And it wasn't in the real world. It was in the isolated, separate, rarefied world of the service."

"Newbury isn't exactly the real world either," she argued.

She had me there, but I said, "It is to me."

"Perfect. I need a friend who's 'real' here. Somebody murdered Ron. Please help me find him."

I shook my head. "I'm sorry, Rita. If I'm going to play detective in my hometown, it'll be to find out who killed my cousin Renny. At least I know my way around here. I'm not equipped to check out Ron's background. You haven't known him that long. Who knows who was gunning for him?"

"Ron was an open book. He didn't have any secrets, aside from me. Now look, Ben, if you're chasing after Renny's killer you'll need expenses. Right?"

"We've already established I could use the money."

"As I understand it, private detectives up here ask twenty-five dollars an hour. I'll triple it—top New York rates—and all your expenses. Phone, trips, gas, lunch, airplanes, you name it."

I had to admire her acumen. She had settled on a tempting figure. I was curious how she knew New York rates, not to mention Connecticut.

"So what's the hesitation? You took my husband's money to take dirty pictures of me."

"I gave it back."

"Catch the killer and you can name your bonus. . . . Ben, will you help me?"

I didn't say I would, though her money would make it easier to chase Renny's killer. All I said was, "Answer a question?" which Rita seemed to interpret as a kind of yes.

"What?"

"Two questions?"

"Go."

"Did you shoot Ron?"

"No." What was she going to say, Yes? Still, I believed her. Not only because of what I had seen of her and Ron. Not only because she could charm my socks off, but because I simply didn't see the violence in her. Maybe I believed that her spooky drawing was the artist's technique she claimed. Yes, I knew Aunt Connie said I was a fool for women. But not this time. Rita Long was not a killer. I'd stake my life on it.

"What's your second question?"

"Can you honestly think of no one better to hire than me?"

"I spoke with a private detective in Torrington. And another in Hartford. And one in Danbury. The Torrington man is a bounty hunter. He recommended the Hartford man, who seemed like a good, solid divorce specialist, but he didn't even know where Newbury was. The Danbury man reprocesses lease cars for GMAC. Business is booming and I didn't trust him to concentrate on my problem. I then telephoned around New York and didn't like anything I heard. Nor did I trust the ones I talked to not to go running to Alex Rose the second they heard my name."

"You didn't give your name."

"Then I thought of you. So yes, I'm convinced you're the man for the job. Will you take it?"

"Secretly, I gather?"

"As long as that makes sense."

"Why would it?"

"I don't want people working against us."

"Like who?"

"The killer."

"Do you have a suspect?"

"Yes."

"Going to tell me?"

"Going to take the job?"

I could think of three reasons to take the job. The money to pursue Renny's killer; the opportunity to spend some time with Rita; and that sensation that killed the cat. Also, Vicky McLachlan was right. I liked dancing on the edges, daring Oliver Moody, Marian Boyce, and Sergeant Bender. I said, "Yes, with two conditions."

"Which are?"

"I want Renny's name cleared; I want his killer. I won't charge you for that time, but if something comes my way I go for it. Renny comes first."

"What's the other condition?"

"You promise that the instant you think I'm wasting your money, you fire me."

"Deal."

We shook hands over the armrest.

"Who's your suspect?"

"I don't know how he did it, but I think it's Jack."

"I just saw Jack's picture in the paper, shaking hands with the President. It said he went for a luncheon. And stayed for dinner."

"I still think it's Jack."

"You mean he hired a killer?"

"However."

"Why? Jealousy?"

"Why not?"

"Why did he hire Rose to prove you were . . ."

"Screwing around? Maybe he wanted to cover himself in case he got caught. He's like that. He's very methodical."

She called Jack Long methodical. Al Bell said he was a cold fish. I'd seen him in action—quick-witted and sure of himself. The thing that didn't quite fit these impressions of Jack Long was the Castle. Rita had told me he had designed it and she had only drawn it. The house was a fantasy—about as lighthearted as you could get building in stone.

"I don't know, Rita."

She said, "Check him out. Start tomorrow night."

"What's tomorrow night?"

"Jack's coming up. I'll give a dinner party."

"You're out a week on bail and throwing a dinner party? That's the kind of behavior the state's attorney would gobble up."

"A small dinner party. Call it supper. You. Me. And Jack."

17

As luck would have it, my first legitimate customers in a month knocked on the office door just as I was locking up to dress for dinner with the Longs. What I saw through the glass made me invite them in: a prosperous-looking late-thirtysomething couple driving a top-of-the-line Volvo with New York plates. They were for real, the fabled dream-house hunters who had kept their high-paying jobs and were ready to go bargain hunting, checkbook in hand.

We discussed what they were looking for and I recommended the Tilden place. I showed them the survey map and a few pictures and in minutes we were in the Olds, hightailing it out to a modest, well-maintained Civil War–era house on ten acres. The stolid Volvo told me they were smart enough to go for the land and expand the house later.

"It's not too built up here, is it?" the husband asked. Both of them had gone gaga for Main Street.

"Well, as we like to say around Newbury, Thank God for the Indians."

I measured the home-hunters' reaction and saw I had read them right. Nervous furrows of the brow at the hint that something untoward would be said of Native Americans.

"Burial grounds," I went on, reassuringly. "The Housatonic Indians buried their dead in Newbury, long before we were Newbury, buried them on raised platforms so wolves wouldn't eat them. When the Feds geared up to drive a four-lane interstate through the heart of them, we got together to protect the Indian sites as sacred ground. The valley's narrow. Thanks to the Indians, you'll never see an interstate within twenty miles of here."

"I'll bet this two-lane road gets jammed up on weekends."

"Worth it," I said. "No condos, no subdivisions to speak of, plenty of open space. Which, of course, is what brings a certain sort of person here who's looking for peace and quiet and a solid investment only two hours from New York."

"We made it in an hour and forty."

"You did? Wow, you must have found a shortcut. You're natives already. Now, the Tilden place starts around here." I slowed the car. "There's a big ash on this boundary."

"How about that stone wall?"

"No, we must have passed the tree while I was talking. We're well within the property already."

"Who owns the land on the other side of the road?"

"That could be yours too. Mr. Tilden's selling it separately, but he'd take a fair offer, save him a fight with the zoning."

When I was good, I was good. They didn't give me a binder, but I went off to dinner sure they would make an offer.

Jack Long met me at his hobnailed door in a flannel shirt and jeans. He invited me into his soaring antique-wood-paneled skylit foyer, looked me in the eye, shook hands, recalled the land trust meeting, and apologized for not wearing a jacket and tie, as he so rarely got a chance to shed his business clothes.

I apologized for being late. "Last-minute customer."

No problem, said Jack. Business was business.

Alex Rose had tagged him a little overweight; actually, I thought, Long was built more along burly lines, with a firm-looking barrel of gut straining his braided leather belt. His jeans were stiff and his shirt a muted red check—your basic country-life catalog ensemble mail-ordered by the wife of a guy too busy to shop. He wore a black mustache—the bushy sort you can get away with in business when you own the company—and funny running shoes.

"Oh, take off your tie," Rita said as she breezed in from the kitchen. "Jack won't keep one in the house." She looked lovely, with her hair swept back in a French roll and wearing the same silvery top she had shimmied out of the night I videoed her—a choice of garment I took to mean total forgiveness for my sins and a symbol of our conspiracy against her husband.

I unknotted my tie and opened a couple of buttons, and we rolled merrily toward the living room. Jack asked what I would like to drink. I looked to see what Rita was drinking. White wine in a near-empty glass. Jack had set a red wine, similarly drained, on the coffee table. But I wanted a few moments alone with Rita, whose sparkling hostess performance could have won admission to The Actors' Studio. So I asked for a bourbon old-fashioned.

Long covered his dismay and hurried off to the kitchen, muttering doubtfully about oranges and maraschino cherries.

I took the opportunity to ask my hostess, "How are you?"

"Oh, fine."

"This is bizarre."

"Go with it." She led me deeper into the living room. For one horrible moment I thought she was going to sit on the couch where we had laid poor Ron's body—or, worse, direct me to sit there. But it was gone—shipped off for cleaning or seized by the cops—and a brand new silk-covered eight-thousand-dollar Henredon was in its place.

"What does Jack think you're thinking?"

"It's never concerned him before."

"But this is—"

"Jack! Do you need help?" she called.

From the distant kitchen came an insincere, "I'm all right, darling."

"Excuse me, Ben. He doesn't know where anything is."

I had been at this party before. Who hasn't discovered their hosts half in the bag and anxious to kill each other? Such struggles behind a scrim of forced gaiety go with the matrimonial territory and usually abate with the arrival of the first course. But "kill" being the operative word tonight, the subtext was extraordinary.

Jack eventually returned from the kitchen, bearing my old-fashioned with a grim smile. Rita fluttered behind him, her eyes diamond-bright. I said, "Thank you."

Rita said, "Jack, my glass is empty."

Jack took it, finished his in a gulp, and plowed back to the kitchen, returning with both glasses inelegantly filled to their brims. I said, "Cheers."

"*Schlange*," said Jack, and Rita murmured, "Cheers."

"How's the drink?"

"Remarkable." It tasted a little of barbecue.

"So. How's the real estate business?"

Oh, it was going to be a wonderful night. I explained to this titan of technology that things were still a little slow in the real estate business. Surprise, surprise. I answered a half-dozen real estate questions and assured him that a unique home like theirs would always command top dollar from the right buyer. And how, I wondered, were things in the electronics business?

"Gangbusters!" said Jack.

"When's it going to filter down to the rest of us?"

"Don't hold your breath."

"Oh, Jack. Don't be such a pessimist."

"I'm not a pessimist," he replied evenly, gazing at some spot in the air beside her left shoulder. "But Ben here's no fool, and with his background he knows damned well what I mean. Don't you, Ben?"

I took a second hideous swallow, wondering how he had screwed up an essentially simple cocktail, and demurred. "As a former 'master of the universe' I'm afraid we enjoyed an overblown rep."

"But you know what I'm talking about. I'm talking about efficiency."

"Ah," I said. "Efficiency."

"And I know you know the price of efficiency." He seemed determined to enlist me against Rita in this stupid conversation.

I said, "Walter Reuther knew it forty years ago: Robots make lousy consumers."

"Exactly," Long enthused, with a triumphant glare at Rita, who looked a little pouty. I had the weirdest feeling that they had both forgotten Ron. But I soon discovered that I was wrong about that.

Long said, "My poor partner—former partner—the guy you found—had a big problem understanding that. His father had made his bucks in the fur trade and had long ago ditched his American factories. Ron just couldn't get that the employee you pay in Hong Kong is going to spend his paycheck in Hong Kong."

I had yet to meet a successful entrepreneur who didn't sooner or later develop a deep philosophical explanation for what was wrong with the world. Although Jack Long's understanding of the economy dovetailed with my own, I couldn't resist asking, "Are you moving your operations back to the States?"

"Damned right."

"I wish you luck."

"Jack's very patriotic," said Rita. "He met the President."

"Patriotism has nothing to do with it," her husband fired back. "A homegrown workforce spends its salary at home. That's why I don't mind the Japanese setting up car plants here. They make jobs. But the bind is that to compete with overseas labor you have to increase productivity, which *eliminates* jobs."

Rita yawned. Jack Long didn't notice. He was ballistic by now. "See this?" He thrust out his left hand. He wore a pinky ring next to his wedding band. It held a tiny semiconductor chip where a diamond would have been. "See this? X-ray lithography. This chip can process more data faster than an entire IBM mainframe. IBM used to operate foundries, assembly plants, paint shops, wire machines—heavy industry—to build a computer. Today they mail you more capacity in an envelope. That's jobs, mister, jobs gone to hell."

"Speaking of which, could I have a refill?" asked Rita.

Long's gaze locked on my old-fashioned glass, still three-quarters full.

"Wine?" Rita prompted.

"Jesus!" Long leaped to his feet. "Worcestershire sauce! I put Worcestershire sauce in your drink. It's supposed to be bitters, isn't it?"

"Traditionally," I admitted.

"Jesus, I'm sorry. Let me fix you a new one." He snatched up my glass. "Rita, you want some wine?"

"Oh, why not?"

And off Jack went, trailed by Rita's enigmatic gaze, which swung toward me when he disappeared through the door. "Well?"

"Well what?"

"What do you think?"

"I think you're both doing a great job of pretending nothing happened."

"That's not so strange."

"It isn't?"

"It's how we live. We're both busy as hell. We hardly ever see each other, and when we do we've got business to discuss. The personal stuff gets pushed in the corner, particularly if it's stuff you don't want to talk about."

"I see."

"I am aware, Ben, that Ron's death is a lot more serious than the usual 'personal' stuff. But this is the pattern. This is how we deal with things. And don't deal with things."

"Rita. Ron was killed, here. You're charged with it."

"Do you want me to cry, right here, now?"

"I'm sorry," I said. "I read you wrong." I got up and looked out the window. There was a thick autumn haze in the valleys, deep blue in the fading light.

"Just stop judging me."

"You're the boss."

"Don't be snide."

"There's deer in your meadow."

Rita jumped up, exclaiming, and joined me at the window. "Oh, beautiful— Jack! Come in here," she yelled. "There's deer."

Jack, bless him, just kept making my drink, and when he brought it in it was excellent. He watched intently as I tasted it. "How is it?"

"Excellent."

"Good. Sorry about that. I really feel like an idiot. Hey, Rita, we gonna eat, or should I shoot one of those animals?"

"Very funny. We'll eat soon. Excuse me, Ben. I've got something on the stove."

"Brace yourself," Jack warned me, loud enough for her to hear. "Rita's taken up cooking. When we moved in she thought the kitchen was a test lab so I could work weekends."

"You do your own engineering?"

"I like getting my hands dirty."

"Rita told me you designed this house."

"Rita exaggerates. She's got this idea that I should be artistic. Ever notice women are like that? They want their men to be everything."

"Heroes," I agreed, shamelessly milking our moment of secret chauvinism to keep him talking. Just as we've all attended parties with our hosts pie-eyed and contentious, so are we not unfamiliar with a wife simultaneously bolstering and taming her slob husband. Often as not it's exactly what the guy needs, though in Jack's case I doubted that he needed any bolstering.

"So who did design your house?"

"Rita did. From a picture in a children's book. I ran it through some architecture software and *voilà!* Jack's an artist."

"Did you train as an engineer?"

Long smiled into a practiced routine he probably kept ready for interviews. "I'm an E.E. from M.I.T. But now that software's the hot thing, I'm a windjammer captain of a steamship, if you know what I mean."

"Like a bowman with a shotgun."

Long flashed me a fast, hard, you're-messing-with-the-wrong-guy look. It lasted about one millisecond—long enough to show he meant it, too brief to escalate to a big deal, like a battleship traversing a silent battery. "Speaking of shotguns," he said bluntly, "what's your take on this mess?"

"I think from your wife's point of view it's a damned serious mess."

"Which aspect? The law?"

"I wouldn't want to go to trial in her position."

"What position is that?"

"You're outsiders. You're wealthier, by far, than any jurors they'll empanel. And, rightly or wrongly, you represent a world many local people find distasteful."

"What world?"

I thought he was overdoing the ingenuousness, so I said, "Call it the Reagan 'Eighties."

"They voted for the faker. Big in 1980. Bigger in '84. Even elected his pet turkey in '88."

"In '80 Reagan promised them a fantasy that Vietnam never happened. In '84 he promised them cheap mortgages. Bush promised the good times weren't over. Today they're scared they'll lose it all. They blame people like you."

"You were part of the 'Eighties, Ben."

"I already had my trial. Besides, new president, new times, new rules, new standards. But you and your house remind them of a past they'd rather forget."

"Maybe we should go for a change of venue."

"Not a bad idea, if you could pull it off. But keep in mind, the judge as well as the state's attorney would like very much to hold the trial right here— Hey, with any luck there'll be no trial. Everybody agrees they've got a thin case."

Long rubbed his face. "Jesus, I hope you're right. I've got my absolute top people on it, but I'm scared. For just the reason you're saying. What if they make my wife a symbol? For God's sake, she's just a woman like any other woman."

That I would argue with.

"I hear you hired Ira Roth. That was a good move. He's never lost a case."

"So he told me," Long replied dryly.

"What does he think about the ballistics conclusions?"

"He's hired an expert witness who swears the shot came from the woods."

"What do *you* think about the ballistics?"

"What do you mean?"

"I gather you're a shooter. And an engineer. What do you think? Could the shot have come from your tower?"

"*I* certainly couldn't have scored a bull's-eye at eighty yards from the tower."

I refrained from remarking that Ron Pearlman's back was bigger than a bull's-eye. "What about Rita?"

"She's a fair shot. But the state's attorney is talking about some pretty fine gun work."

"Who do you think shot Ron?"

"Goddamned deer poacher is my guess. Shot at movement, or sound, the way some of these damned fools will, realized what he did, and faded into the woods."

"That's how I read it," I agreed.

"I'm glad to hear that." Long rubbed his face again. "You see, if Ron had been just an ordinary houseguest, that's how the state police would have seen it too, but goddamned Rita went and spilled her guts to that woman state trooper—told her everything."

That was news to me. Marian Boyce was even better than she said she was. And closer-mouthed than she pretended. I said to Long, "You can hardly blame her. She was really upset."

"Too late to blame her, but thanks to her big mouth, Ron jumped from ordinary houseguest to millionaire's wife's boyfriend."

"And a millionaire in his own right."

"Yeah, right," Jack conceded bitterly. "Born with a silver spoon up his ass."

The rosewood paneling in the stairwell, I recalled, had come from Jack's mother's Park Avenue apartment. "Well, you're not exactly a self-made man either, are you?"

"The hell I'm not. I left home when I was fourteen. I didn't go back until I could buy out my old man."

"Was he proud of you?"

"The bastard was dead by then." Long looked in his glass and saw that it was empty, and that he had probably said too much.

"Interesting," I said.

"How so?" he demanded harshly.

"You and Ron had similar business backgrounds. He was born comfortable too, and he also pushed out on his own."

"Bullshit! His old man gave him the money and told him what to do with it. He was the quintessential preppy airhead. If they weren't Jewish he would have been a trust-fund baby. Since they *were* Jewish his old man wanted him to make a decent mark for himself. Too dumb to be a doctor, so Daddy bought him an electronics factory.

The old man's a pisser, by the way. You ought to meet him some-time. Salt of the earth. Ron was Momma's boy."

"I'm getting the impression you didn't get along."

"I can't stand fakers." He looked into his glass again. "Jesus, how did we get started on Ron?"

"Tell me something?"

"What?" he asked warily, but I had shifted gears, reckoning I had drawn his personal well dry for a while.

"If you're right about the productivity bind, what's your plan?"

Long grinned. I knew he had a plan. It went with the philosophy. "Volume. Build simple stuff you can sell to everybody in such volume that you have to hire more people to handle it."

"Personal electronics?" I ventured, borrowing the phrase from Rita, on the assumption this was the basic Long family line.

"Exactly. Personal electronics. Single phone numbers for every person on the planet. Pocket computers. Digital tape. And a virtual-reality game in every rec room in the country. That's four highly marketable items off the top of my head. We're testing others I can't talk about. I'm going to sell them to every man, woman, and child in America. And then to every citizen in the rest of the world."

"What about the Japanese?"

Long grinned happily. "They can buy 'em too."

Again I said, "Good luck."

Rita hurried in with high color in her cheeks. I couldn't tell whether she was flushed from cooking or had overheard Jack's low opinion of Ron. "Dinner," she said. "In the dining room."

"Christ I'm hungry," said Long. "I'll open some more wine. You want another of those, Ben?"

I told him wine would be fine and followed Rita into the cavern-ous dining room, where beneath the silver chandelier stood a card table set for three. A linen cloth draped halfway down its spindly legs. The silverware was sterling; the fresh wineglasses crystal; and the china, Pottery Barn. I glanced over at the lonesome Empire side-board, and it seemed to glower back disapprovingly.

"Light the candles, Jack," said Rita, racing out as he blundered in with the wine. I approached the table, wondering where to sit, and found place cards written in a clean, Gothic hand.

Jack poured the wine. He noticed me eyeing the label and said, "California. I bought a little vineyard next door to Josh Jensen's."

"That sounds like a wonderful thing to own."

"The candles?" the cry repeated from the kitchen.

"You got a match?"

"No."

He went in search of matches for the candles and I stood there alone—me and the sideboard, which I was feeling affection for. It looked like Newbury's venerable school principal, who taught his students to spell the homophonous title by reminding them that he was their *pal*.

Rita pushed through the swinging door, deliciously backside first, carrying a huge platter.

I lunged to help.

"Thanks, I'm all right. Where the hell's Jack?"

"Looking for matches."

"Jesus Christ." She hesitated, considering the distance of the sideboard from the card table.

I said, "Why not on the table, since there's only three of us? Here, I'll just move the flowers a hair and . . . Right."

She put it down, stood back tentatively, and wiped her brow. She had perfect ears, with a fat diamond stud in each. "What do you think?"

"Beautiful."

"Really?"

Whether she could cook was still an open question, but she was an artist and had arranged the chicken breasts, baked potatoes, and string beans in a parkland of parsley.

"I just remembered, I owe you for the groceries."

"Rita, chicken doesn't last."

"Don't worry, I used yours to experiment."

Jack came back with the matches, complaining, "I can't find a goddamned thing in this house." He lit the candles and finally noticed the platter.

"Jesus, hon. You did that?"

"No, Federal Express from Fraser-Morris."

"Looks great."

Rita sat down. Jack and I took our places.

So far, I had learned a very few facts: Jack disliked Ron; Jack and Rita, whose marriage of nine years resembled one of thirty with its practiced wrangling, had called some sort of blind-eye truce; Jack *said* he thought a poacher had accidentally shot Ron; he claimed he was worried Rita wouldn't get a fair trial. What else did I know? Rita was a hell of an actress. Jack was very nervous. Edgy myself, I proposed a stupid toast:

"Confusion to the state's attorney."

It went down big. Rita's eyes darkened. Jack's narrowed. I amended it to "Cheers" and we drank and fell on the chicken, which was cooked rare.

Rita watched me chew.

I said, "I think I'm familiar with this recipe. You've got a nice touch with herbs."

"The builder gave us a spice rack," Jack explained, then, a bite later, "This is really good, hon."

"Thanks, hon. Ben, did you say you cook?"

"Yes."

"Do you think these same spices would work with veal?"

"Ground veal," I replied, and got a secret smile. I ate around the red parts, thinking how much fun flirting with Rita Long would be if poor Ron hadn't lived and died.

Jack burned his mouth on his potato. She had microwaved them, and the skins were as crisp as wet Xerox paper. The green beans, however, crackled admirably. I complimented Rita on them. She credited the Gierasch farm stand on 361.

"Jack, pour Ben some more wine."

I covered my glass. "Driving." Jack had quietly switched from wine—which he occasionally touched to his lips for appearance sake—to water. Now and then his gaze would alight inquiringly on me. He was wary, maybe even rethinking what I was doing in his home.

"How long you going to stay in the real estate business?"

"Oh, I think I'm in it for the duration."

"You could have a problem."

"How so?"

"It's possible homeowning patterns are changing. We might go back to a situation like England used to have, where people live in the same house their entire life."

"I hope not. But even so, people still marry and die. There'll always be some market."

"But a lot less real estate agents."

"The newer ones could have some problems," I agreed, drawing a smile from Rita. I was sorely tempted to say, Look, Jack, Rita and I will wash up. Why don't you go to New York?

"Did you ever think of getting a job?" Jack asked.

He made it sound more like an insult than my third genuine job offer that week. I suppose I was a little touchy on the career subject, which cropped up nights I couldn't sleep and days my bank statement arrived. But his superior tone did not inspire me to admit that occasionally I did long to get back in the action.

"No," I answered. "My business keeps me busy."

"I'm told you used to be some sort of genius at structuring debt. I'm always looking at new acquisitions—I say buy it before it buys you—I could use a man with that talent."

I pretended to give this absurdity my full interest, before replying, "Keep in mind, Jack, when I worked on Wall Street, debt was the *goal*. I doubt that's your position these days."

"Talent is talent. You telling me you're too old to adapt?"

"I have adapted."

"What are you, thirty?" Jack scoffed.

"Thank you. Thirty-five."

"That's not too old to change."

"Ben is saying he's already changed," Rita interrupted. "He's gone from Wall Street to . . . Main Street. Haven't you, Ben?"

"Right. If you're offering me a job, Jack, I'm flattered. Very flattered. And I'm grateful, particularly if you assume I'm in desperate straits. But I'm not interested in that sort of work anymore."

"What's wrong with it?"

"Mainly, it doesn't go anywhere." I looked across the table at Rita, who gave me a noncommittal smile. Jack, however, laughed.

"You're too young for forty-something angst."

"No I'm not. Wheeling numbers is for the young and dumb. Pass the time, make a ton of money."

"You've got plenty of time on your hands not selling houses and damned little money from what I can see."

"Jack, shut up," said Rita. "That's no way to talk to a guest."

"Relax, hon. Ben and I understand each other. Don't we, Ben?" Fully on the attack now, he hunched over the table, probing for any ambivalence he could turn against me.

"You probably understand me better than I understand you. What do *you* want to be, Jack?"

"Nothing I'd waste time thinking about. I just do it."

"Why bother? Aren't you rich enough already? Why not bank it, move full time to Newbury, and grow flowers Rita could paint? What are you trying to prove? You going to beat your father again?" No way to talk to a host I barely knew, but he'd set the tone. Nor did he seem to mind.

"The fight's not over, man. That's all I'll say. Look, Ben, I'm offering to put you back in the game. You got a ban on you? I'll get it lifted."

I wondered whether he had guessed I was working for Rita and was trying to buy me off. Rita seemed to wonder too. She looked a little worried that I'd succumb to visions of Bentley convertibles, fast women, and Sutton Place digs, so I said, "I'm a country boy, Jack, back home where he belongs."

"Country boy my ass! I know a player when I see one. Guys like you don't sell houses, you sell towns."

"Not anymore. At least when I sell a house it's the beginning of something. I've enhanced the house. When I ran takeovers, people got fired."

"They should have been. Goddamned bloated payrolls were killing us."

"We used to tell ourselves that at the celebration dinner—improving efficiency, raising productivity, streamlining."

"Somebody had to do it."

"Somebody else. I don't want to play God anymore."

Jack snickered. "Sanctimonious bullshit, Ben. Sounds to me like the U.S. Attorney turned your head."

"Jack!" Rita protested. "Apologize. Or I'm leaving the room."

"I apologize. Okay, Rita? I apologized."

"Ben? All right?"

I should have excused myself and gone home before it turned ugly, but I saw real alarm on Rita's face.

"No problem."

Jack said, "Just because I apologized doesn't mean I believe you. Nothing's that simple."

He was right, of course, but I could not abandon Rita, so I tried to smooth it over: "I'll tell you a story, Jack. This happened long before the U.S. Attorney came down on me. . . . Leaving Chanterelle, late one night. Way downtown? Dark, empty streets. I put the client I'm about to gut into his limousine, and after he's gone I discover I'm locked out of mine. My driver's stuck inside, can't get the doors and windows open, dead battery or an electrical short or some damned thing. Anyway, I'm locked out, and this old black beggar comes along and corners me with a paper cup."

"The yuppie nightmare," Jack chuckled.

"Poor guy looked like he hadn't slept indoors since the Korean War. So I peeled off a fifty."

"Generous."

"I'd just tipped a wealthy sommelier a hundred."

"Did the old guy thank you?"

"No. He just took the money and leaned in closer. My driver's banging on the windows, like he's the one with the problem. The old man asks me, 'Do you know what's wrong with capitalism?'

"This was some months before the crash, and I could not for the life of me think of *anything* wrong with capitalism."

"Other than shoddy limousines."

"Other than shoddy limousines. 'Okay,' I said, 'fill me in.'

"He said, 'Capitalism runs just fine at eighty percent.'

"I felt like he'd dropped a paperweight on my head from the top of the World Trade Center. I had never thought of it that way before. Then he explained, 'You boys do real fine at eighty percent, so long as you can pay enough cops to keep the rest of us out of your houses.' "

"Old guy should publish a newsletter," said Jack.

"Yes, well, I was his first convert. That was the night I lost my taste for playing with numbers."

"You know what I'm hearing?" asked Jack. "I'm hearing you lost your money in the crash and got religion."

"No. I got rich in the crash. Morning after the old beggar, I moved all my ill-gotten assets into bonds."

Jack Long stopped sneering abruptly. "You did?"

"Followed my gut. Made out like a bandit."

Jack looked at his wife. "You see why I want this guy on my side?"

Rita said, "I'd hire the old man with the cup."

Jack laughed. "Don't say no, now, Ben. Keep my offer in mind. Hey sweetheart, what's for dessert?"

"Sweetheart" reported there was Oreo ice cream, or lemon ice for anyone concerned about his weight. I had Oreo, and we withdrew to the drawing room, where Jack lit a smokey fire.

"Could I ask you something, Jack?"

"Nothing's stopped you so far. Shoot."

"I saw your picture in the paper. What's it like meeting the President?"

"Less expensive than it used to be under the Republicans. With Bush, grip and grin cost seventy-five thousand bucks to the re-election campaign. This was much more . . . democratic."

"You don't really meet?"

"He shakes your hand, speaks your name, gives you a big hug. This is a warm, huggy guy. You could walk away thinking he knew his ass from a hole in the ground."

"Does he?"

"I frankly don't know. Back with Bush you knew right away you were dealing with an idiot, because while you tried to explain to him that *he* was the leader, he was rattling away about the rotten economy as if his gang hadn't been in charge for the last twelve years. This guy's smart, and he listens. Very smart. Look at the way he's end-run the White House press. Maybe he listens too much, but I'll withhold judgment. And he's tough. Comes out of bare-knuckle politics. I like his wife. Major asset. What worries me is whether he can rise above the people helping him. They're very young. They're ignorant of the past—which might not be terrible. But that young, that close to power, how soon before they believe their own bull-shit?"

Jack snatched up his wineglass and emptied it. "You should have seen his 'inner circle' that night. One of them did the Larry King show. King massacred the puppy, but they sat there telling him what a great job he'd done on King. Total fantasy."

"What does it cost to meet the 'inner circle'?"

"A whiff of cordite."

"Beg pardon?"

"Jack was a war hero," explained Rita. "That always goes down big with the Beltway crowd, no matter who's in office."

"I was not. I was young and dumb." He saw me waiting expectantly and laughed. "I joined the Marines when I left home. Went to 'Nam, very early on. Two tours and I was back in the world by '64."

"He won a Silver Star," Rita said with genuine admiration.

"Yeah, right." Jack shrugged.

"Tell him how, Jack," Rita prompted. Her eyes sparkled, and she leaned closer to touch his arm.

I felt a stab of jealousy at this unexpected insight into the early, better days of their marriage. Regardless of how things had turned out, they had once been hot for each other.

I chalked it up to the aphrodisiac charms of an older man's money, power, and "whiffs of cordite" for an impressionable young woman of twenty.

"Ben doesn't want to hear this," Jack scoffed. "It was practically before he was born."

"I do. I do."

He looked at his empty glass a moment. "I'd trained as a helicopter mechanic. Back in those early days, we could not afford to waste anything. So when we had a chopper down with a blown engine, I jumped in with some parts, installed them, and flew the thing out."

"In," I gathered, meant in the Viet Cong's jungle. I was impressed and said so.

"You do what you have to do." Jack shrugged again. "Before they do it to you."

"Did you have any backup?"

"Forty-five automatic. Brandy?"

"No, I got to drive."

"Oh, don't worry about that," said Rita.

"I need my license."

"No, no, no. Stay the night."

"Sleep here," Jack echoed. "We got an extra bedroom furnished upstairs. No one's using it, now. Right, Rita?"

"Stay. Jack, pour Ben some brandy. I'll have some too."

"You've twisted my arm."

Jack opened a cute little Chinese lacquered cabinet in the corner, came up with three balloon snifters, and cracked a brand new bottle of sixty-year-old Napoleon. He splashed generously into each, handed a smiling Rita hers, passed me mine, and raised his. "Welcome, Ben. Hope you're enjoying yourself."

"Very much." Jack was starting to confuse me. I had enjoyed his take on administrations past and present, and I wondered what else we had in common in our respective world views—he out there on the cutting edge, me snugged up in front of a fire with *The Manchester Guardian Weekly* for facts and moral position, the *Economist* for reality, the *New York Observer* for uplifting gossip, the *New York Times* for kindling, and the *Newbury Clarion* for moving violations.

Jack told funny President Bush and Reagan stories for a couple of rounds, and even a howler about our new Democrat—funny if it were someone else's country—and when he got up to pour a third time, I said, "You amaze me, Jack. You sound like a liberal."

"The hell I am."

"Jack has a short fuse when it comes to idiots, don't you, dear?"

He tossed her a black look and drank. Rita looked at me and gave me a little nod, which I read as saying, Push that button harder. The glint fired in her eyes by Jack's war story had long faded, and she was regarding him again with veiled contempt, which made me inordinately happy.

"I'm curious. You're in the thick of the economy. What would you have him do different?"

"He's overwhelmed by health care and the deficit. He's losing his focus on the main problem, competition. Pump money into research. Make it profitable for businesses to invest in productivity. Pay for the kind of advanced education the Japanese workforce gets. Pay for a Manhattan Project type program to build an electric car. For high-temperature superconductivity. Underwrite a light rail intercity-intersuburban system people would ride."

Sounded to me like Jack Long's LTS Corporation had plans to expand into mass transit and electrotechnology.

Rita asked, "Where's the money to come from?"

Jack said nothing for half a minute. Then he spoke: "From hot-shots like Ben here."

"You want to bring *back* the 'Eighties?"

"I want to bring back 'Eighties energy."

I reached for the brandy.

Very late that night, tucked into the guest room where Rita had tucked Ron, I was blearily fantasizing that she would pop in to see if I were comfortable, when it occurred to me that I still had no idea whether Jack Long had been jealous enough to kill his wife's lover and then cold enough to let her go to prison for it.

The main subjects on his mind seemed to be money and debt. It probably meant nothing, but if there was one thing we learned from Robert Maxwell, Donald Trump, and even Rupert Murdoch, it was that they were never as rich as their bankers hoped.

I heard a soft knock at my door. I sat up, smiled, and called, "Come in," innocently, and not so loud as to be heard down the hall.

Jack walked in with a couple of brandy snifters and a sheepish expression. "Kick me out if it's too late, but I can't sleep, and I really hope I didn't mouth off at you too hard. I like mixing it up in conversation, and then later Rita tells me I've been acting like a jerk."

This was a different, extremely apologetic Jack, and I hardly knew how to take him. "Relax. I had a great time."

"Want a drink?"

"Why not?"

He handed me a glass and sat down in the armchair. He was wearing a silk paisley robe. Where Cary Grant would have knotted his cravat, Jack had bundles of chest hair. I had never met a man so determined not to come from Park Avenue.

"Cheers."

He turned out to be in a confessional mood.

"Shit, let me tell you, Ben, this is crazy time. I'm feeling pulled every which way. Before this hit the fan I was up to my eyeballs buying another Singapore operation. Then Rose calls me and tells me there's a dead guy on my property. Then he calls back and says it's Ron. Then it turns out Rita's sleeping with the bastard. This is not my idea of a marriage. But instead of wanting to shoot the bitch, which would seem reasonable, I'm worried about her trial. I'm worried sick. I got Rose lurching around like a loose cannon and a bunch of farmers hoping to crucify my wife. Anyhow, that's why I can't sleep. And that's why if I got out of line at dinner, I apologize. I been under a lot of pressure."

"Why is Rose a loose cannon?"

"Huh?"

"You said Alex Rose was a loose cannon."

Jack scratched his chest and crossed his hairy legs. "Al's all right. He's doing a crackerjack job backing up my lawyers. I've seen him in a clinch. The man knows when to hit. And he stays on top. He got to me before the cops."

"I don't follow."

"I pay to make sure I'm not surprised. When the cops called to tell me there was a dead guy on my land, I was already heading up here."

"Rose told you?"

"Sure. That's what I pay him for."

"How'd he find out?"

Jack peered into his brandy. "One thing I learned from my old man, when people bring you information, don't ask. It's like sausage. You don't really want to know how they make it."

He struggled to his feet, gathering his robe. "Hey, you're passing out, Ben. Get some sleep."

"Thanks for the drink."

"Don't mention it. Anything you want in the house is yours. Except my wife." He smiled as he pawed open the door, but if it was a joke it didn't quite work, and I felt sorry for him.

18

At dawn I heard a car crunching down the drive; I fell asleep and awoke in daylight to the smell of coffee. Rita tapped lightly at the door and entered with a cup and saucer. "Good morning." She had her hair in a braid and she looked all fresh-faced, as if she'd been walking. I could smell autumn on her sweater.

"Good morning."

"Jack's gone to New York. He had a good time last night. He said to say Goodbye."

"I had a good time too." I sat up in bed, bunched the blankets over my lap, and moved the book to make room for the coffee. "None for you?"

"Be right back."

I washed my face, borrowed somebody's brand new toothbrush, and climbed back into the bed, just before Rita returned. She perched on the deep windowsill, alternating between looking out at the valley and down at me with a smile.

"So? What do you think? Am I crazy? Or is he a killer?"

"I don't know."

"What did he say about Ron?"

"He didn't like him much. Called him a momma's boy."

"Momma's boy?" She smiled a secret smile that said she had a different opinion. "Momma's boy is Jack's lowest putdown. He's a little strange about family. He was dyslexic as a child. They treated him like he was dumb, so he left and showed them."

"I got some of that last night. Anyway, he tore into Ron and got really ticked when I suggested they had similar backgrounds. . . ."

"Vaguely," she conceded. "Except Ron was a happy child."

"He likes Ron's father."

"Nat's a character. Poor man. He's heartbroken over this. It's so sad."

"Did Ron's father know about you?"

"I wouldn't put it past him to guess. But if he did, he kept it to himself. . . . What else about Jack?"

"He came by with more brandy after we went to bed. Apologized for mouthing off."

"What else did he say?"

"He surprised me. He said Rose is a loose cannon."

"I don't *like* Rose, but I wouldn't call him a loose cannon."

"Yeah, well then Jack sort of amended that, talked about how he stayed on top of things."

"What did he say about me?"

I looked at her.

"Boy talk?" she nudged.

"Sort of."

"Don't forget you're working for me."

"Basically he said he wished you hadn't had an affair with Ron."

"That's it?"

"Said he was buying a new Singapore operation."

"So?"

"He said the negotiations were distracting him."

"He's exaggerating. We're snapping it up cheap."

"Is Jack in debt?"

"Of course. How could he do business and not be in debt?"

"I mean really in debt."

"I don't think so."

"You told me you helped Jack manage LTS. You'd know his financial situation, wouldn't you?"

Rita looked out at the valley and considered her answer. "Until a year ago Jack didn't make a move without talking to me."

I doubted that Jack's young wife had played as big a part as she thought. LTS wasn't exactly a family grocery store.

"What happened a year ago? Ron?"

"Before Ron."

"So what happened?"

"Are you interrogating me, Ben?" She looked down at me in the bed. I couldn't make out the expression in her eyes.

"Yes."

"Why?"

"You think your husband killed Ron. And you told me the other day that you think Jack threw you together with Ron. I want to know what's going on with you two. What happened?"

She sighed and hugged her knees.

"*HG* came to photograph the Greenwich house. I, in my *naïveté*, thought they admired my interior decoration. What I got was a bunch of horrible old women acting like they were doing me a favor invading my house. And it suddenly struck me that these gossips didn't give a damn about me or the decor. They were photographing it solely because it was Jack Long's house."

"Your house too. You were partners. Right?"

"Do you want breakfast?"

She was angry. I tried to jolly her out of it. "Getting pretty sure of yourself around the kitchen, aren't you?"

"I've been reading up on toast."

She swung her pretty legs off the windowsill and hurried out the door. I called after her, "Hey? How'd you meet Jack?"

"I was a bicycle messenger."

"Beg pardon?"

She came back and leaned on the door jamb. "I dropped out of school to study at the Art Students League. My parents were really pissed; they wouldn't pay for it. I was supposed to be a lawyer. My father had a hardware store. He worked really hard and wanted me to be something special, which to him meant a professional. So I worked as a bicycle messenger."

"Jack's limo ran over your bike?"

"No, I delivered blueprints up to his office one night, late, and he was alone. And we talked a minute. He was kind of fat and funny-looking, but I was so glad to be in the air conditioning. August and muggy. When I got down to Sixth Avenue they'd stolen my bike. You know, they spray Freon on the lock—freeze it and smash the brittle metal? It had been the worst day, and I was standing there crying when Jack came down with his blueprints. He bought me a new bike and then he bought me dinner and we became friends. Three months later we were married."

Wondering where Jack had bought a bike in the evening, I asked, "Did that redeem you with your parents?"

"Jack was worth about a hundred million then. They thought it was a great idea."

"How'd you go from bicycle messenger to business advisor?"

"Slept with the boss."

"Seriously."

"Seriously, Jack saw I had a head for business. He'd been on his own almost twenty years. He hates partners. But he began to feel he needed a sounding board. He got in the habit of laying out a plan and I'd play devil's advocate."

"That's very unusual in a corporate situation."

"I had been at Columbia. I had to learn a lot of stuff to keep up with him—like what fork to use for salad—but I wasn't dumb. Keep in mind, none of this would have happened if Jack hadn't broken with his family. His parents would long before have found him the right sort of wife. Forks and Junior League and all that stuff that those kind of people need to make a family. A woman who'd breed the kids and manage the houses and give parties."

"Why no kids?"

"He doesn't want them."

"What about you?"

"We had a lot of fun, Ben. We were very busy. And I was very young. . . . I still am." She turned to go. "I wanted a baby with Ron."

I lay in bed awhile thinking about Jack. Fat and funny-looking, Rita had thought at age twenty. Not exactly aphrodisiac. Nor did it sound as if she had gone for the money at that moment in her life.

Rather, she had seen past fat and funny to Long's dynamic energy, and had been charmed by the promise of action. While he, considerably older and wiser, had spotted a winner. Again I felt sympathy for him. How, he must be thinking this morning, had he screwed up?

Smoke drifted up the stairs. I climbed quickly into my pants. "It's okay," I heard Rita call. "It's just the toast." Blue haze hung in the kitchen. She looked flushed but happy as she stuffed black ash down the disposal. "The second batch is perfect."

"Did you love Jack?"

"He was my best friend until Ron."

"Would you call him passionate?"

"He's not cold."

"No offense, but I read you two as a couple long past the jealous-rage stage. He seemed passionate enough about beating his father. He seemed passionate about saving the economy. But he doesn't seem passionate about you. Not enough to kill for you."

"You just told me he wished I hadn't gone with Ron."

" 'Wished.' He didn't sound torn up enough to commit murder."

"He'd kill to win. Didn't you see that in him?"

"No. I saw a guy too happy in his work and too smart to risk the second half of his life in jail. I think when he found out about you and Ron, he wrote you off."

"You're wrong. Jack knows I never ran around on him before. He wants me back. And with Ron gone, he's probably got me."

"Sounds like you've made a big decision."

"Not if he killed Ron."

So that was my job. I worked hard on keeping a poker face, but I was shocked and dismayed. She wasn't as worried as she should be about her trial. She'd leave that to Rose and the lawyers. She was looking ahead, past an acquittal, hoping I could confirm that her five-hundred-million-dollar husband and friend would make a proper partner for the rest of her life.

It was a win-win plan. She could stay with the action, while remaining forever loyal in her heart to the great love of her life. Fantasy? Not necessarily. Romantic? Definitely. Practical? Maybe deep in the recesses of her heart she had left herself an out: If it all hinged on

Jack's not having murdered Ron, who safer to prove that he didn't than an amateur?

"What's your next move, Ben?"

"I have to think about it."

I thought about it all weekend, which was a humbling experience, as I hadn't put my mind to much except selling houses for a couple of years. I wondered some more about Jack's financial situation. But the weekend was no time to gather business gossip; I'd been out of the loop too long to bother people at home. So I posed a question: If Jack didn't kill Ron, who did?

How about Alex Rose, the man in the middle? Security man. Intelligence gatherer. Tame gofer. Was he a rich man's indulgence, or a shrewd operator who protected Jack's back? A loose cannon?

No man is a hero to his valet, cynical Victorians smiled. Did Alex Rose ever wonder how'd the boss get so rich? Or did he leap when the boss hinted how happy he'd be if Ronald Pearlman disappeared?

By Sunday morning at the Drover, I was all over the map. It was still possible, regardless of the lack of police evidence, that some damned fool Chevalley or the like had accidentally blasted Ron from the woods. My cousin Pink might have heard by now. But he'd never tell me, much less the state cops.

Sunday night, I telephoned a portrait painter I'd sold a barn to. I had waited until dark because he once told me, "I have a jealous mistress. Her name is Daylight." He was slurring a little, as if he were two-timing her with another called Chardonnay.

"I've got an art question for you," I said. "When you're painting a face, do you ever do the skull first as a foundation?"

"Foundation?"

"First you draw the skull, then the muscles and flesh, then the skin?"

"Sure. I used to do a series of sketches when I was starting out."

"A series of sketches? What about doing them one on top of another?"

"That would entail a lot of erasing."

"But you could paint over the drawing," I persisted, vaguely aware a lawyer would object that I was leading the witness, "couldn't you?"

"Sure you could," he answered affably. "What, are you taking a course?"

Sautéing a plate of mushroom-stuffed cappelletti, I found myself focusing on Jack again. Maybe it was because money was what I knew best, but I just couldn't ignore the possibility that Jack Long might be in serious debt. I was probing like a player, feeling for rust in his armor.

Six o'clock Monday morning I unlimbered my old Rolodex and started working the phones. Thirty percent of my former colleagues had vanished like ice in August. The rest sounded only mildly chastened, and many seemed to be enjoying a grand old time.

I got some very wary Hellos—and some even warier inquiries as to how I was doing—until I assured them I was not looking for a job. That they took the calls at all was less a matter of friendship than fear. It was widely known that I had declined to cooperate with the Securities and Exchange Commission and wildly rumored that I had told the United States Attorney to take a hike—which wasn't remotely the language I had used when I found myself emptying my pockets on his desk. But people wondered what I knew, and if I had changed my mind about spilling it. So they took my calls and promised to keep their traps shut about my questions. Unfortunately, they didn't have much in the way of answers.

LTS was privately held, so Jack Long was legally permitted to play it very close to the vest. No public offerings, no stock, therefore no prospectus, no SEC filings, no analysts' reports. That didn't mean Long didn't borrow money, but he was privileged to borrow it quietly. A full morning's work on the phone—sixty calls—got me the names of several institutions that *might* act as Long's bankers. Rita was paying the telephone bills, so I kept dialing. Finally, Bob Mayall, a savvy independent investment banker who was more of a friend than most, asked *me* a question.

"Why don't you call Leslie Harkin?"

I had known in the back of my mind that her name would surface in one of these conversations. I hadn't looked forward to it.

"Are you still on the line?" Mayall asked.

"Yeah, I'm here. I doubt she'd take my call."

"She owes you at least a call, Ben."

"Is she back from London?"

"Via Tokyo."

"I thought the Japanese were out of money."

Mayall sighed. "Back in the woods, do you remember when the Lexus came on the scene?"

"Good-looking automobile."

"Yes, well, what the Japanese taught themselves about finish and performance to build the Lexus and the Infiniti, they are now translating down to ordinary cars. Low-end luxury-quality Toyotas and Subarus are going to blow what remains of Detroit out of the water. The Japanese are merely catching their breath. Leslie Harkin is up to her shapely butt in Silicon Valley, running M&As paid for by Tokyo."

That was news to me, and grim news for Silicon Valley. Back when, Leslie Harkin had frolicked by my side in the Rustbelt. There wasn't a machine tool shop in the state of Michigan she hadn't put into play at least once. To many a battered trade unionist she was the she-devil incarnate. And since I'd been the she-devil's boss, they lit bonfires the night I went to prison.

I did not want to confront Leslie, and yet she looked like my best source. Like a train whose locomotive had jumped the tracks, I was joining the wreck, like it or not. "Is she vulturing on her own?"

"Where have you been?"

"Home."

"You never heard of Harkin & Locke?"

Before I could comment on that grim alliance, I heard a scream from the barn.

19

Four seconds after ripping a pocket on the kitchen doorknob, I burst into the barn. The cars were on the ground floor, quiet in the shadows, the Mealys' apartment up a rickety interior staircase.

"Don't!" Alison screamed. Janet shrieked. Something fell heavily overhead, shaking dust from the rafters.

I took the wooden steps three at a time. Their door was smashed open, sagging on a broken hinge. Through the little living room I could see the kitchen: Mrs. Mealy crawling across the floor; a large man rearing back to kick her; Alison clinging to his leg, screaming, "Don't, Daddy!"

Tom Mealy had won parole.

He faced me as I came through the door. When he recognized me, he balled his fists. "You're screwin' my wife," he slurred, spit trailing from his heavy lips.

"No," moaned Mrs. Mealy, dragging herself over the linoleum.

He whirled on her, aiming another kick. He was tall and broad, with arms as big as my waist, but he was drunk, so I took a chance and went straight at him, inside the big arms, hoping to do quick damage to his gut. Tom tried to bearhug me. I butted him until he stopped trying and kept on hammering his belly. His anger turned to shock, then bafflement as his legs gave way.

I had been taught the hard way to finish a fight. Punching his neck as he went down, I launched a kick at his head to make sure he stayed there.

Alison flew at me, her little body all desperate bone and muscle, clutching my leg, pleading, "Don't hurt him, Ben."

Adrenaline was popping through my skin and I was breathing hard and fast. Tom eyed me blearily from the floor, trying to gather his legs.

"Don't," I warned him.

He gave it up and sagged on his back, his face going slack as he closed his eyes. I pried the child off my leg.

"Alison. Take your mother to the house. Can you walk, Janet?"

"I'm okay. I'm okay."

"Draw her a nice hot bath and call Dr. Greenan."

"No."

"Janet, let's just make sure you're not hurt."

But she insisted she was fine, just a little sore—Tom hadn't really meant to hurt her. He was just drinking and sometimes he got that way when he drank. "I can't afford the doctor," she concluded. "I'm fine."

She was, in fact, white as the kitchen wall. Her cheek was swollen and there was blood on her lip. I insisted that Steve Greenan look her over. "No," she whispered, explaining that the doctor would tell Trooper Moody and Oliver would arrest her husband. I looked at Alison and saw that this warped logic made equal sense to her.

"Ben, don't you understand? They'll send him back to jail."

That struck me as a terrific idea, an opinion I couched carefully and gently, as I caught my breath. "Maybe that would be better for a little while until he calms down. They can help him there."

"Detox didn't work last time," said the eleven-year-old.

"Hush," said her mother.

I looked at the big, inert form on the floor and tried to figure out some way to protect his family. One thing was for sure: I wasn't going to New York that afternoon. For that I felt relieved. Tomorrow, with any luck, we'd get a forest fire. Or maybe the river would flood.

"All right," I said. "Go over to my house. Take a hot bath, lie down. I'll talk to him."

"Ben, don't hurt him." Alison had seen another me, and the fear on her face told me it would take a long time to convince the child that all I was, was a survivor. When I leaned over to kiss her hair, she shrank back. "Promise," she demanded.

"Don't worry. There's no more fighting today. Go on now. I'll just sit with him and sober him up and get him out of here. Okay?"

She stared, clear-eyed and anxious.

"I promise. Go. And put some ice on your face, Mrs. Mealy."

They went at last, with fearful glances, as if I would carve him up with a breadknife and stuff the parts in garbage bags—another terrific idea.

Tom opened his eyes.

I stepped out of reach.

"They gone?"

"They're gone."

He fingered his nose and winced. Closed his eyes and lay silent. I didn't remember hitting his nose. Probably when I butted him.

"Wha'd you hit me with?" he mumbled.

I didn't answer.

"I'd have taken you easy if I wasn't drunk."

"You wouldn't have had to if you weren't drunk."

"You screwing my wife?"

"Who told you that?"

"Heard it at the White Birch."

"From some old friend you met an hour ago?"

"Screw you."

"When'd you get out, Tom?"

"Last month."

"Took you a whole month to come home to beat up your family?"

He said nothing.

"Where you living, Tom?"

"By the river."

I had heard that somewhere ten miles downstream the homeless were camped. "You working?"

Tom Mealy opened his eyes. He was far from sober, but getting slammed around unexpectedly can clear the head. "They hit me with a DWI suspension when I was waiting for sentencing. Got a year to go before they give me my license back."

That was reassuring. Sometimes the system actually worked. Would that the parole board had read their man as accurately as the traffic-court judge.

He was too drunk to reason with, but maybe I could scare him. I said, "Tom, I'm sorry, but I've got to call Trooper Moody."

He sat up on the floor, looking around wildly. "No."

"Yes. You would have killed your wife if I hadn't come along. You terrified your daughter."

"No. They'll send me back for violating parole."

"Maybe we can get you into a program."

"No way."

"Sorry."

"Hey, what business is it of yours?" he demanded belligerently.

I watched his feet. "You've put Alison through hell. She was just starting to unwind from last time."

"What do you mean, last time? Wha'd that kid tell you?"

"It was in the newspaper, you idiot."

"Oh, yeah . . . It didn't really happen like that. I didn't mean nothing. Anyway, you got no right to interfere with my family."

"Don't stand up, Tom."

"What?" He paused on one knee, reeling a little.

I said, "Your family isn't here to protect you now. I'll massacre you if you stand up." I had taken no satisfaction in what I had done to him before, but I was angry now, remembering how Alison had shied from me, and I think he sensed that. He tried a hard glare anyway but couldn't hold on to it.

"Will you go into a detox program, or do I call Trooper Moody?"

"I ain't going in no program!" he shouted. "Give me a break. You don't know what it's like."

I didn't know whether he meant jail or being a drunk. All I knew was that I was getting nowhere fast. "Tom, if I give you a hundred bucks, will you get on a bus and go to Florida for the winter?"

"There's no snow in Florida. I'm a snowplow driver."

"Then go to Alaska. Just out of Connecticut."

"For a lousy hundred bucks?" he asked with a crafty smile. *"Five hundred."*

"I don't have five hundred."

"Then I'm staying."

That tore it. I yanked him to his feet and marched him out and down the stairs before he realized we were moving. "What are you doing?" he whined.

"We're going to Trooper Moody."

"No." He dug in his heels. He was too big to drag. I wound up to kick an ankle, but he suddenly began to weep, sat down on the wooden steps, and cried.

"Come on, Tom."

"Please don't make me go back."

"Tom, I got to. You're just going to get drunk again and come and cause trouble."

"I won't."

"You know you will."

"I won't. I swear it."

"I've got to protect your kid. Do we go quietly, or do I have to call Trooper Moody? You don't want that. You know what he's like. Better to just turn yourself in."

Tom Mealy knew what I meant. An arrest by Oliver Moody under the wrong conditions could make what had occurred upstairs feel like a friendly arm wrestle. He dried his eyes, and when he looked at me they were suddenly surprisingly alight with hope. Hope, and the crafty look I had seen a moment before.

"If you let me go I'll tell you something about the guy who shot Renny Chevalley."

"What?"

"You gotta give me the hundred bucks too. Hey, let go. You're hurting my arm."

I was gripping it like a vise—not to control him, but in amazement. *"What?"* I shouted again. "What do you know?"

"Leggo!"

I let go. By the light that spilled in through the window over the cutting garden, I could see a parade of ideas lurch across the drunkard's face. My heart sank. He didn't know what he was saying. "What?" I repeated.

"You let me go."

"Only if you leave the county."

"I'll go to Massachusetts. I got a buddy up there."

"Fine." I would have preferred a more distant state, but he held the cards now.

"You going to give me the money?"

"Not till you tell me what you're talking about. What guy? Did you see him?"

"Buddy of mine did."

"Where?"

"On the Morris Mountain road."

"He *saw* him? What did he look like?"

"I don't know."

"Why didn't he tell the cops?"

"Yeah, right."

"Where is this guy?"

"By the river."

"Take me to him."

"First the hundred bucks."

"The minute he shakes hands with me. Not before— Get in the car."

He climbed into the Olds. I opened the barn doors and drove out. "Put on your seatbelt."

Tom Mealy did what I said and gave me directions to his piece of the river. I swung by the bank to withdraw a hundred dollars, then stopped at the General Store for three packs of Marlboros and extra matches. Tom fell asleep, mouth open, reeking and snoring loudly. I reached under the seat for my radar detector, which is thoroughly and completely illegal in the state of Connecticut, and floored it.

Eight and a half minutes later, I spotted the overgrown logging road that Tom had instructed me to look for. I nudged him hard in the ribs. Several nudges and a few bouncing potholes later, he woke up. Eventually he remembered why he was in my car.

"Right past that oak."

The tree in question was spiraled like a barber pole with blazing red poison ivy. Several turns down roads I didn't know, and we stopped in a small clearing, which, to judge by the litter on the ground, was a parking lot for active practitioners of safer sex.

"Now what?"

"We gotta walk."

I left the car unlocked—anyone who wanted to break in had privacy enough to open the windows with a chainsaw—and followed Tom Mealy into the woods. We walked a quarter-mile on a deer path, me worrying about ticks. Tom stopped. I looked around. Just dense growth. He opened his fly, watered some of it, and resumed walking.

Ahead, the tree canopy thinned, marking the bed of the river. The deer path descended steeply until we found ourselves on the open bank. The river was deep here, deceptively smooth as the current raced.

"Where's the barn? I heard they were living in an old barn?"

"Some guy tore it down. Sold the beams."

"How'd he get it out of here?"

"Made a raft." Tom gave a low whistle. At an answering whistle he said, "Come on," and headed down the bank, ducking low limbs. A hundred yards of that brought us to a little meadow, at the back of which, hard against the woods, was a twelve-by-twelve blue poly tarp pitched lean-to style. Three people were sitting cross-legged under it, watching a fourth try to start a fire.

"Wha'd you bring?" asked the one woman.

Tom looked abashed. "I forgot."

"Jesus, Tom, you were supposed to bring food."

"I was drinking."

"Who's this?"

I was wearing my tweed jacket. Old as it was, it looked a little out of place. The men and woman under the tarp were wearing dirty blue jeans and hooded sweatshirts. The guy building the fire—who looked oddly familiar to me—was upscale by comparison, with cleaner blue jeans, a moth-eaten sweater, and a bright green nylon windbreaker of the kind they sometimes give away at a Salvation Army prayer meeting. Burn scars speckled the backs of his hands.

"He wants to talk to you," Tom told him.

He was about forty-five—a weatherbeaten forty-five—with a walrus mustache and a gentle but weary look in his eye that reminded me of Mrs. Mealy. His movements were economical and precise. He finished piling squaw wood and lighted it with the last match in his book. It flamed instantly, igniting the larger wood he had arranged above the dry twigs. Then he looked up with a lopsided smile and said, "I didn't do it, Officer."

"I'm not a cop."

"I still didn't do it."

I looked at the others, who were watching curiously, and back at him.

"Could I have a little of your time?"

He considered that, gravely. I kept thinking I knew him. I knew I knew him, but I couldn't place the face. I opened a pack of Marlboros and passed them over. "Like a smoke?"

He took one out, lit it in the fire, and passed the pack to his friends.

"Keep 'em," I said, and walked to the river. He bent his head in discussion with Tom a moment, then joined me. "Tom says you're paying him a hundred bucks for me to talk to you."

"I'm paying Tom a hundred bucks to go away and stop beating up his wife."

"Someone told him you're screwing her."

"Someone's full of it. I gave them the apartment in my barn."

"Tom's a menace," the man said quietly.

"I'm Ben Abbott, by the way." I stuck out my hand.

"Oh, I know you, Mr. Abbott," he said as he took my hand in a rough grip.

"I'm sorry. You look familiar, but I can't place you."

"My name's Ed Hawley. I cook at the Church Hill Diner. You come in for breakfast now and then."

"Of course. Oh yes. But what are you doing here?— I mean, why are you living outdoors when you have a job?"

"Security deposit and first and last month's rent up front," he answered. "I'm still getting it together."

I must have stared. I thought I knew something about the ways of the world, but I hadn't put much thought into the fact that a guy with a steady job couldn't rent some little apartment someplace. He mistook my puzzlement for sympathy. "Hey, no problem. I almost got it saved up. With any luck I'll get indoors this winter. As long as I keep my job."

"How long have you been outside?"

"Ten, eleven years. . . . I had a little drinking problem. It's getting better."

I stood there feeling ignorant. He watched me placidly. I could see the booze lines in his face now. He had put it away over the years. But I'd seen him at the diner since I got out of prison, so he had obviously gotten his act together enough to keep a job. I said, "I don't have it with me, but I'll certainly slip you a hundred if you tell me what you know about my cousin."

"I'd appreciate that. Very much. But I didn't see much."

"What did you see?"

"Well, I didn't understand it at the time, I only put it together when I saw a paper next day at work. You know, about the airplane?"

"Right."

"I saw a guy in a car."

"Where? Where were you?"

"Up near the top of the Morris Mountain Road."

"How'd you get all the way up there? Do you have a car?"

Ed Hawley smiled. "Two or three, but it was the chauffeur's day off."

"So how'd you get up there?"

"It's a long story."

"I don't understand." I was trying to be patient. Hawley seemed intent on spinning it slowly.

Which he did, explaining that to supplement his short-order cook income he tried to get day work, hitchhiking down to a street corner in New Milford where contractors and the like hired laborers from the down-and-outers who gathered there at dawn. A farmer on Morris Mountain—a man I knew, as a matter of fact—had offered him five dollars an hour to drive fence posts. Hawley had taken it, but they had had a falling out near the end of the day, with the farmer refusing to pay all the money because he hadn't sunk enough posts and Hawley contending that the particularly stony land had slowed him down. It had turned into a shoving match, and when the farmer threatened to call the police, Hawley had run for it without any money at all.

"Eight hours I gave that man. Eight hours. Didn't offer a bite of lunch. I had to ask permission to drink from his hose. Anyway, I got out of there quick before he got some friends and came looking for me. So I'm walking down Morris Mountain Road, figuring I got a long walk to go because there's no cars up there at all. I saw a pickup coming down and ducked in case it was the farmer. . . . So I'm walking along."

"What time?"

"Three-thirty. I know because I started working at seven."

"Go on."

"A little white plane comes in low, looks like it's going to crash in the trees. Disappeared. I didn't hear a crash or see any smoke, so I figure he made it. Course, I didn't know there was a airstrip up there. Ten minutes later I hear this car screaming down the road. He comes around a curve and I see he's not the farmer, so I stick out my thumb. Guy goes by me at sixty."

"What did he look like?"

"I saw sunglasses and a hat."

"What kind of sunglasses?"

"Wraparound. Doper shades."

"What kind of hat?"

"Cap. Baseball cap."

Great. If there was a man in Newbury who didn't own at least one cap, I hadn't met him yet. Many kept a clean one at home to wear at the supper table.

"You saw nothing of his face?"

"Not behind that fancy smoked glass."

"The sunglasses?"

"And the car windows."

"What kind of car?"

"Old muscle car. Camaro, maybe."

"Why 'maybe'?"

"Well, it looked brand new. But of course they don't make 'em like that any more. Do they?"

"No, they don't. Did you see the license?"

"Connecticut plates," he answered. "Something HAL. Three numbers and HAL. I remember the HAL because that was the name of the computer in *2001*."

I slapped his shoulder and shook his hand. I was sure that the three numbers preceding HAL could be found in Marian Boyce's computer.

"I really appreciate this, Ed."

"Yeah, well, he was your cousin. If I had known, I would have told you sooner, I guess, when I saw you at the diner. But I didn't figure a Main Street guy for being a Chevalley. Man, when some of them eat we have to hose the booth out."

"I really appreciate this. Now look"—I gave him my card—"stay in touch. You say you have some of your rent and deposit saved up?"

"Some."

"Well, maybe I can find you something you don't have to put up so much. I know some people looking to rent space, and maybe I could talk them into reducing the up-front money if I vouched for you. When do you work next?"

"Tomorrow."

"I'll bring your hundred in the morning. Soon as the bank opens."

"You know, that might have been some kid out joyriding."

Ed was right, but I thought he was trying to answer his own second thoughts concerning why he hadn't told the police. I pressed the rest of the cigarettes into his hand and we walked back across the clearing, where Tom Mealy stuck out his palm for his hundred dollars.

I drove him to New Milford first, to put him on the Pittsfield bus. I told him not to come back to Newbury drunk. And if he wanted to visit Alison sober, call me first and I'd set something up. I gave him the money and he lurched up the steps, belching and grumbling. The bus driver looked thrilled to see him, and he thanked me warmly when I bought Tom's ticket.

I passed the bus on the first short straight and tore across the county to see Marian Boyce.

20

Trooper Marian welcomed me to the Plainfield barracks with a big handshake. "What brings you to Monster-woman's Lair?"

"I got a partial license number from a car leaving the airstrip the afternoon Renny Chevalley was shot."

"From whom?"

"Homeless guy walking down the road."

She invited me in. The detective room was as bright and snappy as Jack Butler's Church Hill Insurance Agency. They had WANTED posters instead of happily insured family portraits on the walls, and the staff wore guns, but the neat half-partitions, the industrial carpeting, and the coffee machine all promised the same dedication to a secure night's sleep.

Marian's temporary office could have belonged to a CPA with a brilliant secretary. On her desk was a pencil, a phone, and a notepad. A computer waited. Beside it a lucite frame held a photograph of a little boy high-fiving the camera.

"This guy have a name?" Marian asked.

"Why don't we check out the number first?"

"Why don't you tell me the witness's name?"

"If it looks good I'll give you his name. If not, why bother the poor guy?"

Marian gave me a wintery look. I gave her one back.

"HAL, old Camaro probably. Dark. Black or blue."

Marian shrugged, poked her computer, and punched HAL into it. "Sit," she said. I sat, inspecting the little boy while she frowned at her screen. He had her chin and her eyes. He'd make a good cop when he got a little older, if he learned to sit on his smile.

Marian frowned some more as blocks of information scrolled up the screen. "That's Jason," she said.

"How old is he?"

"Five."

"I didn't realize you had a child."

"I reserve him for the second date."

She touched a key and the scrolling stopped.

"Find something?"

"You're not going to like it."

"What?"

"Well, once we eliminate the HALs that aren't Camaro look-alikes, we get down to one 1973 Camaro, navy blue, 337 HAL."

"Who owns it?"

"It's registered to the Frenchtown establishment Chevalley Enterprises."

"What?"

"It's Renny's car."

"No. He doesn't drive a Camaro. He leased a four-door Blazer when the kids were born."

"He registered the Camaro two weeks before he was murdered."

"Oh, Christ. One of his restorations."

She made some notes, hit some keys, and turned from the screen. "Okay, let's have the witness's name."

"Ed Hawley. He cooks at the Church Hill Diner in Newbury. Don't screw it up for him."

"Contrary to what you may think, I am not in the business of getting witnesses fired from their jobs. Neither is Sergeant Bender. If you don't mind too awfully much we'd like to discuss with Mr. Hawley anything else he might have seen. Like the numbers 337, or even the face of the driver."

"I asked. He didn't."

"Thank you, Sherlock, but we'd like to ask too."

"Sorry. I'm really disappointed. I thought this would lead to something."

"At least it suggests your cousin expected to land at that strip."

"And the guy who shot him stole his car."

"Could have happened."

"Where do you think it is now?"

"I've already asked the computer for abandoned-car recoveries." She gave me a goodbye look.

I looked at the picture on her desk.

"Where's his dad?"

"My husband was a trooper too. When I filed an affirmative-action suit for unfair disciplinary procedures, the force retaliated by eliminating his resident post. Lost the house that came with it. A neat little saltbox like Trooper Moody's. Began to seem like my fault. We split."

"Marian? Can I ask you something?"

"Try me."

"If it was a drug thing, do you think the guy planned to kill him, or was it a sudden fight?"

"Sorry, Ben. I can't discuss it."

"Come on, Marian, all I'm asking is whether you think it was a premeditated double cross or a spontaneous quarrel."

"I'll listen to your theories. But ours are not your business. Thanks for coming by. Appreciate the witness."

"Show your appreciation. Answer one question."

"What?"

"Did Renny's plane crash into that tree landing or taking off?"

"Taking off."

"Was he shot through the windshield?"

"No more questions. We're even."

"No, no, no, Marian. We're even on the witness. You still owe me for the other night."

"You owe me, fella. Bender wanted to bring you in while we checked out your gun permits. So did that jerk you decked—nice hit, by the way. Stupid move, but nicely done. They teach you that left cross at Leavenworth?"

"Prep school."

I left, thinking that the existence of Renny's car at the airstrip, which suggested that Renny had planned to land there, sort of fit Marian Boyce's drug-delivery theory. Sort of. But he had crashed his plane into a tree while trying to take off? Trying to escape? Or heading back to Danbury to return the plane as promised? Leaving his passenger a car to drive away in. So why was the coke aboard the plane? It made no sense to unload it at Danbury Airport in front of Chernowsky. Why hadn't he unloaded it in the privacy of Al Bell's hilltop airstrip?

I was also curious how he got the Camaro up there, so I swung through Frenchtown on the way home and asked the mechanics and the women who ran the front office at Chevalley Enterprises if they recalled whether Renny had towed the Camaro the day or so before he died. He had not, on their shifts, and the night tow-truck driver confirmed that Renny hadn't taken the wrecker out after business hours. So if he didn't tow the Camaro up Morris Mountain, who had given him a ride back when he dropped the car?

I had a feeling I knew who, though prying it out of her might be impossible. It meant putting off my New York City trip another day. Another day without seeing Leslie. With luck, Jack Long, Rita, and Alex Rose would all confess to Ron Pearlman's murder, and I'd never have to go.

The wise man calls on a Jervis woman when her father, sons, and brothers are away. The safest bet is the first day of hunting season. I couldn't wait till then, so I tried twelve noon—time, I hoped, for Jervis men to be down at the White Birch for their morning beer.

Gwen's branch of the clan lived in a crowd of trailers circled like prairie schooners in the deep woods, far beyond Frenchtown, on the edge of the Housatonic Reservation. In the center area of beaten earth, children fought. Washing hung in the cool air. Beyond the trailers were cars and trucks up on blocks. Women called their children inside as I parked beside Gwen's rust-eaten '79 Ford pickup. My Chevalley connections were worthless here: Jervises draw no distinctions between Frenchtown and Main Street.

Her tin door had buckled at the lock and someone had bolted on a couple of lengths of pressure-treated two-by-fours to straighten it out. A fair-sized crack remained between door and frame, stuffed with a pink towel. I knocked a few times. "Gwen, it's me. Ben Abbott."

"I know why you're here," she greeted me. Her old bathrobe would have looked ratty on a woman with a lesser body, but at forty Gwen was still all curves and angles, full-breasted, narrow-waisted, long-legged. To describe her as sullen would ignore her sadness.

"I'm real sorry, Gwen. I miss him and I know you do too." She'd hung in to school until tenth grade, as she'd been repeatedly left back, finally giving up when I was in seventh. Puberty had propelled me in her direction with a six-pack of Bud Pinkerton Chevalley bought for me. She wasn't sullen back then, just a big, warm, open girl-woman. She'd lived a hard twenty years since. But at noon in an old bathrobe and missing a front tooth she still radiated sex, and I caught myself staring into those deep dark curves, remembering how fortunate I had been that she chose to be my first.

"May I come in?"

"No."

"I've really got to talk to you, Gwen."

"About what?"

"Renny."

"Why?"

"I'm trying to find out who killed him."

She just stared.

"He wasn't running coke, was he?"

"Cops think so. See how they trashed my door? Busted into every trailer. Frightened the kids."

"Search warrants?"

"Oh, they had all their papers. Left real disappointed, though."

"Renny wasn't running coke, was he?" I asked again.

"People here are really pissed."

Gwen stared some more. Then she said, "Take me for a ride. I'll get dressed."

She came out in tight jeans and a loose sweatshirt. She'd run a comb through her thick red Jervis hair, which she had chopped short. It used to fall to her waist. The night she initiated me it was in a braid, which she wrapped around my neck, further scaring the hell out of me. She noticed me looking and said, "I was going to grow it out for him."

We got in the Olds. "Where would you like to go?"

"The mall."

I knew she meant the new little mini-mall down Route 7. The Danbury Fair Mall was as distant and intimidating to her as Fifth Avenue. Staring into the bright autumn woods that hugged the dirt road, she lit a cigarette and said, "He was one sweet explosion after another."

"How'd you hook up?" I still couldn't believe it. Renny was not exactly a ladies' man.

"My damned truck stalled over on 349. Renny happened along in his wrecker. Jumped me," she said with a smile. "After that we jumped each other every chance we got."

"Wha'd your husband think?"

"Last I heard he was humping an oil rig in the Persian Gulf. Checks stopped in May."

"Renny give you money?"

"Screw you, Ben Abbott."

"I meant did he help out?"

"What do you want to talk about?"

"Did Renny have any problem with your brothers?"

"Pete ran him off the road down in Morrisville. I spoke to Daddy and he ordered a truce. Said I'm old enough now to run around with who I want."

"That sounds uncharacteristically mellow of your father."

"Daddy's got arthritis. He's slowing down."

"Pete taking over?" I didn't say "the business," but she knew I meant the stolen-car chopping, the cigarette smuggling, the distribution of uppers and downers to the truckers, and the fencing of stolen goods. Years ago when the Hunt brothers of Texas cornered the silver market, the Jervises turned a pretty penny melting down antique candlesticks from every unguarded house in the county.

"Little Bill," she answered. "Pete's got a drinking problem."

"Good choice," I said. Little Bill Jervis had beaten a triple-murder rap back in 1978. Some Hell's Angels from Derby had tried to cheat him in a drug deal.

"How are the kids?"

Gwen brightened. "Josie's in the army. She made corporal."

"When'd she join the army?"

Her expression darkened. "Those bastard MacKays would put it in the paper."

I wasn't surprised; the MacKay family's *Clarion* trumpets school, sports, and agricultural achievements, a balanced town budget, and a social order where people know their place. Also, rumor had had it that Scooter's sexual initiation had proved a disappointment all around.

"What about Rick?"

"He'd get a pipeline job if he could find his dad. . . . Little Bill's leaning on him to drive a truck."

"I'm sorry to hear that." The word was that the Jervises' Canadian cousins stole cigarettes, which the Newbury Jervises delivered to the United States, neglecting to declare them at the border.

"Yeah, well, Rick's not stupid, maybe he'll . . ."

We left that hope hanging until we finally reached a blacktop road. I hated to admit it, but part of me had to wonder whether Old Man Jervis had intervened in the Pete-Renny dispute for business reasons, such as protecting a valuable coke-flying pilot.

"So what do you want to know about Renny?"

"Pillow talk," I said, knowing that a direct question would turn her off forever. A long, slow afternoon would have to run its course.

"What?"

"The stuff he'd tell you and no one else."

"Jesus, scared me a minute there, Ben. Thought you meant doin'-it talk."

"I'll bet he would have told you if he was flying coke."

"He wasn't."

"Are you sure?"

"Ben, when's the last time you've been really hot for somebody?" She gave me a motherly look—Mom passing on the facts of life. I could have said "twenty minutes ago" staring at her in her bathrobe, but that wasn't the "hot" she meant.

"Couple of Fridays ago."

"Well, think back and try and imagine something you wouldn't have told her."

"That's what I mean. Pillow talk. And you're saying you're sure   would have told you if he was flying coke."

tive."

"W.   if he were working for your father? Would he still tell you?"

"Why not? Daddy and me get along fine." I glanced over at her. She was regarding me with mild puzzlement, a reminder that even though she was glad Josie was in the army, and she worried about Rick, Gwen was very much a Jervis. And it was true that her father, a man not known for soft spots, had always had one for his youngest. I reminded myself, too, that she, and most of the clan, spoke well—maybe they read the Bible at home or something—which could throw you off and fox you into thinking they were just ordinary middle-class people who happened to live in trailers. They were not. They were Jervises.

So my problem was this: She might be telling the truth. But if Renny had been working for her father, she might be lying. She didn't owe me anything. Nor was there any hope of bringing him back.

We got to the mall. It had a grocery and a drugstore, a toy store, a video rental, a liquor store, an ice cream shop, and a lot of unrented space. While I went to scout out some coffee, Gwen ran ahead. I found her in the toy store. The saleswoman was very nervous, following Gwen closely. She calmed down when she recognized me from several failed attempts to rent the dark stores on either side of hers.

We went to the ice cream shop, then strolled the empty drugstore and the grocery. I asked Gwen if I could buy her anything. She said she had everything she needed, though she did want to browse the videos. I bought a used copy of *Sea of Love*. Gwen wandered.

Back in the car, as I pulled out of the parking lot, she said, "Look, Ben."

I looked. She lifted her sweatshirt. I thought she was flashing me. And indeed, I caught a lovely glimpse of her full, round breasts. But flashing wasn't her intent. Out of her sweatshirt tumbled a couple of video cassettes, some pricey shampoo, perfume, several tins of pâté, and a teddy bear.

"Hey, you stole—"

"You wuss!" She laughed.

"You used me for cover."

"Did not. You kept getting in my way."

"How'd you do it?"

She lifted her sweatshirt again—not high enough—and showed me an interior layer of cloth elasticized around her waist.

I turned the car around.

"Where you going?"

"Back to pay for that stuff."

"No way."

"My money."

"No."

"Gwen, I'm weird about stealing, okay? I don't like it."

"I'm weird about paying. Turn around."

"I'm not going to rat on you, I'm just going to pay."

"If you don't turn around, *now,* I'm going to jump out of the car." She opened the door. The road roared by at forty. I saw she meant it. I pulled over and stopped.

"Jump."

"If you pay I won't tell you about Renny."

"Tell me what?"

"Take me home."

She picked up her shampoo, opened it, and sniffed. "Oh, wow. You gotta smell this, Ben."

I turned the car around, again, and headed back to Newbury. She held the shampoo under my nose until I sneezed. Then she scrutinized her teddy bear.

"What are you going to do with that?"

"Sleep with it," she muttered, suddenly dark.

She opened the perfume—the venerable Madame Rochas— dabbed her ears, glanced sidelong at me, and ran some under her sweatshirt. I remarked that my car smelled like a cathouse.

"What were you doing in a cathouse?"

"It was a navy ritual. Tell me about Renny."

"What?"

"You told me you knew more about Renny."

"I did?"

"Goddammit, Gwen."

"Okay, okay. God, you should see your face. You're so serious."

"I am serious, about Renny. I thought you were too."

"Ben, your cousin was your friend. He was a lot more than that to me. Okay? Let me be sad the way I want to be sad."

"I'm sorry."

"You bastard in your big white house. I hate you."

"I'm sorry, Gwen. I'm really wired about this."

Silence the rest of the way to Newbury. Silence down Church Hill Road, past the Grand Union, past the afternoon motorcycles outside the White Birch Inn, past the old train station. Silence all the miles to the junction with the Jervises' dirt road.

"Stop."

I shut off the engine. A shotgun echoed in the hills. Someone jumping the season. Gwen grimaced. "Deer meat till April."

She gazed into the deep woods. I watched her tongue probe the hole in her front teeth. "Gwen, give me a break. All I'm trying to do is clear Renny's name."

"What the hell for? Who cares? He's dead."

"He cared," I said. "He worked like a dog for respect."

"He worked for money. He wanted to be rich."

"Of course he wanted money. But he wanted respect too."

"*You* want respect," she countered.

"I *have* it."

"Jailbird."

"I'm still an Abbott," I replied. "It goes with my big white house."

"Screw you, Ben Abbott. You think he was just like you. He wasn't like you at all."

I sat back comfortably and draped a hand over the wheel. Another shotgun boomed, closer. Gwen ignored it. "Gwen?"

"What?"

"Do you know what a *chevalier* is?"

"No," she said sullenly. She had come closer to graduating high school than anyone in her family and was very defensive about words she didn't know.

"Well, I didn't either until they put me in the day school. A *chevalier* is a French knight."

"Any connection to *Chevalley?*"

"Direct. *Chevalley* comes from *Chevalier*. Originally, back in Colonial times, Renny's name would have been *René*. When I learned that, I jumped on my bike and pedaled like mad down to Frenchtown to tell Renny he was really René Chevalier: René the French knight."

"I'll bet you made his day."

"He decked me."

"Ha!"

"Took me totally by surprise. Renny never got in fights. Hit me so hard I saw stars."

"Good for him."

"I said, 'Wha'd you do that for?' You know what he did?"

"Started crying."

"He told you?"

Gwen gave me a look of disgust. "No. But that's what he would have done. You made him feel like garbage."

"Well, that's what I'm trying to explain. He was hurt. All this nonsense about names and position really bothered Renny."

"Easy for you to call it nonsense."

"That's the point. He cared. So I'm going to clear his name."

"That ought to make him feel better."

"I'm also going to get the guy who killed him."

Gwen touched my hand and pulled me deep into her eyes. "Tell me who," she said, matter-of-factly. "I'll take it from there."

"No thanks. I'll take it to the cops."

"I can wait," she said, in the same matter-of-fact voice, which I took to mean that Renny's murderer would face Jervises in jail.

"But first I have to find him," I said. "Which is why I need your help. Did you give Renny a ride back when he dropped the Camaro at Al Bell's field?"

"We met up there to screw."

"Friday night?"

"One of the nights."

"And you left his car?"

"Yeah."

"Did Renny say why?"

Gwen hesitated. I said, "Gwen, if the cops ever find the Camaro, are they going to find your fingerprints?"

"Footprints." She smiled.

"What?"

" 'Footprints on the dashboard upside down': You know the song?" She hummed *Humoresque.*

"Did he say why he was leaving the car?"

"No."

"Well, didn't you ask?"

"What the hell would I ask for?"

"Gwen, didn't it seem strange he'd leave a mint-restored Camaro up in the woods?"

"You think old Al would steal it?" Gwen scoffed.

"It just seems to me you'd at least *ask* how he was going to get it back."

"My mouth was full."

"What?"

"Renny was driving."

"Oh."

We fell silent. Until she asked, "What are you smiling about?"

"You and Renny. He was always afraid of girls when we were kids."

"Betty Butler was his first."

"You're kidding."

"He was a late starter."

"I guess so. Wow."

"I never met such a grateful man in my life. Just my luck."

"You think he was running dope, don't you?"

"No."

"Then why didn't you ask about the car?"

"I don't ask men their business. I wasn't raised that way."

This made a certain sense, and just then, as if to emphasize her point, the hemlocks on the edge of the dirt road parted and out stepped a Jervis teenager, wild and lanky as a coyote. He froze when he spotted my car.

Gwen waved. The kid turned back into the trees and returned carrying a shotgun. He was trailed by old Herman Jervis himself, the head of the clan.

"Oh shit!" Gwen whispered. She jumped out of the car and approached her father warily. That she was his favorite did not exempt her from the occasional backhand swipe of a bony hand if he was crossed.

Well into his seventies, Herman Jervis slouched on a wide-legged stance, baggy green pants sliding down his skinny hips. He might have looked like a harmless old woody. But a red scar slanted down his face from temple to jaw, and his eyes brimmed with cold intelligence and contempt for everything he saw.

He jerked his head at the kid, who handed him the shotgun and slipped back into the woods. Then he addressed Gwen, who listened, head down. I couldn't hear what he was saying. When he was done, he lit a cigarette. Gwen came back and leaned in the window.

"He wants your car."

"What for?"

"He shot a buck. Wants you to run it back to my place."

"Oh, great." I could just imagine Oliver Moody cruising by me with an out-of-season deer on the roof. Not, I could see, that I had a lot of choice in the matter. The boy staggered out with the deer on his back, its front legs in his hands, its horned head over his—a prime way to get shot in the woods, as he looked exactly like a deer himself. Ignoring me totally, he heaved the dressed carcass, bouncing the Olds on its springs. Old Man Jervis approached, pulling a rope from one of his deep pockets as blood started trickling down my windshield.

He gave the Olds a sour look. "Goddamned new cars—nothing to tie on to."

My "new" car was eight years old, but I didn't see much point in correcting him. "Here. Pass it through." He shoved a rope end in my window and indicated I should pass it to Gwen, which I did. We passed it over the deer a couple of times until the old man allowed it would hold.

"Get going."

"Want a ride?" I asked.

"Nope. When you get to my daughter's place, you lend her a hand hanging it."

"My pleasure. I'm Ben Abbott, by the way, Mr. Jervis."

"I know who you are."

"Can I ask you something, Mr. Jervis?"

Gwen, who had climbed back into the car, gave a little inward hiss of alarm, but it was too late now. Her father broke open his ancient double-barrel, inserted fresh loads, and snicked it shut.

"Like what?"

"Would you know if my cousin was flying drugs?"

"Yup."

"Was he?"

"Nope."

"Thank you. I'll get your buck home."

"Sonny."

"Yes, sir?"

"You ask the wrong man questions like that, he'll blow your head off." He rounded the car, trailed by the kid, and plunged back into the woods.

Gwen exhaled. "You are out of your mind. You are *crazy.*"

"We understood each other."

Gwen snorted. "You didn't even hear the warning."

"What warning?"

"Don't ask Bill."

"Your brother?"

"Jesus, you're over your head, Ben. He probably just saved your life."

"Wait a minute. Does that mean Renny might have been working for Bill and your dad didn't know?"

"He said he'd know and he said Renny wasn't. Which I told you all along. You asked two of us now. Go look someplace else."

"Gwen."

"Your car's getting bloody. You better take me home."

I drove her home to the trailers and parked under a tree that had a hook and chain hanging from a low limb. I took off my jacket and shirt and wrestled the carcass onto the hook.

Gwen returned from her trailer with paper towels for the blood and a cold beer. "You better get going before the boys get home."

I cleaned off, dressed, and drained the beer. "Thanks."

"No more questions?"

"You told me not to ask."

"That never stopped you before."

I got in the car. She had undergone some transformation when she went for the beer. The edge of anger that had underlain her all afternoon was gleaming in her eyes. "Ask," she said.

"All right. Renny left his car because he knew he was flying into Al's field. Did he tell you who his passenger would be?"

"No."

"But he knew, didn't he?"

"Yeah. He knew."

"But you think it was someone in your family. That's why you've been lying to me."

"One of my people," Gwen confessed.

"And you're caught in the middle. You'd never tell who."

"I don't know who. If I did, I'd kill him."

I started the engine. "You're wrong, Gwen. It wasn't your family."

"Are you kidding, Ben? Soon as they learned we're running around, they went for him like flies on honey. A pilot! A real live pilot humping their sister."

"I thought Pete ran him off the road."

"I told you, Pete drinks. The rest of them were tickled pink. I swear, if my husband had come home from the Gulf they would have drowned him in the river."

"No," I said. "Renny played it straight."

"They would have given him anything."

"No. He hated being at a disadvantage. I lent him a few bucks for the garage. Drove him crazy. Finally insisted on giving me a new engine. No way he would have let your people get control over him by doing something illegal."

"*I* had control over him."

"I gather that ran fifty-fifty."

Gwen nodded. Tears slipped from her eyes, down the lines in her face.

"If you hear anything, would you let me know?"

"Are you sure what you said, that it's not my people?"

"Positive. It just couldn't happen that way. Partly for the reason you just said. If he had flown coke—which I'm sure he didn't—they wouldn't kill the golden goose. Would they?"

"No."

"It had to be a paying passenger, Gwen. Somebody local he'd leave his car for. Somebody he trusted."

I was half a mile from the trailers when I spotted headlights in the woods. It looked like I had left Gwen just in time: "The boys" were coming home. They were angling along one of the two-rut tracks that joined the dirt road. But when they reached my road they turned right and continued on ahead of me.

"Son of a bitch."

My own headlights revealed a long, dark van similar to the one that had blasted Connie's Lincoln. I hit the gas to pull up for a closer look and hung tight on his tail until a curve in the road gave me a glimpse of its battered right side. Same van.

I edged closer, to read the mud-spattered license plate. Brake lights flashed and he stopped dead. The Oldsmobile's brakes are good, but not great, and I came within six inches of smacking his bumper. Before I could wonder, What next?, pickup-truck roof-rack lights blazed on behind me. I had not seen the second vehicle following me with his lights out. I had six inches of maneuvering space in front, six inches in back, and thick woods on either side.

21

Doors thumped. I locked mine. Someone rapped hard on the driver's-side window, and when I did not open it fast enough, someone else smashed the opposite glass with a shotgun butt and pressed the barrels against my temple.

"Open the door."

"Just take it easy," I said. "You can see both my hands, right here on the wheel."

"Open the door."

Very slowly, I reached and pressed the lock release, unlocking all four doors with a thud much softer than my heartbeat.

"Get out of the car."

Slowly, keeping my hands conspicuously in view, I opened the door and climbed out, relieving the pressure on my temple.

"Turn around."

They helped me with that one, turning me roughly to face the truck lights. I was blinded. I sensed one of them circle the car and knew he had when the shotgun touched my head again.

"Step away from the car."

I stepped sideways until he said to stop.

"Put your hands behind your head."

I raised my hands, clamped them around the back of my head,

and waited, distinctly aware of my exposed front and my elbows pointing at the sky. We all knew they were going to hit me. I was the only one who didn't know where. I guessed an elbow. Off by a mile.

A second shotgun whipped across my gut—a direct hit to the solar plexus that slammed me to the dirt, retching for air. When I could breathe again, one of them shoved a shotgun muzzle against my lips.

"You hear me, Abbott?"

"I hear you."

"Got anything to say?"

"Yeah. I don't know why you're doing this."

"Guess."

"Shoot the son of a bitch, for chrissake. Let's get it over with."

"No, wait. I want to hear this."

I couldn't see their faces. If I had to guess, I thought the one baiting me might be Pete Jervis. I could smell beer. The impatient one was just a lanky stick figure against the glare.

"Guess!" yelled the first, and I was pretty sure it was Pete. A familiar something crazy in his voice.

"Shoot him."

"Speak." Pete pulled the shotgun back an inch so I could move my lips.

I said, "I also don't know why you ran me off the road the other day."

"Same reason."

"Come on, Pete. Let's do it and go home. I'm fuckin' freezing."

I knew that wasn't Bill, which was both good and bad. Good because Bill was undoubtedly a murderer several times over. Pete, on the other hand, drank, and when he drank he got crazy. It was Pete who had run Renny off the road.

I said, "I don't know why you're doing this. But you'll bring a shitstorm down on yourselves if you kill me."

"You already brought a shitstorm down on us, you son of a bitch."

I asked him what he meant and got a gun barrel in the groin for my temerity. It was a little while before I could douse the pain enough to think. When I started thinking, the fear threatened to overwhelm me.

"Admit it," said Pete, "and we'll let you go."

And invite me home for supper too, I thought. I knew he was lying, and fear spiraled down to despair. We were miles from the nearest house. Even Ollie didn't patrol these woods. They'd bury me in a hole in the ground and disappear my car in a Waterbury chop shop.

I began to feel a strange peace. I'd read somewhere that people attacked by tigers all admitted the same sudden loss of will to resist. Maybe Heaven was simply the end of the fight. Maybe I'd meet Renny there, maybe Ron Pearlman. Maybe we'd feel sorry for the ones we'd left behind. I heard a voice at a distance—my own, it turned out, some other part of me, ever the friendly salesman—negotiating the last breath.

"Pete, whatever shitstorm came down on you, it can't be as bad as this, and frankly, I don't know what you're talking about."

I think it was the conversational tone that slowed him for a brief moment. I certainly didn't plan it, and he certainly didn't expect it. I couldn't see his face, but I could see him move his head to look at the other guy as if asking, Is this character real?

It was the best chance I'd get in my life. I slapped the gun barrel. Pete yelled. The double-barreled twelve-gauge bellowed fire into the ground. I rolled, fell in the shallow ditch beside the road, scrambled onto my feet, and ran past the pickup-truck lights into the dark.

"Get him!"

Another weapon roared. Buckshot whistled, fanned my face, and spattered the trees. I ran with all my strength. I was going in the wrong direction, back to the Jervis camp, but the first thing was to put distance between me and the guns. I got fifty yards. A flashlight smacked me in the eyes. I found myself looking past it, down the barrels of a break-breech Savage into the disdainful gaze of Herman Jervis.

"That was real cute, sonny. Now you will turn around, very slowly, and go back and finish talking to my boy."

I felt like he had ripped me open with his deer knife and drained all my blood. I shambled back to the pickup, the gun prodding my spine. This time I got a good look at Pete, and the other guy, whom I'd never seen. Pete was red-faced and shaking with rage.

"You son of a bitch."

"Explain," said Herman Jervis. "Why'd you sic the cops on us?"

"I didn't."

"You're going around stirring things up about Renny Chevalley. State police raided my camp."

"I never mentioned your name or anyone in your family."

"Pete hears you did."

I looked at Pete Jervis and got mad. "You can hear a lot of things at the White Birch. Guy the other day heard I was sleeping with his wife. A dumb drunk named Tom Mealy. It wasn't true. What you heard wasn't true either."

"You son of a bitch," Pete said again.

"What, exactly, did you hear?" asked old Herman.

"You gonna listen to him instead of me?"

Herman looked at him without saying a word. Pete shuffled his boots in the dirt. "I heard Ben Abbott was going around checking up on Renny. Heard he was asking everybody how coke was brought in."

"Jesus Christ," I said. "You've been talking to Freddy Butler."

"I'm not saying who."

"You tried to kill me on the word of *Freddy Butler?* You son of a bitch. You wrecked my aunt's car. Almost killed her."

Old Herman jabbed me hard in the back with his gun. "Shut up."

"Who?" he asked Pete in a gravel-pit voice.

"Freddy Butler's a good guy, Dad. I trust him."

"Go home," said Herman Jervis. "You too," he snapped at the skinny one. "And you too," he said to me. I hurried to my car, brushed the broken glass off the front seat and got in. The engine was still running. As I put it in gear, Herman rapped on my window. I lowered it.

"You be careful around my daughter, sonny. She's got plenty of sorrow in her life."

"I understand."

"I don't mean don't call on her. Just do it right."

"Well, we've been friends a long time."

The old man's interest had already shifted. He said, "Like I told you earlier, my son Bill calls the shots now. Don't cross him."

As it was pretty clear that the Jervis clan had had nothing to do with Renny's death, I already planned to avoid all Jervises on general principles. But I didn't tell old Herman, who might have taken it the wrong way. So I promised him I wouldn't cross Bill and drove home to drink something.

22

They had a long memory at Le Cirque, and a table ready.

I noticed a higher percentage of ladies lunching since the Drexel Burnham mob had dispersed. Their increased presence made for a prettier room, though oddly more decadent, perhaps because most of the Drexel boys never fully understood what they were selling.

Otherwise the New York I saw on the walk from Grand Central didn't seem all that changed. Recessionary malaise was notably absent. Traffic was dense as ever; Madonna, naked, couldn't have nailed an empty taxicab. There may have been fewer construction sites blocking the sidewalks, though, and the women definitely looked younger.

Alex Rose arrived for lunch glowering suspiciously, an expression that neatly complemented his camouflage. In his pinstriped suit and Brooks tie, he looked like a truculent lawyer, or a wary pension-fund manager. Perfect.

I myself was resplendent in an Italian midnight-blue double-breasted suit, vaguely redolent of mothballs, and a Sea Island cotton Dunhill shirt. On my wrist was a gold Piaget moon watch I should not have accepted from an arbitrager. Little Alison could have attended a week of boarding school for what I had paid for my necktie.

"I don't get this," Rose said, looking around the lavish room. "Wha'd you hit the lottery?"

I didn't tell him it was Rita's lunch tab.

"Like I told you on the phone, I got nothing new on your cousin."

"I figured after we talked you might make a call or two."

"Well, as a matter of fact, I did talk to a guy at LaGuardia."

"And?"

"Renny Chevalley took off at two-fifty that afternoon."

"Thank you."

Ed Hawley had seen the plane at three-thirty. Forty minutes to Newbury, nonstop. Thank you very, very much.

We ate a sumptuous lunch—écrevisses, ris de veau, and crème brûlée—saved Rita some money on a Muscadet with the entrée, then blew it all on an '85 Chambertin with the main course.

I pumped him a little about the detective business and learned a lot. Rose was increasingly mystified as to why I had invited him, but he was an ebullient talker once he got wound up. By dessert, he'd packed my brain with the latest P.I. basics, from sweet-talking data out of credit-rating companies to infinity bugs that transmitted conversations on telephonic request.

"There are no secrets," he assured me with childlike glee. He was, however, no fool, and both wine bottles were removed containing plenty to cheer the kitchen. He had noticed people watching us while we ate, and when I had paid the check, he said, "You used me for cover, didn't you?"

I denied it, of course.

He noticed me moving stiffly as we left the restaurant.

"Whudaya still sore from the accident?"

"Somebody bent a shotgun on my stomach."

Rose laughed and slapped me on the back, reminding me of another sore spot. "Welcome to the P.I. business, fella. Who'd you piss off?"

"An innocent bystander."

"That'll teach you to mind your own business." He laughed again.

"How'd you happen to tell Jack Long that Ron had been shot before the troopers called him?"

"I keep telling you, Ben: You got to make your connections, man.

I pay the security company. I write the checks. They owe me. They know damned well that if I don't hear everything to do with Mr. Long's house, I hire a new alarm company."

"How'd they find out? There was no alarm."

Rose stopped laughing, and his cockeyed wink hardened into an unpleasant squint. "They got a radio scanner. They monitor the state police channels. You ought to buy one, Ben. Keep in touch."

My next stop was the midtown offices of Harkin & Locke. Buddy Locke, my second protégé. I had phoned ahead for an appointment and been told that Ms. Harkin's schedule was booked for a month. I had told her secretary I was coming anyway. It was a heavy-security building on Fifty-seventh between Fifth and Sixth, but, as I assumed, the lobby guards had orders to let me up.

Harkin & Locke's reception room had three features: a stunningly beautiful blonde greeter, a heart-stopping view of Central Park, and a single article of Japanese sculpture that, if I knew its owners, had probably been looted from a Kyoto monastery.

"Oh, Mr. Abbott. Ms. Harkin has just gone into a meeting."

"That's okay. I brought a book."

I sat across from a guy who was reading the *Wall Street Journal* with desperate nonchalance. He assessed me over the top of his newspaper. I wanted to tell him I was not job-hunting competition, but if he was any good he would scope that out for himself.

I *had* brought a book, and I opened pleasurably to the first page of the new Patrick O'Brian novel. When the receptionist interrupted me an hour later to tell me Ms. Harkin was still in the meeting, I expressed my gratitude. It was approaching five o'clock when she interrupted me again. I asked if I might have a cup of coffee. It arrived in Limoges, which pleased me, because among the many things I had taught the two pirates behind the door was to go first class. Buddy Locke's instincts leaned to canned soda, while Leslie quailed at the thought of giving anything away for free.

"Mr. Abbott?"

"Yes?" I marked my place in the book.

"Ms. Harkin is expected at the Downtown Athletic Club at six, but she can squeeze you in for a moment right now."

"Terrific. Hang on one paragraph." I finished the chapter, laid the novel reverentially into my briefcase, and followed the blonde into Leslie's office. She was on the telephone, of course, her back to me, looking out the window.

"She'll be with you in a minute," whispered the receptionist.

"Who's that?" I whispered back, indicating a beefy guy in a tight suit who occupied a straightback chair in the corner.

"I think he's with security."

Leslie spun her chair and hung up the phone. "Thank you, Doreen."

Doreen went out the door, fast. The security guy emitted a cop stare, which was wasted on me. Leslie Harkin had my full attention.

I hadn't seen her in the five years since the trial. To say that she strongly resembled Rita Long would be to say that all raven-haired, beautiful women looked the same. Both women radiated their personality, but what shone through their beauty was quite different. Need a guide across a foreign city, ask for Rita Long. Need an escort through a hostile one—or brain surgery in a hurry—hire Leslie Harkin.

Physically, Leslie was slimmer, leaner in the face and in the body. She was a few years older than Rita and definitely looked it, her narrow brow and cheeks aging early from overwork, too much jet travel, and too many nights of shorting sleep.

All the same, she was a vigorous woman, and I had the impression that if she could stay in bed for a month she would wake up gorgeous again. Her most compelling feature was her strange violet eyes. She had a trick of widening them suddenly, and I had yet to see a guy in a meeting stay aboard his train of thought when she zapped him.

I thought I had developed partial immunity to the Leslie Look after she plea-bargained my ass into the U.S. Attorney's lap. But my heartbeat, which had revved at the sight of her familiar silhouette, redlined when she faced me. I had been nuts for her in bed and awed by her ferocious intelligence. If that wasn't love, she still stirred my soul, and I knew in an instant why I hadn't had much success in trying to hate her.

"What do you want, Ben?"

I still didn't hate her, but I very much wanted to beat her at her own game.

"Is the bodyguard for me?"

"What do you think?"

"I think you have a guilty conscience."

"Are you accusing me?"

"I'm chasing some information. Everybody says you're the one to ask."

"What do you want to know?"

"Nothing I want King Kong to hear." King Kong stirred. I said to Leslie, "Tell him I won't hurt him if he behaves himself." I said it with a smile aimed at her, a smile that asked, What is this crap? Leslie looked at her watch, and I knew I had won. "Thank you," she said to the guard. "That's all."

"You sure you're okay?"

"Get out of my office."

He blinked and left.

"Leslie, why would you fear me?"

"Ben, I'm busy. Ask your question."

Before I could, the telephone buzzed. She answered it without apologizing, and talked machine-gun style for five minutes. She hung up, looked at me, and it rang again. Another five minutes, this time in Japanese. When she hung up, I said, "I'm impressed. When'd you learn Japanese?"

"What do you want to know?"

As I opened my mouth, she looked at her watch—for real, this time. "Christ, I gotta get downtown. Come on, we'll talk in the car." She left, firing orders at secretaries and assistants, trailed by a vice-president who held papers for her to sign, and me.

Her car was a Rolls-Royce limo, which, last I had heard, was running two hundred and seventy-five thousand. "You're doing well."

"You know the Japanese. They love their brand names."

"What does Buddy drive?"

"Dodge Viper."

"I'm jealous."

We settled into the car, and the cell phone tweeted. She picked up, again without an apology, and sing-songed in Japanese. At Houston Street, she hung up with a hearty *"Banzai!"*

"Ask," she said to me, writing a note in her datebook.

I said, "What do you know about—" and the phone rang. That conversation was still going when the car stopped dead in heavy traffic at Canal Street. A homeless guy approached, rapping the window with a battered paper cup. I lowered the glass.

"What are you doing?" asked Leslie. I took her phone, gave it to the guy with the cup, and closed the window.

"What? That's a two-thousand-dollar telephone!"

"I'll give you mine. Now will you answer my goddamned question?"

"You gave him my phone."

"I'll give him your datebook next. Will you shut up and tell me what's going on with LTS?"

She said, "I hear you're trying to put LTS into play."

I must admit enormous satisfaction in manipulating my former love and protégée. Only a killer pro on the scene, who specialized in electronics, could confirm Jack Long's financial strength. But it had occurred to me over the weekend that Leslie wouldn't give me the time of day if I came on as an amateur detective and simply asked whether Jack Long was riding as high as he claimed. Whereas a deal in the works would make my questions potentially valuable, especially if it sounded like a deal she could move in on.

It had been a safe bet that some sort of rumor would get around after last week's Rolodex party. I had engineered today's conspicuous lunch with a mysterious stranger at Le Cirque to give the two-hundred-phone-call-a-day crowd plenty of I-told-you-so ammunition.

"Well," I said, "don't believe everything you hear."

The phone was forgotten. Her eyes gleamed like tropic dawns. "What do *you* hear?"

"You first."

"Okay. Get this, Ben: Jack Long goes to Ingersoll at Salomon, like maybe he's interested in floating a high-yield bond."

I said, "I gather you're not involved."

"What do you mean?"

"That's not exactly news."

"Oh yeah? How about the fact that he's sucking up to the Flying Dutchmen?"

"Come on," I winged it again. "He's been in bed with Holland Brothers since God knows when." Interesting. It sounded like Jack Long was looking to borrow hard money. Be it junk bonds or a private loan from the usurious Holland Brothers, he'd pay the high interest businessmen paid only when no one else would lend at normal rates. With rates low and money going begging, maybe—just maybe—LTS was suffering.

So far this was like shooting fish in a barrel. Not because I was any smarter than Leslie Harkin—nobody was—but in some dark crevice of her psyche Leslie would always be *my* protégée, *my* employee, and therefore could not imagine herself any more clever than the day we met. Also, she was still hungry, while I didn't care. It gave me a longer perspective and a decided advantage. Could I use it now to get her to spill again? I debated appealing to her vanity, and chose, wisely, greed.

"I'll hop out here. I'm meeting a guy." Her car was creeping past Trinity Church at the foot of Wall Street.

"Wait. What are you doing, Ben? I didn't even know you were back. Did they lift your ban?"

"Nice talking to you. Say hello to Buddy. Tell him I want a ride real soon in that Viper."

"Ben, what in the hell are you up to?"

"Just getting along. Driver, stop here."

"No. Ride down with me. I'll have him drop you back. It's just a couple of minutes. Please, Ben. We should talk."

I shot my cuff and looked at my Piaget. She looked surprised I hadn't hocked it. "Okay. I'll ride along. He'll wait."

"So what are you doing?"

"It's just exploratory. No big deal."

"You want money?"

"I don't even know how much I need at this point."

"Ben, you name it, we'll raise it."

"This might be a little steep for conservative Japanese these days."

"Let me be the judge of that."

I said nothing. Leslie said, "Think about it." I said I would.

"What set you off?" she asked. "Long's Hong Kong deal?"

She was watching my reaction intently now. I assumed she meant Ron Pearlman's factory. But I didn't know the electronics field like she did, didn't know what other big deals Jack Long was juggling, didn't know diddley.

"The Hong Kong deal sounded expensive," I ventured. "Made me wonder how badly it exposed him."

"Big question," Leslie fished back. "What's his payment schedule? Right?"

I sort of nodded. So far Leslie hadn't even paid for my train ticket, much less lunch. "One of the big questions," I replied vaguely. Too vaguely. All of a sudden she smelled a rat.

"Wait a minute. Didn't Ron Pearlman get killed up where you live?"

"Shot."

"That's what started you?" Scorn stalked across her face, and her eyes dimmed down to shadows.

I laughed at her. "Yeah, right. The idea popped into my head two weeks ago."

"Do you know his payment schedule?"

Rolls-Royce is famous for a quiet car. No automobile in history was quieter than this one at the moment, nor its inside icier. I looked Leslie straight in her violet eye. "No, I don't. And neither do you."

"Want to bet?"

"You know rumors. It's a closely held company."

"I have a source."

"Your source doesn't know. Jack Long is not the kind of guy to share that with anybody, unless you're sleeping with his accountant."

"You know Long?"

"Sure. We had dinner the other night. Straight shooter. Hates partners. Probably wouldn't tell his own wife what he owes or when he owes it."

"End of this year. Less than three months. December 31."

Bingo, I thought.

"Bull," I said. "You're guessing. I'll guess next June."

"Eighteen months after they closed the deal. Notes. Something like two hundred twenty-five million."

I said, "He doesn't seem worried. The man's talking expansion into Singapore."

Leslie beamed. Dawn was back in her eyes.

"I *knew* you were running a deal," she said triumphantly. "You're putting him in play. Come on, Ben. Let us in on it. We'll spook his bankers."

"I don't think so, Leslie. I'm not really looking for partners."

"Because I testified against you?"

I gave her an unsmiling look she could interpret any way she wanted.

"You don't trust me."

"Should I?"

"Jesus, you want revenge. You hung this deal in front of me to make me feel bad I can't be part of it. Well, let me tell you something, Ben: Buddy and I will run this one by you. We'll leave you in the dust."

I had to remind myself we were discussing a fantasy. I had no deal, no plan to take over LTS. It would be funny if Harkin & Locke destroyed LTS or themselves trying to make my fantasy happen. Not so funny if my name got attached; technically, just sitting in Leslie's Rolls-Royce violated my SEC ban. Not at all funny if Jack Long was innocent. "Drop me here."

Her limousine raced off—in search of a pay phone, so she could call Buddy Locke and start raking Long's bones.

I went down to the subway wondering if I had created a monster. I telephoned Jack Long's office from Grand Central. Jack greeted me in a country-neighbor voice, subtly implying that last weekend's job offer had been dinner-party talk.

I said, "Try to keep my name out of it, but you ought to know that my old playmates Harkin and Locke might make a move on you."

He waited half a second too long to laugh. "I'll eat their lunch."

23

I got home aching all over and thoroughly depressed. I'd done well in New York, and I should have felt elated. But first on the train and then in the car from the Pawling station, a sense of rejection commenced to linger. I felt old and out of it. Even the delicious scent of wood smoke drifting in the cold autumn evening failed to lift my spirits, and when I retreated into my library and built my own fire, the walls closed in like the night.

Funnily enough, the deal to snatch control of LTS that Leslie imagined me running just might be a way to get back in the game. I didn't know whether I was afraid to try, or was finally listening to Aunt Connie nattering in the back of my head that Long produced jobs and wealth and what right did I have to steal his creation?

I supposed I should report to Rita, but the more I thought about it, the less I had to report. In fact, it was likely that she could have told me half, at least, of what I'd learned from Leslie. Strange she hadn't told me that Jack was scrambling.

I wandered into my office and checked the answering machine. The Volvo couple I'd shown the Tilden Place to the night of the Long dinner had called, politely, to say they'd decided on a house in Salisbury instead. I was shocked. I'd really convinced myself they had fallen for the Tilden place. It made me wonder what I was doing wrong. The economy wasn't any hotter in Salisbury, but some agent up there had managed to close a sale.

The second message was from Rita, and she sounded depressed too, saying, "Ben, please call. Anytime. I'll be up late."

"Hi. I just got back from New York."

"Have you eaten dinner?"

"No, I was just getting hungry. I had a big lunch."

"Would you bring a pizza?"

An evening with Rita certainly beat sitting around alone rehashing my relationship with the fast lane. "What do you want on it?"

"Anything."

"You don't sound so great."

"I had a very depressing visit from Ira Roth. They're really going to indict me."

"Did Ira say that?"

"I read between the lines."

"He's not known for his bedside manner, you know. He just goes out and wins."

"I think I know how to read lawyers," she replied tartly. "He's worried."

"I'll be there in an hour."

The Castle was lit up like the Plaza Hotel—windows blazing, spotlights scouring the lawns, fairy lights winking on the walks. "Up here," Rita called from the turret. "The door's open."

I carried the pizza through the house and up the steps into the cold tower. She was sitting in the observation room dressed in a wool shirt and down vest. "I can't stand going indoors tonight. Okay to eat out here?"

"If you don't mind ice on your pizza."

She made room on the table for the box and handed me a beer. "How'd it go in New York?"

"When people talk about Jack's Hong Kong deal, do they mean Ron's chip factory?"

"Probably. It was the biggest and the most recent out there."

"Did Jack really pay two hundred and fifty million to buy Ron out?"

"Yes."

"With a big note due?"

"Yes."

"With something like ten percent down, with the remainder due in eighteen months? December thirty-first?"

"I think so. I wasn't really in on the final details. But December thirty-first sounds about right. Hey, you're pretty good, Ben."

"At New York rates I'd better be. Thing is, nobody but Jack knows exactly the situation. Did he rewrite it? How's he intending to pay? There's a hundred variables, but my gut tells me he's got a problem. So does the gut of a shark I was talking to today."

I opened the box, cut through the steaming cheese with my pen-knife, and lifted out a slice. Rita bit into it with a moan of pleasure.

"Do you have a copy of the contract?"

"Not here."

"I'd like to read it. I want to see where Jack's head is at. . . .What's he going to pay Ron's family with?"

"He was hoping to pay cash. That was the whole point, to buy him outright."

"Could he pay him in stock if he couldn't get the cash?"

"Ron had the option to accept stock."

"Would he have?"

"Sure. As long as LTS looked good. Which it does."

"Are you sure about that?"

"I'm not sure about anything anymore."

"What if Jack couldn't raise the money? Would he lose the ten percent?"

"All twenty-five million dollars."

"Have you read the contracts?"

"I read the deal memo. We agreed to pay Ron two hundred and fifty million dollars for his Hong Kong operation, plus a two-and-a-half-million-dollar management fee yearly, for five years."

"What?"

"What's so strange about that?"

"Jack made a big point of saying Ron was a pampered dilettante. Why would he want him for a manager?"

"Ron insisted. It was a dealbreaker."

"Why? Just to get the fee?"

"Ron was not a dilettante. He wanted to keep his Hong Kong connections. It's a hot city. Who knows what'll happen after the Chinese take over in '97? Ron intended to run the operation while he scouted out new opportunities."

"That must have driven Jack crazy."

"He didn't love it."

It struck me that a dead Ron meant that not only Jack got his wife back, he also got rid of a thorn in his side.

Rita disagreed. "Except now he's scrambling to replace Ron to run the operation. It's a real mess. You know about flash chips?"

"I know people are hoping to get rich out of them."

"Well, that's where Ron's operation was going. So are IBM and Sony."

"Lousy time to lose a manager."

"Even one making love to your wife," Rita agreed.

"I still want to see the contract."

"I'll get someone to fax it to me. I can't leave the county."

"Don't let Jack know."

Rita smiled. "I have friends."

She called me at noon the next day. "Got it."

"Be right there."

Their three-thousand-dollar laser fax had printed a perfect copy on twenty-pound white bond. I sat at Jack's own desk, an inlaid nineteenth-century secretary, and read the ten-page document word for word, as my father had taught me, to save money on lawyers.

I made one note. When I finished the last page, I read the entire document again. Then I took a head-clearing turn around the lawn and read it a third time. I found Rita in the kitchen, staring blankly at a tag-sale copy of Julia Child.

"Did you read it?" I asked her.

"As it came off the machine."

"Did you see what I saw?"

"Yes. The bastard murdered him."

Assuming he was broke, the contract gave Jack Long a powerful motive.

If—said a little escape clause on the last page—Ron Pearlman was unable to accept his five-year management contract, LTS could cancel the deal and get its ten percent deposit back.

With Ron dead, all bets were off. Ron's heirs—his father, presumably—still owned his piece of LTS. But Jack was off the hook. He didn't have to pay two hundred and twenty-five million bucks on December 31.

The money business is built on belief and leaps of faith. Jack knew that if he had failed to make his payment to Ron, his banks would have taken a closer look at his entire indebtedness, disliked what they had seen, and called his loans, retiring him to the same hands-tied limbo to which they'd sent Donald Trump and Robert Maxwell and several hundred lesser lights: no more acquisitions; no more private loans; no more shots at cornering markets in flash chips.

Rita looked sick.

"You didn't know about this?" I asked.

"He must have negotiated it after the memo."

"But how did he shoot Ron from Washington, D.C.?"

"He paid Rose to shoot him," said Rita, and I had to agree that was probably the way it went down, though I still wondered if Rose did it on his own, betting that Jack would be pleased and reward him. "Who do we tell?"

"First we tell your lawyer," I said. "Give him something to fight with."

24

Ira Roth's father had owned a feed store next to the freight station. He'd had a reputation during the Great Depression as a soft touch, and another after World War Two as a financier of harebrained manufacturing schemes. He died around 1970, flat broke, loved and admired. Ira, whom the old man had hounded into law school, had spent his life overhearing remarks to the effect that he just wasn't quite the gentleman his father had been. That was all Rita's defense attorney and I had in common.

Twenty-five years older than I, Ira was rich, vigorous, and driven. He wore splendidly old-fashioned three-piece suits, florid neckties, and a trademark gray fedora. He could make a quiet stroll down Main Street look like the third reel of a Frank Capra movie where entered the savior or the villain, take your choice. He kept his main office in Plainfield, by the courthouse, and lived on a splashy Western-style horse farm on Morris Mountain, not far from Rita's. He was pugnacious, as a good trial lawyer should be, and quite convinced he was the smartest man in the state, which probably didn't hurt either. As a child I had found him intimidating. As an adult I had a better sense of his complexities, and still found him intimidating.

"First of all," he said, when we called at Open Gate Farm, "what is Ben doing here?"

"He's with me," said Rita.

"He's a witness for the prosecution. Ben, I can't see you."

"He stays," said Rita.

"Mrs. Long—"

"He stays."

Ira said, "As I told you, Mrs. Long, when your husband retained me, I have my best successes with obedient clients. Trust me or hire a yes man."

Rita looked at me. I said, "We have a theory that Mr. Long hired a private detective to kill Ron Pearlman."

"In a fit of jealousy?" the lawyer asked scornfully.

"No. To nullify a contract."

Bushy gray eyebrows rose a fraction. We had his attention. "To nullify *what* contract?"

"Ron Pearlman dead means Long doesn't have to pony up a heap of money. There's an escape clause in the buyout contract, and it looks like Long might be in fiscal trouble. If he had to honor the contract, his banks would have shut him down."

"That's very interesting. Are you proposing a Carolyn Warmus defense?"

"What's a Carolyn Warmus defense?"

"The defense theorized that Ms. Warmus's lover had actually shot the victim and framed Carolyn to avoid getting caught."

"But didn't they find her guilty?"

"I was about to mention that."

He beckoned us into the house. We took chairs in a little sitting room off a two-story living room the size of a paddock. Ira turned his formidable attention to Rita. "It's a tricky tactic, Mrs. Long. If the jury thinks you're trying to weasel out of it with smoke and mirrors, they might easily conclude that you conjured up a farfetched tale simply because you have no other defense. In other words, guilty. Next case."

"But I do have some defense, don't I? Isn't this worth pursuing?"

"Look at it from the state's attorney's point of view. He has a choice of convicting you—discovered on the scene, with a gun and fingerprints. Or your husband—who, sadly, does not project the image of a jealous fiend—and who happened to be shaking the President's hand in Washington, D.C., the day the victim was shot."

"What about a hired killer?" I asked.

"Ben, do you mind my asking your interest in this?"

"I think Rita's been set up."

"Is there something between you two I should know when I'm pleading your case, Mrs. Long?"

"We'll keep you informed," said Rita. "Come on, Ben, let's go."

Roth stood up.

I said, "Ira, can Mrs. Long count on attorney-client confidentiality?"

"Of course," he snapped.

"Sorry, but it had to be asked."

"I'm not for sale," Roth replied. "You can trust me, Mrs. Long. If you don't, you can have your retainer back, minus costs. Ben, a word with you, please?"

"I'll catch up," I said to Rita, who pushed through the door and hurried down the porch steps to her car.

"Ben, I implore you to be careful. This is a very delicate case. Perception is all. If I can't quash it on a technicality, that sexy-looking woman is going to face a jury of overweight, middle-aged citizens who are going to seize, consciously or unconsciously, a chance to redress all their personal disappointments since high school."

"The husband's P.I. did it."

"Don't make it worse for her. If the prosecution gets wind of you running around accusing her husband, they'll paint pictures of multiple infidelities that I will not be able to keep out of the trial. It's going to be a circus anyway. Try to avoid joining the animal act."

"I hear you, Ira, but I get the feeling you're looking through a narrow lens."

"That's my job, Ben. The last thing I want the jury to see is the big picture. . . . By the way, Ben . . ."

Here came a very big "by the way."

"Have you told anyone about that videotape stunt Rose paid for?"

"Only Rita."

"Keep it under your hat."

"Rose told me I'd have to testify."

"Under no circumstances! You're a prosecution witness who saw the body. If you care for that woman, keep your mouth shut about that tape."

"Fine with me. Rose threatened to force me to testify."

"I know. That was the single dumbest idea Jack Long's so-called lawyers proposed. And they proposed some doozies. I want nothing in that courtroom that makes the woman look kinky. I'll have my hands full with the slut image."

"She's no slut."

"I'm afraid it won't help to quote you on that."

"Ira? I just remembered something."

"What?"

"I told Vicky McLachlan."

"How about Scooter MacKay? He could print an insert for the *Clarion.* Or do a mailing."

"Only Vicky. I'm sorry. I forget. It was sort of . . ."

"Pillow talk?" Ira growled.

"Pre-pillow talk."

"Well, it would be nice for Mrs. Long if you pillow talk Vicky into keeping it under her hat."

"We're not talking any more."

Ira looked thoroughly disgusted and echoed Alex Rose: "With friends like you, Mrs. Long won't need enemies."

"Can you talk to Vicky?"

"I'll have to reflect on that. Vicky's a smart woman. She knows that testifying about your pre-pillow talk won't be the finest moment in her career. But if the state's attorney somehow gets wind of your escapade, and subpoenas Vicky, she will tell it straight and true."

"She doesn't owe me anything," I admitted.

"It's not that. She's too smart to lie. . . . Or too honest. You're sure you didn't tell anyone else?"

"Positive. But Ira, Rose knows. And if he's protecting Long to protect himself, what's to stop him from blabbing it to send Rita down the river?"

"Look at the bright side," Ira said grimly. "That would pretty much validate your theory that Long hired Rose to kill Ron Pearlman."

"Very funny."

"While I get to tell the jury, She's not a kinky slut, it just looks that way."

"Do you know about the picture?"

"What picture?" Roth asked in a voice that didn't like surprises.

I described Rita's drawing of Ron.

"A skull instead of a face? Where is it?"

"Disappeared."

The lawyer sighed. "She probably hid it."

"She swears she didn't."

"Well," he said carefully, "I would hope that someone who has influence with her would persuade her to make damned sure it stays hidden. Better yet, burn it."

He opened the door for me. "How's your Aunt Connie?"

"Hanging in there."

"Please give her my regards."

"Thanks. Ira, how bad are Rita's chances?"

"About as bad as yours were when you went down."

"She didn't do it."

"Well, she has one advantage that you didn't."

"What?"

"Counsel."

"I had lawyers up the wazoo."

"Always wondered why you didn't call me. What was the matter? Didn't trust a country lawyer?"

"I considered it, Ira."

"I'd have gotten you off."

"Maybe I didn't want to get off."

"But you were framed."

"I know, Ira." I'd been pondering this since New York, trying to understand why I didn't hate Leslie Harkin for selling me out.

"You didn't break the law."

"No."

"So why didn't you call me?"

"I broke the spirit of the law, Ira. I plundered. I deserved to go down."

"That is your crazy aunt talking Puritan claptrap."

"Clean slate, Ira. I'm not guilty anymore."

Rita was huddled in the car with her arms crossed tightly. "Now what?"

"He'll follow up—quietly, I think."

"Did he say that?"

"No. But he has to follow it up."

"I'm scared."

She said she was scared, but she acted more like mad. Flooring the Jag, she scattered rooster-tails of Ira Roth's driveway gravel. All the way home she treated me to a blistering critique of her lawyer. She dished his taste in furniture—yecho-modern; his horses— swaybacked; the roofline of his ranch house—which she characterized as Wild West so-what.

Actually, Ira had invested a fortune in creating an authentic Western spread, much as she and Jack had done Ivanhoe. Nor were they alone in grafting wacky fantasies onto the countryside. Ira's immediate neighbor inhabits a Norman farmhouse, and the guy over the hill, Reg Hopkins of Hopkins Septic fame, lives in a Tudor cottage under a roof he learned to thatch himself. Of late I had been noticing a lamentable penchant for stucco tricked up to resemble Santa Fe adobe. On the plus side, most of the so-called contemporary architecture was hidden in the woods.

When Rita finally noticed I wasn't responding, she screamed at me. "Would it be too much goddamned trouble for you to investigate where Alex Rose was when Ron was murdered?"

"My next step," I assured her. "I'm going to check out your alarm company."

"Why?"

"Jack told me Rose reported that Ron was shot *before* the state police called. When I asked Rose how he knew, he said the alarm company told him they'd heard it on their police radio. I'll believe him after I talk to whoever called him."

"You're wasting your time," said Rita. "The alarm company has strict orders to report to Rose every time there's a problem. He tele-phoned me on 'raccoon night' twenty minutes after I hit the panic button."

"Hmmm. I thought I had a way to trip him up."

"He wouldn't be that stupid. Come on, Ben, you've got to find out where he was the afternoon Ron was shot. Force him to give you an alibi. *Then* trip him up."

Wondering how I would go about doing that, I picked up my car at her house and drove home.

Trooper Moody was waiting in my kitchen, out of uniform. He wore heavy boots, work pants, and a commando sweater stretched tight as shrink-wrap around his enormous chest. I liked him better in trooper gray, which promised, however falsely, that he would be constrained by the peacekeeper's oath.

"Who let you in?"

"Jailbird, you've got problems."

He kicked my feet out from under me, picked me off the floor, and threw me a long way into the dining room.

25

I skidded across waxed chestnut and crashed into a heap of chairs. Oliver loomed in the doorway.

They taught us to box like gentlemen in prep school. The navy was in the killing business. The rule at Leavenworth was Destroy. But in all three institutions, a good big man usually beat a good little man. Oliver Moody had me by half a foot and one hundred pounds. If he didn't know all my dirty tricks, he was tough enough to absorb punishment while he puzzled them out. I looked for a weapon.

It had stood on the mantel since the house was built—a heavy brass candlestick made by William White, who had come over on the *Mayflower*. I mapped a route to it, under the dining table, and looked elsewhere before he noticed.

"Don't get up. You just lay there and listen."

"I listen better on my feet."

"Remember what happened last time you got up when I told you not to."

Like yesterday.

"I remember you made me cry in front of my friends."

"Somebody had to teach you little bastards respect."

We were hacking around on a Saturday night—Renny and me and

Scooter and the Butler boys—and suddenly there was the new resident state trooper, staking out his territory with a measured beat of bootheels drumming on the grange-hall porch. He was twenty-five, fresh out of the military police, and knew how to inflict savage pain without leaving a mark.

"Remember what happened to your vehicle?"

Oliver Moody went red. I got ready to roll under the table. But then, to my surprise, he regained control of himself and, instead of bounding into the dining room to kick my head in, whipped a flat, silvery object out of his pocket.

"Recognize this, jailbird?"

"Looks like a TV channel zapper, Ollie," I answered, concentrating on not looking at the candlestick and worrying how hard to hit him with it. I'd wreck my own life if I killed the man. But if I didn't hit him hard enough to knock him cold, Oliver Moody would break my arms and smash my teeth with it at his leisure.

"It's a remote control for a Sony camcorder."

"What?"

"Lets you make videos of yourself."

"So?" *That* was what he had found in Rita's woods. The damned thing had fallen out of its nest on the camcorder. I hadn't noticed it and neither, apparently, had Rose when he got it back in the mail. I didn't like how pleased with himself Ollie looked. "So?" I asked again.

"It's from a camcorder purchased in New York City at Grand Central Camera by a guy named Alex Rose."

"So?"

"Alex Rose is a private detective."

Boy did Ollie look happy. I said, "So?" again.

"Two weeks ago Alex Rose was in your Oldsmobile when I issued you a summons for speeding."

"I remember now. I was showing him a house. But I don't recall introducing you."

"The Mercedes Benz parked in your driveway belonged to Mr. Rose."

"Oh, I get it," I said from the floor. "Rose dropped his remote control while you were giving me a ticket. You found it and ran a license check on his car to find his address in order to return it. And just to be sure it was really his, you went all the way to New York City on your day off to confirm the serial number at the store where he bought it. I'm impressed. Way beyond the call of duty, Ollie. Public service *par excellence*."

"*You* dropped it, jailbird."

"Me?"

"You know where?"

I looked at him like he was nuts.

"*You* dropped it in the woods behind the Long house the night before Mrs. Long's boyfriend got shot."

"You're losing me, Ollie. If the remote control belongs to Alex Rose, wouldn't any normal human being conclude that *Rose* must have dropped it in the woods behind the Long house?"

"Rose was watching the Sox on Lori Match's TV."

Lori Match owned Matchbox, one of the last old-fashioned tourist homes in the area. It was on Church Hill Road, with a discreet neon sign that glowed TOURISTS.

"Rose stayed in Newbury?" I asked. "Stayed the *night?*"

"Never left the house. I noticed the Benz parked there and checked with Lori."

"He told me he was going back to New York."

"Guess he lied."

"So?" I still didn't know what Ollie wanted, but I knew that as soon as I got rid of him, I was going to ask Lori Match where Rose went the next morning.

"So you tell me, Ben."

"Tell you what, Ollie?"

Ollie pulled a black, leather-covered sap from his jeans. "Tell me you went back the next day and shot the boyfriend."

"Are you out of your mind?"

"I didn't hear you, Ben. Tell me again."

"Oh for chrissake, Ollie. It's the 'Nineties. Cops don't beat up white people in their own homes."

"It's my afternoon off. I'm playing poker with some of the boys at the barracks."

I got scared. Ollie may have been stupid, but there was nothing quite as frightening as a bully with a plan.

"I figure it went down like this," he said. "First Rose pays you to videotape his boss's wife screwing around."

"Why would I do that?"

"You're broke. You're behind in your taxes. So you tape 'em screwing—or you try to, 'cause they spot you and call me and you run off in the woods. So Rose says, You screwed up. I won't pay you unless you shoot the guy."

"*What?*"

"You figure, what the hell. The money's good. You don't know the guy. You sneak in the house and steal one of their guns."

"It's got burglar alarms like Fort Knox."

Ollie smiled. "Maybe somebody *gives* you the gun. . . ."

"Who?"

"I'll get to that. . . . Anyhow, you shoot the guy like it's a hunting accident."

"Ollie, go bounce your cockamamie idea on Sergeant Bender. Just don't be surprised when he laughs."

"You want a laugh? I'll give you a laugh." His reptile eyes never left my face as he switched the blackjack from his right hand to his left and reached back into the kitchen and produced a large, two-by-three artist's sketchpad. He flipped the cover, revealing a penciled landscape—a meadow with a split-rail fence. "See this little signature at the bottom of the picture?"

"Can't see that far from the floor, Ollie."

"It says 'Rita Long.' See? 'Rita.' 'Long.' "

"Where'd you get it?"

"Landfill."

"What?"

"Found it in a mini-dumpster of construction garbage. Guess whose?"

"Newbury Society of Artists' ?"

"Longs'."

"Were you picnicking in the dump? Or did someone happen to give you a tip? Like maybe an anonymous tip? Like maybe someone called in the night and heavy-breathed, Check out the Long garbage."

"Check this out, jailbird." He flipped back the landscape and there was the sketch of Ron Pearlman, naked, with skull.

"What's that supposed to be?"

"Chest and legs remind me of the boyfriend who got shot."

"Could be anybody."

"You know what I think?"

"No, Ollie, I don't."

"I think she's bent."

"Mrs. Long?"

"Look at this thing. She's nuts."

I recalled Rita's explanation and my friend the painter's opinion and tried to keep it simple for the man with the blackjack. "The picture isn't finished, Ollie. It's like looking at the frame of a house. House isn't finished until you nail on the shingles, right? She didn't draw his face yet. That's all."

Ollie didn't buy it for a second. He knew a naked man with a fleshless skull when he saw one. And he had strong opinions about the sort of woman who would draw such a picture.

"Nuts. Whack-o. This proves it. I think they had some fun and games. Think it got out of hand. Maybe he hurts her more than she wanted."

"Ollie," I interrupted. "Not everyone's concept of 'fun and games' involves pain."

I might as well have interrupted an avalanche.

"—hurts her more than she wanted," he repeated. "She waits until he turns his back the next day and blows him away."

He sounded so damned sure that even I found myself wondering: Did Rita shoot Ron? Were Rose and Jack Long madly scrambling to keep her out of jail? If you bought her drawing for what it looked like—forget art, forget technique—it raised the awful question: Who knew what was in the woman's head?

"Kind of lets me off the hook, doesn't it?"

"Not if she gave you the gun."

"Where's my fingerprints?"

"You wore gloves."

"No," I said. "Something's wrong here. Ollie, what do you want?"

"I want you as a witness."

"Witness to what?"

"To her screwing her boyfriend. To being weird enough to kill him. What are you protecting her for, unless she paid you to shoot him for her? Cop a plea, Ben. Save yourself."

"You looking for a promotion, Ollie? Is that why you're playing detective?"

"You think I can't move up?"

"It never occurred to me. I thought you liked it here. . . ."

The fear that flickered on his face looked as out of place as a Mc-Donald's on Main Street.

"Jesus Christ," I said. "That's it. The budget." He wasn't stupid, he was desperate, and in his desperation he had surrendered the moral high ground.

I stood up slowly. He watched me, carefully, but made no threatening move.

"The budget?" I asked again. "Right?"

"Goddamned town. Worked here twenty years. Now they want to save a couple of bucks on my house."

I almost felt sympathy for him. Connecticut's budget was a mess, thanks to the recession, the Reagan deficit, and a tax code that had worked wonders in the eighteenth century. The state had cut county funds and the counties were dumping the towns, forcing the towns to slash school programs, ignore potholes, and raise dump fees. Another way to save money was to stop paying for a resident state trooper, hoping that when crime happened the troopers would fan out from the county barracks. Which they would, with all the fine perception of an invading army, many hours after Ollie would have restored order. So, for the sake of some forty-nine thousand dollars a year, some people in Newbury advocated firing Trooper Moody.

It had happened in neighboring towns already. Ollie would lose his town-supported house and be transferred to some godforsaken part of the state where, in his late forties, he would have to start from scratch cowing the natives.

Better—much better—to help the state's attorney crack a big

murder. Get promoted to a nice, air-conditioned office. Up his pay. Increase his pension.

I said, "You haven't shown Bender and Boyce that remote control yet, have you?"

"Not yet."

"Or the picture?"

"I'm still building my case."

"Jesus Christ, Ollie, you're taking a hell of a chance withholding evidence. Isn't it your job to report evidence as you find it? They're the investigators. You're the donkey."

"Screw you."

"You're also so far off base you're in the skybox. Rita Long didn't kill Ron Pearlman. Neither did I."

"Says you."

"We didn't *both* do it."

"The state's attorney says *she* did it. I'd give my left ball to tie you in."

"First you say I killed him for Rose. Then you say *she* killed him. Then you say *I* killed him for her. You can't have it three ways, Ollie. You're just not thinking this through."

Oliver Moody put down the sketchpad and switched his blackjack back to his right hand. "I'm not worried. You'll clear things up for me."

"How you going to explain the bruises?"

"That Oldsmobile of yours is going into a tree. It won't kill you, but you'll be banged real bad."

I hit the floor, rolled under the table, and came up beside the mantel, candlestick at port arms. "I hope you get a desk job out of this, Ollie. You'll have trouble walking when I'm done with your knee."

I saw him calculate the potential cost. Again, he switched hands with the blackjack. This time he reached down and drew his ankle gun. "Put it back, turn around, and face the wall."

"No."

"Ben, I'll kill you."

"In my own house? Out of uniform? I don't think the poker players will cover you quite that far."

I tried to read him while he thought it over, and could not. I began to sense that I had misunderstood him all these years. He was much more dangerous than a bully. He was a sociopath in uniform who needed his badge and gun like I needed air.

The little pistol had such a small bore it looked like it would shoot needles. An assassin's gun. The low-velocity bullet tumbles through the brain. . . . After twenty years, how much could he still hate me for the logging-chain caper? Plenty, I feared. After all, the memory still made *me* smile.

My expression rattled Ollie. I think it began to dawn on him that maybe he wasn't the only crazy in the room. "Ollie," I said, "you can shoot me and wreck your career. Or you can let me help you."

"Why would you help me?"

"We can help each other. Put the gun down. Here. See?" I returned the candlestick to the mantelpiece and faced him with my hands open. "You know damned well I didn't shoot Pearlman. I know Rita didn't. 'Cause I know who did. Just give me a couple of days before you turn in that drawing. I'll give you the killer. Your collar. You take him to the state's attorney."

"Why would you help me?" he asked again.

"We're even." In truth, he still owed me his smile for Renny.

"We're not even."

"Let me tell you, Ollie; when I'm through, you'll be so grateful you'll kiss my ass on the flagpole."

"You mess with me you can kiss your ass goodbye."

"We're getting off to a great start. Want to put down the gun, please?"

He holstered the gun, pocketed his blackjack and strode to the mantel. He snatched up William White's candlestick, twisted it like a paperclip, and threw the ruin on the table.

"Twenty-four hours."

26

The White Birch Inn, Newbury's biker bar, is not as scary inside as the chopped hogs in the parking lot look, because the owner, Wide Greg Wright, is even scarier than *he* looks. Every now and then some busybody petitions the town to shut him down on general principles, but Greg is careful not to give the town cause. He's a firm host. On duty every day from noon opening to two A.M. closing, he saunters among his guests, chatting, smiling, laying a light, friendly hand on men and women alike.

As I entered, an argument broke out at the pinball machine. Greg sauntered over, smiling, finding time to nod hello to me, and asked the tattooed disputants was there a problem. Both men were much taller than Greg, but it developed there was no problem.

I found space at the long bar, ordered a beer, and watched everybody do tequila shots for a while. Eventually Greg came by and asked how I was doing. I told him I wished the house business was half as good as the bar business.

Then I said, "I'm looking for a guy named Alex Rose."

"I tend not to remember names," said Greg.

"I was just talking to Lori Match. Alex Rose stayed at the Matchbox, night before the cookout. Lori said he wandered over here next morning."

Wide Greg looked genuinely surprised. "I don't get much trade from Lori."

"I'm not surprised." Though diagonally across Church Hill Road from the White Birch, the Matchbox's clientele tend to be elderly, middle class, and sedate, the sort of tourists who, when you get stuck behind one during leaf season, make you wish your car was equipped with a laser obliterator.

"Lori said she told Rose about the cookout, but he said he preferred a cool, dark bar. Saturday two weeks ago?"

"I tend not to remember names."

"I showed him a house the day before."

"Oh yeah?"

"The Richardson place. I thought he liked it. But he never got back to me, and I lost his number."

"That's a bitch." Wide Greg motioned the harried bartender. "Give Ben a new beer."

"Cheers. Thanks. Big guy, barrel chest. Looks like he's been around. Expensively dressed. When I saw him he was wearing a jacket with a shooting patch."

"Doesn't ring a bell."

"Damn. I figured cookout day would have been kind of quiet for you."

"They came pouring in once they filled their guts. Fire Department would do a lot better if they'd serve beer."

"Well, you know, family and kids and all that."

"Hey, no skin off my back. I made out like a bandit."

"I put extra salt in the burgers, figured to give you a break."

Wide Greg laughed. "It worked. The beer was flowing like, like beer."

"Yeah, but earlier, while we were still cooking, it must have been pretty empty. I thought you might have noticed a stranger."

"Ben. You see, the thing is, my customers—many of my customers—have made a personal decision to maintain their privacy. They count on me to hold up my end, which is no problem, because I tend not to remember names."

"Wait a minute, Greg. The guy doesn't ride. He's a private detective from New York. He stopped in, from what Lori told me. I'm just curious how long he stayed. "

"A private detective?"

"That's what he told me."

"In my place?"

"I guess they need a drink like anybody else, right?"

"Son of a bitch. I don't like that. I don't like that at all. Wha'd you say his name was?"

"Alex Rose. Expensive clothes. Big guy. Face like a boxer."

Wide Greg chuckled to himself and shook his head ruefully. "I'll be damned."

"Did he ask questions?"

"His name isn't Alex Rose."

"What do you mean?"

"Al *De*Rose. French name, he said."

"He called himself *Al DeRose?*"

"Yeah. He rides down in New York."

"He's got a bike?"

"Yeah. Showed me pictures. Custom-built Harley looked like it ran forty thousand dollars."

"You sure it wasn't just a picture?"

"No. He fit right in. Talking with a bunch of the guys. He had a ball. Drank your cousin Pink under the bar."

"Wait a minute."

Something didn't compute. Drinking Pinkerton Chevalley under the bar would take many, many hours. But I had seen Pink at the cookout around two o'clock—stone sober. While Lori Match told me that Rose had read the morning papers on her porch until the White Birch opened at noon.

"Was he in and out?"

"Never left. Opened the joint and shut the joint. Hell of a guy. But I'll tell you one thing, Ben, I just don't see Al DeRose as homeowner, if you know what I mean."

"Homeowner?"

"You said you was showing him houses—"

"Wait, wait, wait. Just bear with me a moment. You say he came at noon and stayed all day until two in the morning?"

"He left about midnight, actually. Had a burger and a pot of coffee for the road, fired up that big Benz, and outta here. 'Scuze me a minute."

Wide Greg homed in on a conversation which had been heating up down the bar and walked someone to the door. I couldn't believe it, but believe it I had to. My prime suspect had a perfect alibi. No way he could have shot Ron Pearlman.

Wide Greg returned.

"I've been thinking about what you said about Al DeRose being a P.I. If he is, he was on vacation. The man never shut up long enough to ask any questions." He furrowed his big flat forehead, thinking back. A smile revealed a mouth of perfect teeth—unusual in a biker turned bar owner. "Hell of a good day. Funny how one guy will really perk a place up. Not that we usually need perking."

I was quietly going nuts. This made no sense at all. Why had Rose stayed overnight in Newbury? Why had he spent the day in the biker bar? Why, when we spoke on the phone that day, did he not mention he was right around the corner in Newbury?

"Did Rose make any phone calls?"

"Oh yeah. The man was wired like NASA. Beeper. Cell phone. Of course, the cell phone didn't work down here the bottom of the hill. Kept asking for change—checking in with his answering machine."

27

Hurrying up Church Hill Road, heading home from the White Birch to inform Trooper Ollie that Alex Rose was our man, I had to admit I had almost believed that Rose owned a custom-built Harley-Davidson motorcycle. I had even believed that he rode under the *nom d'asphalt* Al DeRose. (There is a gold-plated gang of rich New Yorkers who cruise in the mythic wake of Malcolm Forbes.) But I stopped believing when I learned about the phones. Last time *I* spent fourteen hours in a bar, I did not sully the atmosphere by calling my machine for messages; might as well take your tax returns to the movies. Alex Rose stood by to help the killer.

Okay. Alex Rose hadn't shot Ron Pearlman personally. But he had waited close by to back up a professional killer he had hired on Jack Long's orders. Hands-on management, as it were. If the murderer got in trouble, Rose was there to help him out. Maybe even provide the getaway.

I kept telling myself that. It sounded good at first. But the more I repeated it, the more I felt like one of those investors who tries to predict the bond market by the charts. They always come up with some logical-sounding reason for their choice. All it requires is a leap of faith.

I finally recognized my leap of faith. My logic was impeccable, so long as I assumed Alex Rose was stupid.

If *I* accepted a job from Jack Long to kill Ron Pearlman, would *I* take the risk of hiring somebody else and then hang around Newbury until the job was done? No, I would not. And neither would Alex Rose. If he or I were cold-blooded enough to accept the job, we would have the good sense to avoid a conspiracy by doing the deed ourselves.

That cleared that up.

Except why, if Rose didn't need an alibi, did he go to the trouble of establishing an alibi? No human being—with the exception of a brain-dead Jervis, or Wide Greg, who owned the joint—would voluntarily spend an entire day in the White Birch Inn. Why had he stayed? All day? All night? Why do business by beeper and pay phone?

Attaining the crest of Church Hill, I caught my breath, waiting to cross Main Street. On the other side was the Yankee Drover. Now there was a bar to spend the day in. Quiet. Decent food. Women wandering in without tattooed escorts. High on the ridge line of Main Street, a great place to use a cellular phone. Why hadn't Rose just come up the hill and made his calls from a nice cozy booth that enjoyed easy access to the bar and crystal-clear reception?

A passing car beeped. I waved first, looked second. Vicky McLachlan, of all people, a little wave, a cloud of chestnut hair, a blurred smile, and gone. Made me feel good.

Of course cell-phone calls were expensive: charged by the minute, incoming as well as outgoing. But guys with an S-class Mercedes don't count pennies. . . . Unless, of course, of course, of course, he did not want telephone calls recorded incoming on his cell-phone bill.

Rose was Jack Long's gofer. He was loyal and obedient, but not stupid. What if he had been ordered to stand by? What if his *boss* ordered him to stand by in Newbury? What if he is sort of innocent? What if he suspects a killing might be on Long's agenda? He obeys orders. He stands by. But he covers his ass at the White Birch— alibi—*and* an excuse to his boss: Sorry, boss. The cell phone musta been out of range. I checked my machine in New York in case you tried to call me. Out of range, in case an incriminating call had come in: Help, help, the boss needs help. But, no cell phone. Rose erases his answering machine and presents a bar owner and several motorcycle gangs as witnesses he was indoors all day minding his own business.

Right.

And what would happen if I braced him and asked, Long hired his own killer, didn't he? You were afraid he'd involve you if something went wrong. The private detective would laugh in my face: Successful businessmen don't hire killers.

To which I might add, Especially businessmen who hate partners.

I knocked on Scooter's back door. Eleanor answered and told me he was sneaking a cigarette behind the barn. I found him sitting on the woodpile, gazing dreamily at the smoke. It was nearly dark, the night coming on cold.

"Can I see your files?"

"What files?"

"Press releases for the issue before last."

"Which ones?"

"Could I just see them without telling you which ones?"

We had been neighbors since we were born. There are things I don't like about him—I think he's a snob, and I think he occasionally abuses the power his newspaper gives him—and I'm sure there are things he dislikes about me. But in the narrow way he looks at the world, I'm near the middle of the picture. Scooter could assume that when the time came fifty years from now that he needed an iron lung to sneak a smoke behind the barn, I'd squeeze my wheelchair through the hedge to pass the time.

"What's in it for me?"

"I don't know. You want to scoop the dailies?"

"Not really," he answered after a moment's reflection. "But it would be nice to know I could. . . . Come on, I'll walk you over to the office."

Scooter's father had computerized the *Clarion* while the *Daily News* and the *New York Times* were still setting linotype. When I was in prep school his office was already entirely modern, even though the terminals sat on scarred wooden desks that reeked of ink. By now they were in third or fourth generation. Still hard to believe, as the *Clarion*'s quaint barn-red clapboard building with its white shutters and double-hung windows looked more like a used bookstore than a newspaper office. As we entered the cozy wooden foyer, I could feel the floor trembling from the big presses in the reinforced concrete press room below.

"Paper to bed?"

"Grand Union flyers," said the publisher, leading me into the editor's room. "Tell me who wrote the story and I'll point you to their files for that issue."

"You did."

Scooter grinned. "I thought so. You're looking up Jack Long, aren't you?"

"Do I have to answer that?"

"There's the file. Use my desk. Put it back where you found it. Coffee down below. Charley'll get it for you."

The White House press releases were written in a breathless style preceded by a stern warning not to release the information early. The embargo lent importance, I supposed, to the banal announcement that the President had hosted a party of business leaders, as they were called, in the Rose Garden. There were photographs of a striped luncheon canopy and a whole slew of pictures of Jack Long shaking the man's hand. The release appeared to have been forwarded to each of the shakee's local newspapers. Obviously, editors of the *New York Times* had not gathered around it boggle-eyed, but here in Newbury, Scooter got to fill damn near a full page with pictures and text.

A second release relayed the news that Jack Long had dined that same evening with a group dubbed "the President's closest advisors." It included an informal photograph of Long surrounded by bright young men and women in sweatshirts watching television in a book-lined study, while eating—I swear this is true—TV dinners on trays. It did not say what they were watching. Nonetheless, I almost broke a finger in my haste to dial the contact number on the cover sheet.

"P.R.," answered the person at the White House.

"Donald Dodson, please," I asked, naming the contact listed.

"Dodson here."

"Mr. Dodson, I'm Scooter MacKay of the Newbury, Connecticut, *Clarion*. We're writing another story about a visit to the President two Saturdays ago."

"Got a file number on that release?" Dodson interrupted. I gave it to him. He got back on the phone. "Who we talking about here?"

"Jack Long. Supper with the close advisors."

"Right."

"They're watching TV."

"Yeah?"

"What are they watching?"

"Huh?"

"What show?"

"You mean what are they watching on TV?"

"You didn't say in the release."

"Gee, I don't know."

"Our readers might wonder why Mr. Long went all the way to Washington, D.C., to watch television."

"Well, it was something political, you can be damned sure. People don't sit around here watching sitcoms. Hang on, I'll suss it out."

I listened to the minutes tick by on Scooter's phone bill. If it wasn't the Larry King show, I would walk up to Main Street and ask Oliver Moody to throw me in front of a truck.

"Hi. Sorry it took so long. I had to find what time they were watching."

"What time?"

"The supper ran from about nine to midnight."

"That late? What are they watching?"

"A special edition of 'Larry King Live.' "

"Are you sure?"

"Yes."

"Absolutely sure?"

"Yeah, you see, Zack Bowen was King's guest that night. The

group watched, and then Zack returned from the studio and joined them for brandy and coffee—well, say 'dessert' if you don't mind. I'm sure it was dessert."

"How'd Bowen do on Larry King's show?"

"Massacred him. King didn't know if he was coming or going."

"Thank you very, very much."

"Listen, don't quote me on that 'massacred' thing. Your Mr. Long attended a private supper, if you know what I mean. Totally off the record. No point in offending Mr. King just because he wasn't so sharp that night, is there?"

Dodson laughed. And I laughed and promised him that the *Clarion* would never betray a confidence. "By the way, what went on between lunch and supper?"

"What do you mean?"

"Well, Mr. Long lunched with the President and supped with his advisors. What did he do in between?"

"It looks to me like he went back to his hotel and changed."

"How do you figure that?"

"In the photos I'm holding he's wearing a different tie at supper."

I laughed again. "Boy, you'd make a great detective." (Though hardly in the class of my Great-aunt Connie, who, perched beside me alert as a bluejay on our drive to Renny's widow, had fancied there might be a connection between the two killings.)

I wasn't surprised I had missed the change in neckties. The laughs had come hard and brittle. I was getting cold inside.

"Anything else?"

"Yes, one question: What was the President's schedule after lunch?"

"You realize, Mr. Scooter, that I can only give you his official schedule."

"I just want to know what time he left lunch."

"Oh, that's easy. The President was outta there by twelve-twenty."

"Twenty after twelve. Did the guests stay much longer?"

"They were free to go once he said goodbye. Of course usually they hang around until the Marines frog march them to the door. Don't—"

"I won't," I promised, and hung up.

Colder still, I had one more question for one more person.

After dark was a hell of a time to call on Gwen Jervis. I would have preferred driving a tank instead of the Olds, but I didn't have one. And a bulletproof vest instead of down, but I didn't have one of those either. When I reached the end of the long dark trail through the woods, I turned on the interior light, kept both hands in plain view on the steering wheel, and parked slowly beside Gwen's pickup truck.

A bright light on a pole in the center of the trailer circle switched on. The woods beyond its glare were black. I got out slowly, sure I was being watched, slowly climbed the wooden steps to Gwen's door, and knocked.

She opened it and stood there swaying drunkenly. It took her a moment to recognize me, and when she did she gave me a big smile and ran a hand through her tangled hair. "I knew you'd be back."

"I got a question."

"The answer is No. At least not for a long while. I got a way to go before I forget him."

Saying that that wasn't what I had come for didn't seem like a good idea. So I said, "Can I ask you a favor then?"

"Try."

"Tell me who Renny's airplane customers were."

"The cat doctor was the main one."

"Cat doctor? A vet?"

"No, the doctor with a cat."

"Right. Danbury–Block Island. Who else?"

"A stockbroker in Roxbury. Renny landed right in his back yard. And a guy who had horses over in Pawling. What was his name? Packard, something, Packards. Hey, you want to come in?"

"Who else?"

"The new guy in the Castle. What's his name? You know, the guy whose wife's boyfriend you found. The one who got shot."

I should have listened to Connie.

"Hey, why you want to know?"

I was ready to kill, but I didn't want Gwen doing it for me, so with my last ounce of rationality I said, "Who else? Who else did Renny fly?"

"Oh, jeez, I don't know, Ben. Oh, yeah, he flew Scooter to a convention once." She laughed. "Renny said Scooter puked in a thunderstorm. Poor Scooter. Made Renny promise he wouldn't tell. Never could do anything right."

"Good hunter," I said, easing toward the car.

"Oh yes, now that you mention it. The man was a hunter. But you know what?"

"What?"

"Hey, where you going?"

"I gotta go."

"Really?" She followed me down the steps. "You know what about Scooter? He was a lousy shot. Everybody said so. But he got so close it didn't matter. Pink Chevalley told me Scooter could have left his bullets home and clubbed them to death. Where you going?"

"Gotta go, Gwen. Talk to you soon."

"Man, you look weird tonight."

"Right." I started the Olds.

"Jeez, you're coming down with something." She touched my cheek. "You got a fever."

"Yeah, I'm hot."

"Well, you take care. Get into bed or something. You still screwing the politician?"

"Just friends."

"Hey, thanks for coming out to see me. . . . Screwed up lonely as hell out here some nights. You got no idea how crazy it gets."

I said I did and drove home, counting for the hundredth time the hours it took to travel from Washington, D.C., to Newbury, Connecticut, roundtrip.

28

One o'clock shuttle hits LaGuardia Airport before two. Fifty minutes to find Renny and take off in his rented plane. Three-thirty, land on Al Bell's field. Shoot Renny. You are now the only person in the world who knows you are in Newbury.

Rev up the plane and run it slow into a tree. Scatter a plastic bag of cocaine, indicting a kid from the wrong side of town for drug smuggling. Drive down Morris Mountain in Renny's Camaro. Park behind the barn I parked behind and sneak into your own house. Take your wife's gun, wait for her boyfriend, shoot him in the back. Put back the gun and get Renny's car before Rita gets home at four-thirty. Drive two hours to LaGuardia Airport, where you catch the seven o'clock shuttle to Washington—paying cash again—and arrive in Washington in time to shower and change in your hotel and return to the White House for TV dinners with the President's men.

I stopped at Renny's garage and dialed the pay phone by the light of the Chevalley Enterprises sign. Alex Rose probably slipped in here with the forty thousand in cash to finish the job Long had started on Renny's reputation. Boss didn't tell him why, just told him, Do it, and he did it.

The Plainfield state police barracks duty officer told me Trooper

Boyce had gone home. I found her card in my wallet and called her there. The little boy answered.

"This is Mr. Abbott. May I speak with your mother?"

He dropped the phone on something hard and yelled, "Mommy!"

Before I could say, "I know how Long killed Ron Pearlman," she said, "I can't talk to you, Ben. I've been cited for fraternizing with a convicted felon."

"You're investigating a murder."

"It's political. It's bull. But until I go through a hearing it's a blot on my record. My lawyer says I can't talk to you."

"Wait. What rooms did you find wiretaps in, in Long's house?"

"Goodbye, Ben. Sergeant Bender's handling the case."

"Tell him he'll find Renny's car at LaGuardia Airport."

She had already hung up on me.

I considered calling Bender but decided not to. He was probably the one who had filed the complaint. Fine. I didn't really want their help anyway.

I continued driving home, and when I was high enough up Church Hill, I called a number I had entered somewhat optimistically in the car phone's memory.

Rita answered sleepily. I said, "Go to the guest room where you made love with Ron. I'll call you right back."

"Why?"

I hung up, gave her a moment to walk to the guest room, and dialed again.

"Why?" she started to ask, and I cut her off.

"Jack killed Ron."

"Can you can prove it?"

"I'm waiting on one more piece. Day after tomorrow I can tell the cops."

Jack Long called me nine o'clock the next morning.

"Ben? Jack Long. Hope this isn't too early."

"At my desk, paying bills." Barefaced lie: I'd been staring at the telephone since seven, praying that Alex Rose still checked the bugs he had installed for the Rita-Ron gaieties. "Say, how'd you make out with Harkin and Locke?"

"No sweat. . . . Listen, this might sound a little strange, Ben."

"Try me."

"Rita and I don't think we can go on living in that house—because of everything that happened there. Do you understand what I'm saying?"

"Sounds like you're putting it on the market."

"We are. We'd like to give you an exclusive but we feel obligated to Fred Gleason."

"Understood."

"We'd like you to share an exclusive."

"Let me think about that. I'll have to talk to Fred."

"You do that. In the meantime, we're going to need a place to live. Alex Rose told me about an old estate you showed him."

"The Richardson place."

"Sounds interesting."

"Jack, it's a nice house, but it's not a thirty-seven-room stone mansion on a hundred acres."

"Rita and I want to downscale a little. Maybe we need a simpler life. The kind of place we could manage alone."

"The Richardson place needs gardeners."

"Gardeners are fine. I just don't want a house full of live-in help, if you know what I mean."

"Would you like to see it?"

"How about this afternoon? Around three?"

"The light's real pretty around three."

He arrived at my office at ten after. To my surprise, he had brought Alex Rose. Rose was back in his shooting costume. Long wore a windbreaker and a baseball cap that almost made him look local. Both men looked nervous.

"Sorry I'm late. Damned pickup truck almost ran us off the road."

"Where's Rita?"

"I wanted to look myself first."

I glanced at Alex Rose, and Long said, "We had stuff to discuss, so we drove up together. You want to wait here, Al?"

"I don't care."

"You can grab a beer at the Drover," I said. "Or ride along. Maybe we can find you a house too."

"Yeah, right, me in the country. What the hell, I'll come along. If it's okay with you, Mr. Long?"

Long replied, "Suit yourself," as if he couldn't have cared less.

We got into my car, Rose scrunched up in the back seat, Long in front beside me. Alison Mealy careened into the drive on her bike. "Ben!"

"Catch you later."

"They're giving a special computer course at school. Can I take it?"

"Sure. If it's okay with your mom."

"It's seventy bucks."

"We'll talk. Later."

"Hey kid?" It was Rose, lowering his window. "Check this out." He passed her his electronic notebook.

"Oh, wow!" She sank cross-legged on the lawn, instantly immersed. Rose grinned until he saw Long shoot him a dark look. Rose reached out the window. "Sorry, kid. I better take it back now. I got stuff on it."

Alison's face fell.

"Hey, I'll mail you one. One you can keep."

She handed it back, with a wary look.

"Don't worry, I'll Fed Ex it. It'll get here the day after tomorrow."

"Let's go," said Long, and I began to wonder whether the two men might have different agendas. As I pulled onto Main Street, they checked the traffic.

"You guys okay?"

"Yeah," said Long. "I swear that damn truck was following us. Gone now, looks like."

"I'll watch for him," said Rose.

There were no pickup trucks on my agenda. I figured they'd annoyed a drunk who'd taken a dislike to Rose's Mercedes. The road was clear at the edge of town. I hit the gas and ran it up to ninety. "Consider him lost."

"You're going to get another ticket." Rose chuckled.

"Not today," I said, belatedly draping the radar detector from the rearview mirror. In a few short minutes we reached Academy, headed down it a little more sedately, and onto Richardson Street. It hadn't rained for a week, and we churned up a huge dust cloud. The maples had turned a soft amber gold. If I didn't haul some firewood out of here soon, I'd be chainsawing in the snow.

"This used to all be Richardson land, but it's been sold off. The house has six acres, with another fourteen available."

"Think I could buy what's been sold off?" Jack asked. "I don't want some son of a bitch building in my front yard— Jesus, look at that tree. What is that, Ben?"

"Shagbark hickory."

"I want that."

"Comes with the hayfield."

He gazed around appreciatively. "The views aren't as good as ours, but damn, this is a nice piece of land."

"Some people say buy the horizon, some say build your own view."

"Yeah, I could move my barns out here. Hey Al, isn't this great?"

Al Rose was peering out the back window, trying to see through the dust cloud. I'd been watching too, but I had not seen any pickups.

"Here we go."

"Oh wow! This is great. Look at that house!"

"Adlai Stevenson used to visit his mistress here."

"Adlai Stevenson had a mistress?"

"So they say. Her estate was out there, through the sycamores."

"How close?"

"Quite a ways. We're all alone here."

We got out of the car. I pulled out my keys.

"There's a beautiful brick keeping room that overlooks the skating pond. I swear on a winter day you can still smell the hot cocoa."

"Ben, we gotta talk."

Long was watching me intently. Rose had wandered back toward the road, still watching for the phantom pickup truck.

"You're not going to make a bid without seeing the inside, are you?"

Jack called, "Al, why don't you wait in the car? Ben's going to show me the back of the house."

"You sure?"

"Yeah, wait here. Come on, Ben, show me the skating pond."

We walked up the overgrown brick front walk. Laid in a herringbone pattern, barely detectable through the grass in the cracks, it split at the front steps and continued around both sides of the house. I forged ahead to the left-hand path and led Jack Long between the sunroom and the overgrown rose gardens. "Tell Rita there's probably old varieties growing here you couldn't buy today. But you see what I mean about a gardener."

"Sure."

We continued around behind the house and stopped on a slate terrace between the keeping room and the silted-up skating pond.

"That used to be the tennis court." I indicated to the right. "With the cherry tree in it."

"Ben, let's talk."

"All right, Jack, we'll talk. I gotta be frank."

"I agree. Cut the bull."

"I represent the estate."

"What? What estate?"

"Ellie Richardson's estate. Her heirs have no interest in this land. They just want some money. So I'm really representing you, as the buyer, in that I have a chance to sell you property at a very reasonable price, recession or no recession."

"Don't fuck with me, kid! And don't try your head games on me. We gotta talk. And you know damned well what we gotta talk about."

I turned away from him and walked closer to the house. He caught up and took my arm. "You know, Ben, you do a lot of deals, you never know which one's going to bring you down. You don't even think about it. You can't operate if you think that way, right? You know what I'm talking about, you've been there."

"Where?"

"Taking chances."

"Yeah, I've been there."

"All those balls in the air—one falls, so what? You toss another. Then one day—no different than any other day—you reach for another and it's not there. . . . I still cannot believe that of all the deals I cut, Ron Pearlman's factory would bring me down. If you told me that two years ago, I'd have laughed in your face. You know what I mean?"

"I know one thing, Jack. When businessmen spout philosophy, they're through. You drop the ball, you pay the penalty."

"You do what you have to do," Jack shot back. "Assholes pay the penalty. Let's talk."

"About what? Shooting your partner in the back?"

"He was fucking my wife."

"Bull. *I* would have shot him for that. Or maybe I would have just waited for her to get tired of him in hopes she'd come home. But that's not why *you* killed him."

"Oh yeah? Why'd I kill him?"

"The payout. Like you just said, the deal was bringing you down. You didn't have the money you owed him."

"So what do you care? I did what I had to do."

"You left your wife holding the bag."

"She'll get off. That'll be the end of it. Rita's tough. She can handle a trial. So, what do you want?"

"We don't have anything to talk about. You killed my cousin to cover your tracks."

"For crissake, I didn't know he was your cousin. I didn't know you. He was just a pilot, for crissake. Dime a dozen. Hey, I'm not saying things didn't get out of hand. They got out of hand. That's why I'm explaining to you. I'll make sure his family's taken care of. Scholarships for the children, you name it. Set up trusts. You'll be the executor. And it goes without saying, name your own price too. . . . I assume you're the only one who's put this together, right?"

"Rita has a fair idea of what you did."

"I'll deal with Rita."

I looked at him. He looked me straight in the eye. "Last chance, Ben. What do you want me to do?"

All I wanted him to do was say out loud that he had murdered Ron Pearlman and Renny Chevalley, and he had pretty much done that.

"Hey, I'm not a monster. I just told you, things got out of hand. One crazy step led to another."

"The hell it did. You planned every step."

"You do what you have to do."

"Renny Chevalley was a good man."

Long reached into his windbreaker and came up with a gun. Surprise, surprise. Then around the house there came a real surprise—Alex Rose running flat out. "Hey, you said you were going to pay him off. What are you doing with a gun?"

I said, "He can't pay me off."

"Think that through, Ben. The man's holding a gun. Hear him out. Mr. Long, this is getting out of hand."

"Wait in the car."

A red haze had been working up and down in front of my eyes since yesterday. It rose now at Rose's "out-of-hand" remark, blindingly. The gardens, the house, Rose and Long, all but disappeared. I actually considered trying to take the gun from him. Long tucked it closer to his body.

"Come on, Ben. You're a player. You're one of us. Isn't there any way we can work this out?"

"Stick the gun in your mouth, pull the trigger, I'll consider us even."

"Go wait in the car," Long said to Rose.

"Mr. Long, you're making a mistake."

"I'm only talking to him. Go wait in the car."

Rose shifted from foot to foot like a worried bear.

"Now!" Long's voice cut like a whip.

Rose stepped back. "Okay. I'll wait. See you guys in a minute." As he turned, he said, "Jesus Christ."

Oliver Moody, who had finally heard enough, stepped out of the keeping room, both hands wrapped around his automatic. In full uniform and Smokey Bear hat, he looked nine feet tall.

I had neglected to warn Ollie that Jack Long had been a Marine. While Ollie, who should have known better, made the mistake of thinking rich men were soft. Long caught him flat-footed.

He launched his burly frame into a flying leap, hit the terrace rolling, and came up shooting with remarkable accuracy. The state trooper got off a round that went wild as he pitched forward, blood spraying from his neck.

"Jesus!" yelled Rose. "You shot a cop."

I was stunned. Oliver Moody on the ground was an impossible sight.

"You shot a cop," Rose yelled, his voice rising in panic. "You're crazy. You shot a cop."

"That didn't happen," said Long, eyeing me as he knelt coolly and picked up Oliver's pistol. "What happened was a shootout between our resident state trooper and his old enemy, the realtor convict. Tragic how these country feuds turn bloody. . . ." He turned to me with the smile of a man who knew that finally, a very messy situation would be contained. "Sorry about this, Ben. Like he said, it's really gotten out of hand."

I looked to Rose. No help there. He wasn't smiling, but he looked relieved. Long's story would sell if they could just iron out a few details. Drive my car back to my house. Get in their car when no one was looking. And drive away.

Long aimed Ollie's gun at me. I felt my legs shaking and couldn't stop them. "I thought you hate partners, Jack."

"You lost me there, Ben."

"You kill me and you've formed a lifelong partnership with your tame detective. He'll have this on you forever."

"Bullshit," said Rose.

"No problem," Long agreed. "Al got caught in the crossfire." He raised Oliver's gun and it boomed like a cannon, twice.

29

Long's first shot surprised me almost as much as it did Rose, whose jaw dropped like a brick when the bullet sent him reeling backward. The second shot was a little wide, tearing bloodily through the detective's arm and spinning his body in a complete circle before it landed. I dove on top of Oliver Moody.

I would have much preferred to run Long's gears with my pocketknife, but the distance between us was too great to reach him before he blew me to pieces with Oliver's sidearm. So it was the trooper's ankle gun or nothing, provided I could extract it from the holster and figure out how to disengage the safety, very quickly.

I got one break. Long mistakenly assumed I was hiding behind Oliver's body. He took a second to step closer and aim, and in that time I got my hand up Oliver's pants leg and around the Beretta, before Long tumbled. He snapped a shot. The slug whanged slate chips in my face, and then I was jerking on the trigger.

At Leavenworth NRA chapter meetings, all members agreed: Shoot. Shoot. Shoot. Don't ask. Don't aim. Just keep shooting. My mentors would have been proud. I figured out the safety and pulled the trigger over and over and over again. Long must have felt like he was back on his helicopter over Viet Cong territory. Bullets sprayed all around him. He threw his hands up as if to shield his face, and one of my shots finally caught him in the arm. He cried out, turned, and ran.

I grabbed my knife, started after him, slipped on Ollie's blood, and fell on my face. Before I could get to my feet, Jack Long was around the house with a twenty-yard lead. I charged after him, rounded the house, and saw him running for my car. Suddenly he skidded to a stop as a rusty '79 Ford pickup burst between the hedges that screened the road and roared up the rutted drive.

Jack Long ran. The pickup truck veered, cut him off, hit him with an enormously loud *boom,* and threw him thirty feet across the weed-strewn parking lot.

Long hit the ground, rolling like a log. The truck spun on a dime, spewing dust and gravel. Long tried to stand, dragging himself up on one knee, throwing up his arms and screaming in terror as the truck knocked him down again and ran him over. Red brake lights flared, then backup whites, and it backed on top of him and stopped.

Gwen Jervis jumped out. Ignoring me watching from the corner of the sunroom, she knelt under the truck and gazed silently into Long's face.

I heard a deep and desperate cry from the back of the house, an angry plea. *"Ben!"*

I ran back to Ollie. Blood spurting, he struggled to stand. I gentled him down in my arms, found a terrible gouge in his massive neck, and tried to squeeze it shut.

My fingers kept slipping on his blood. I took off my jacket. The tweed cloth was too rough. I pulled off my sweater and jammed the smoother wool into the wound.

Movement. I looked up.

"What—"

"Saw your dust." Gwen Jervis, who had not been quite as drunk as I had thought the night before, took in the scene with a cold glance.

"Grab the phone in my car. Call for an ambulance."

Instead, Gwen knelt. "Let me look. . . . I'll do him, you call." Her hands were shaking, but they clamped surely on the wound. "Make it two ambulances. There's a guy out front got run over by a pickup truck."

There was dead calm in her eyes. "Fell right under my wheels. Twice."

I ran to my car and telephoned 911.

Thirty feet down the drive, Jack Long sprawled under Gwen's truck like a scarecrow blown off its pole. Newbury answered. I told them they had better bring the Morrisville and Frenchtown ambulances too. Then I knelt for a closer look at Long. His eyes flickered with light for a second, pale, dim, and fading fast.

The wheels had crushed his chest. His voice bubbled thin and bloody. "Why'd she run me over?" he asked. He looked bewildered.

I told him she did what she had to do and went back to help with Oliver.

The body count had dropped a full basis point in my absence. Alex Rose was sitting up. Ever cautious, the detective had worn a bulletproof vest under his fancy shooting jacket. His arm was going to hurt a long time, as were his cracked ribs, but he was not dead. In fact, he was hoarsely gasping a story he thought we ought to present to the cops. I told him to make up his own story.

"Hey, I didn't know he offed Ron."

"Not a clue?"

"Okay, so maybe I suspected, but that's not the same as knowing."

Gwen looked over, with Ollie's blood on her face. "Ask him about Renny."

"I was about to."

"I didn't know anything about Renny."

"Didn't you wonder why Jack told you to stash forty grand in Renny's closet?"

"I didn't do that. I swear it. Jack must have."

I exchanged a look with Gwen. We must have looked dubious, because Rose protested indignantly, again. "I never touched the money." Too indignantly, I thought. So did Gwen.

"Then what are you lying about?" she asked.

Rose thought a moment. We heard a siren on the wind. "Jack asked me to buy him a few grams of coke. That's all I did."

"And never made the connection with the coke in Renny's plane?"

"Not right away. . . . I'm sorry. There was nothing I could have changed. The man was running his own program."

I looked at Gwen, who shrugged. As far as she was concerned, Alex Rose was nothing.

"And you just kept hoping it would all work out?"

"Come on, Rita woulda beat it."

I wondered whether Rose would have come to Rita's defense when the trial went against her. A waste of breath to ask.

"How'd Jack get your balls in his pocket?"

"Goddamned economy. In 1989 my outfit billed four million. 'Ninety-one, four hundred thousand. Last year I would have gone Chapter Eleven without my LTS retainer."

The Newbury volunteer ambulance arrived first, Danny Butler driving, Cathy Chevalley the nurse. Both had done trauma courses, but they were afraid to move Ollie, so they radioed for the Life Star helicopter, which lifted him out before dark. By then we had a lot of bad-tempered state police on the Richardson place, including Bender and Boyce, who were clearly not talking to each other.

Gwen answered their questions with practiced ease, repeating simply that she had just come driving down Richardson Street, intending to pick apples from the abandoned orchard, and this guy ran out in front of her truck. "Hit him, threw him, and ran over the poor bastard." She probed the hole between her teeth and reflected, "It was a terrible experience."

The cops looked at me. "That what you saw?"

I wasn't a liar. Telling the truth was the foundation of the "Puritan claptrap" that Ira Roth had accused my "crazy Aunt Connie" of drumming into me. What Ira hadn't understood was the beauty of principle: the sheer simplicity that swept aside ambivalence and doubt. Connie taught me never to ask, Should I tell the truth?; she taught me that I must.

I looked at Gwen, who was as alone and fearless as a hawk that soared on instinct. She gazed back, asking nothing.

"What did you see, Ben?"

Like I told Jack Long, you drop the ball, you pay the penalty. I had made mistakes. I had paid the price. I paid for principle—paid willingly, even gladly. Clean slate, I had told Ira, though in my heart, at least, I had to wonder if I had spent coin that wasn't only mine.

"Ben?"

"I had my hands full with Trooper Moody. I thought he was a goner until Gwen came running and got the bleeding stopped." (Something else Connie taught me: If a job's worth doing, it's worth doing right.)

A flinty-eyed state police captain who had battled Jervises his entire career asked dryly, "You've had experience with gunshot wounds, Gwen?"

"Hunting accidents," Gwen confessed.

Dark set in, and we all adjourned to Town Hall, where the police set up a temporary HQ. The state's attorney himself came down from the county seat, and he was clearly less interested in Gwen's story than mine. Ollie had choked out a statement on the flight to the hospital, confirming the essence of Jack Long's confession. Now he was tubed and trached in Recovery, and his doctors would permit no more interviews until tomorrow. Alex Rose had either been on the wrong side of the house or unconscious in the grass. That left me as the state's attorney's best witness to the events that appeared to turn his case against Rita Long into low comedy.

He was not a happy man. Nor was he pleased when Ira Roth bustled in in full three-piece regalia, assuring me *sotto voce* he was working *pro bono*.

The state's attorney said, "Let me get this straight. This man claims—"

"My client asserts."

"Your client asserts that Jack Long shot Ron Pearlman in order to nullify a contract that would have ruined him financially. He further claims—asserts—that to maintain the illusion that he was in Washington, D.C., all day of the murder, Jack Long shot your client's cousin, Renny Chevalley, the pilot who flew him to Newbury, and made it look like a drug deal gone bad."

"Where'd the coke come from?" asked Sergeant Bender.

"Certainly not from my client."

"Since he knows so goddamned much about this case, could your client possibly assist us in our inquiries?"

"He'd be delighted, if he could. But how could he possibly know about cocaine? He had had only a passing acquaintance with Mr. Long at what I recall was a land trust meeting. Is that right, Ben?"

"That's right. We shook hands."

"Do you recall whether Mr. Long had bags of cocaine with him at the land trust meeting?"

"Oh for chrissake, Ira!"

"Point being, Mister State's Attorney," Ira answered his old foe, "you're asking the wrong man. Just as you're trying to stampede a grand jury into indicting the wrong woman."

"Your other client."

"If I didn't know better, I'd fear that the rule of law was under siege in Plainfield."

"Goddammit!"

"Give thanks to Ben Abbott, Counselor. Better now than getting laughed out of court. And he clears up the Chevalley mystery, on which your people have not distinguished themselves, wouldn't you say?" He turned to me without even asking the state's attorney's or the police's permission, and said, "Ben, may I offer you a lift to your car?"

"It's impounded," growled Marian Boyce. "I'll drive him."

Ira said, "Can I trust you, Trooper, not to intimidate my client while you have him alone in your automobile?"

"You have my word," said Marian, and turning to Bender, she asked, "Do I have your permission?"

"Yeah, yeah, yeah."

"In writing."

"Where to?" said Marian, once we were in her car.

"The Castle."

"I thought so, Mr. Romantic."

"Does she know yet?"

"I told them to hold off. You'd tell her."

The front door was open, the house dark but for a single light atop the turret. I made my way to the stairs by the glow of appliance clocks, smoke detectors, and security code pads. I climbed, footsteps echoing. Rita was on top, in the observation nest, seated at the little table and staring out at the night. Beside her sat a bottle of champagne on ice and two empty glasses. An Ithaca Deerslayer lay across her lap, sister to the weapon that had killed Ron Pearlman.

"Jack?" she asked as I reached the top of the stairs.

"Ben."

Her shoulders sagged. "Did you kill him?"

"No. Renny's girlfriend ran him over with her truck."

"Did he suffer?"

I recalled his scream. "Briefly."

"He deserved to."

"Yeah, right. What's the gun for?"

"He said we had to talk."

"Who's the champagne for?"

"A man I used to love. Want some?"

"I'll pass. Maybe I can bring a new bottle one of these days."

"Not too soon."

I started down the stairs. My Aunt Connie was right. I was a fool for women. But this one would save me from myself.

"By the way, there's a wiretap on your guest-room phone. Just so you know."

"I disconnected it."

"When?"

"When you told me about the video I realized that Rose must have installed a tap."

"It's not working?"

"No."

"But I called you on that phone last night and—"

"I figured you were sending Alex Rose a message, so I called him up and told him."

"Why?"

"I knew you were bluffing about proof. That meant you were bluffing Jack. Right? To force him out in the open. Right?"

"You knew he'd come after me?"

"Obviously, you had a plan."

"What if I didn't?"

She patted the Deerslayer. "I did."

30

Connie and I gave an orphans' Thanksgiving. We invited Ed Hawley, and Alison and Mrs. Mealy, and my mother, and Vicky McLachlan, and Rita.

The morning was bitter cold. I put the top down for the Fiat's last ride till spring and froze my hair off. By ten o'clock we were back in the garage, oil drained, battery disconnected, and a cover ready to pull on when the engine cooled.

Connie had insisted on cooking the turkey, so I hustled across the street to give her a hand. I'd been popping in and out all week. Last night we'd set the table and arranged the flowers. As soon as everything was good-to-go, I drove out to Frenchtown and picked up my mother, and we called on Renny's mother. When we got to Connie's, Vicky had arrived with a lovesick Tim in tow. Ours, she confided, was one of four politically necessary Thanksgiving dinners they'd be dropping by.

Alison and her mother slipped in almost unnoticed and tried to hide in the kitchen. Poor Janet Mealy was absolutely overwhelmed by Connie's mansion, while Alison had already informed me that her new braces, which she swore hurt like Klingon torture, made her smile look like the front of my Oldsmobile. Connie chased them into the drawing room. There, sitting with a simple elegance in a Salvation Army thrift-shop suit, was Ed Hawley, who addressed Janet as "Ma'am" throughout the afternoon.

Rita Long arrived late, flushed from the cold, as beautiful and exotic as a Russian princess. She presented Connie with an enormous basket of glacéed fruits. Connie thanked her courteously, even as her back stiffened at the extravagance.

At the table, however, she warmed to Rita, admiring how the young woman drew Mrs. Mealy, Alison, and Ed into the conversation. Twice Connie cast me unusually approving glances, and once I caught her nodding subtly at my mother, who didn't quite get it. Rita charmed her too, of course, coaxing her into a gardening discussion and even writing down the Latin names for perennials my mother touted.

Rita was the last to leave after dinner. At the door, she said, "Will you take me house-hunting tomorrow?"

"For real?"

"I've decided to stay, but not in that house."

"Do you know what you want?"

"Something nice and cozy."

I'd believe that when I saw it. She was a very wealthy widow, sole heir to Long Technical Systems, which had a good chance of surviving Jack's death thanks to Ron's canny father and some managerial people I'd recommended. I promised if she came by in the morning I would show her a few places.

I had prepared a list of "cozy," and we spent Friday morning going from one cramped cottage to another, had lunch at the Drover, and visited some bigger places in the afternoon. I was about to invite her home for a drink when she said, "Show me the Richardson place again."

"I don't want to go out there."

"He was my husband, he wasn't yours. Nobody you loved died out there."

"*I* almost died out there."

She returned her warmest smile and asked, "Did it ever occur to you you don't *want* to sell the Richardson place?"

"No."

"Then show it to me."

"You're the customer."

I headed out Route 7, fast, because the days were getting very short and we'd lose the light by four-thirty. Rita was sitting with her head back on the seat, hair shimmering like black lacquer, debating the pros and cons of the houses we'd seen.

"I like your house," she said suddenly.

"Not for sale. Besides, you wouldn't want to live on Main Street. You can't run around naked with the shades up."

"But at least you don't get raccoons making videos."

"Sometimes they come in the house. Slip down the chimney."

Ahead, a quarter mile, someone had parked a hay wagon on the shoulder. I got a little warning tingle in my scalp and hit the brakes.

"What?" she cried, thrown against the seatbelt.

"Speed trap."

We eased by Ollie at forty-four.

I waved. One finger.